# THE COLD KILLER

ROSS GREENWOOD

Boldwood

First published in Great Britain in 2021 by Boldwood Books Ltd.



Cover Design by Nick Castle Design

Cover Photography: Shutterstock



A CIP catalogue record for this book is available from the British Library.

Paperback ISBN 978-1-80048-472-6

Large Print ISBN 978-1-80048-473-3

Hardback ISBN 978-1-80280-977-0

Ebook ISBN 978-1-80048-475-7

Kindle ISBN 978-1-80048-474-0

Audio CD ISBN 978-1-80048-467-2

MP3 CD ISBN 978-1-80048-468-9

Digital audio download ISBN 978-1-80048-470-2

Boldwood Books Ltd
23 Bowerdean Street
London SW6 3TN
www.boldwoodbooks.com

*For Sharyn Rutterford*

1974 – 2021

*A loving wife, a great friend,*
*a fabulous singer, and a wonderful mum.*
*Dearly missed, never forgotten.*

The happy family is a myth for many.

— Carolyn Spring

# 1

## DI BARTON – NOVEMBER 2019

Barton's mouth salivated in the queue at McDonald's. He was next in line and could almost taste the Big Mac meal he was about to purchase. DS Shawn Zander stood beside him, and he was also grinning. When life challenged Barton, Barton headed for McDonald's, and, at least for a while, all was right with the world.

Barton felt his phone vibrate in his pocket. He slipped it out and answered the call.

'Detective Inspector Barton speaking.'

He listened for a moment, then frowned.

'Can you say that again? Did you say sore?'

Barton's eyes widened.

'Okay, location, please,' he said.

He repeated the street back. 'Westwood Park Road. Is that the address I think it is?'

Control confirmed that it was.

'Brilliant,' Barton replied without enthusiasm. 'Zander and I will be at the house in five minutes. Remind whoever reaches the scene first not to attempt any heroics. Nobody approaches until we arrive. Keep the neighbours in their houses.'

Barton stared at the milkshake machine with pained sorrow, but he'd be back. Well, he hoped he'd be back. It wasn't every day he took a call like this.

'Come on, Zander. I've received an urgent call.'

Zander quickly strode after Barton and they got in Barton's pool car. At 11:15 a.m., the traffic was light, meaning blues and twos were unnecessary.

'What's happened?' asked Zander when they were on their way.

'Do you remember the film, *Texas Chainsaw Massacre*?'

'Yes.'

'Well, Peterborough might be having one right now.'

# 2

## DI BARTON

Barton knew, with his colleague's driving, they would be at the scene in less than five minutes, so he spent the time quickly running through with Zander what Control had told him.

'Right,' he said. 'A woman heard shouting outside her house and looked into next door's front garden from an upstairs window. She could see her neighbour threatening an old man with what she called an electric saw.'

'Why are we involved? Aren't uniform dealing?'

'They're en route, but there's a burst water main next to the car park near the town bridge, so we've been requested to attend. They know I'm always interested when it's to do with Mr Spencer.'

'How long for Armed Response?' asked Zander.

'Twenty minutes.'

The address was well known to both men. Archibald Spencer lived there. He had been one of Peterborough's most notorious and elusive criminals for around a quarter of a century, and he was a real blot on the department's record. They'd caught and charged his cronies, cousins, and even his son a few years back, but nothing ever connected directly to the main guy and no one would dish the dirt on him. Five years ago, an ex-girlfriend had grudgingly offered to assist an investigation, but she'd vanished. You didn't need to be a detective to guess her fate, but Archie, as he insisted on being called, had been in Spain since the week before she disappeared.

'Let's hope we get him bang to rights. It'd be weird if we got him for arguing over something like overhanging trees,' said Zander.

'Maybe his lovely wife, Poison, has finally driven him mad.'

Barton smiled as Zander curled his top lip at the thought of meeting the delightful Evie. Meanwhile, Barton wasn't going to count his chickens. It definitely didn't sound like anything Archie would get up to on his own front lawn. Nothing was straightforward with this man. Decades ago, during a pub brawl, Archie spat in a young PC Barton's face, which led to Barton giving him a skull-juddering thump. The cheeky prick complained after, which resulted in the CPS deciding not to proceed with the case against Archie. It was only handling stolen goods back then, but Archie soon moved into the big league, and Barton had learned a lesson about losing control.

Westwood Park Road was one of the richest parts of Peterborough City. You needed the best part of a million to live there, and Archie owned the biggest plot, which had huge iron gates to keep everyone out. They were open when the detectives arrived. The drive was winding and bordered by three-metre laurel trees. It wasn't possible to see beyond them and Barton swallowed as he heard a small engine revving from the direction of the house.

A response van pulled up behind them. Three young men in uniform got out and rushed over. Barton quickly explained the situation and the officers looked nervous once he'd finished speaking.

'You three stay here,' said Barton. 'Secure the street. Shut it fifty metres up each way for the moment. People can drive other routes without too much hassle. Nobody in or out until the ARV turns up. I'll keep Control up to date.'

Barton grabbed a baton and some PAVA incapacitant spray from the boot of his car and beckoned to Zander to follow him through the wrought-iron gates. Policing was never a fair fight, but this was ridiculous. Still, he suspected that an altercation involving a chainsaw wouldn't last long, although God knew what scene they would come upon.

They strode down the tree-lined drive, which bent around to the side of a big Georgian house. It was peaceful, just the sound of their footsteps, until the revving started up again, which was now louder and intermingled with shouting. The noise still sounded a little distance from them, and when they reached the end of the lines of trees the two men who came into view were fifty metres away.

Barton hadn't seen Archie for a couple of years. They knew he'd been up to no good in Puerto Banús in Spain, because they'd heard rumours the drug squad had been sniffing around and Archie's name had come up.

Archie appeared to have developed an addiction all right, but to food. The years had been unkind, but he was still tall and broad-shouldered. He looked like a bloated ex-pat in baggy chino shorts and a Hawaiian shirt, whereas the white-haired old man opposite him was about five and a half feet tall and frail. His ancient suit hung off his narrow frame but, despite that, he waved the hammer he had in his right hand with real malice. Barton also detected a flash of steel in the left hand. Archie had the chainsaw revving and was prodding it at his foe to keep him at bay.

'Stay back,' shouted Archie Spencer.

'You deserve to die, Spencer. Unless you talk.'

Barton opened his mouth, but closed it again. The scene felt so unreal that it was hard to think what to say.

'Drop your weapons,' roared Zander next to him.

Barton and Zander stepped forwards but circled around the two men. The older man glanced over, but Archie kept his gaze and chainsaw pointed directly at his aggressor. Barton was familiar with the look of reckless desperation on the old man's face, but before he could shout out an order the man turned and swung the hammer at Archie. The saw roared in reply. The hammer arced through the air and Barton cringed when he saw there was a hand and forearm still attached to it. Barton and Zander hurtled forward.

The injured man looked at his stump of an arm for a moment and staggered forward a step towards his assailant. Archie's eyes narrowed. Barton recognised the same evil sneer from when he spat in Barton's face all those years ago.

'Back! Back!' roared Archie.

A short woman, well over-dressed for a Tuesday morning, appeared from around the rear of the house towards them. She stopped behind the combatants, glared, then hollered at the older of the two men. Barton couldn't make out anything over the roar of the revving chainsaw. The old man staggered another step towards Archie and raised the small knife in his remaining hand.

Archie's face fell – clearly even he didn't relish what he might have to do. He took a big stride to the side but could go no further due to a large statue of a horse. Zander was less than ten metres away, Barton fifteen.

'No,' shouted Barton, Zander and Archie.

The old man lurched forward, his remaining arm swinging. Archie looked away as he raised the saw, which Barton imagined tearing into the aggressor's stomach. Archie bared his teeth as the blade spun furiously.

Zander was there and grabbed the wrist of the hand holding the knife, then yanked the man back. The saw blade spun in the air. Barton seized the biceps of the stump and together they held the collapsing man up. Covered in blood, Archie held his weapon aloft in both hands. Then he turned to face the police.

# 3

## THE COLD KILLER – FRIDAY 8TH NOVEMBER

It's Friday teatime. The smell of fish and chips pulls me out of my prison cell and I stroll towards the servery. I can immediately tell something's wrong. It's too quiet. I search the faces of the men who are lined up for everyone's favourite evening meal of the week. Nobody meets my stare, but that's not unusual. I stroll to the hatch where the food is passed out. I don't queue, I never have. The servery worker holds out his hand for my plate, which I give to him. The silence is like a building dark cloud while he goes about his business.

I step back and peer up at the top landing. There are four youngsters in a line at the bottom end of the wing. They all have eyes on me as they lean against the railings. It's a modern group: white, mixed race, black and Asian. Peterborough's been a multicultural city for a long time and, in here, they all want a piece of me.

Prison is normally a hive of activity with a loud and constant, almost tangible, noise. Prison is a sea of danger where the threat of violence rules the waves. The con behind the counter clears his throat. I step forward and take my plate off him, then stare down at what he's given me. The wing holds its breath. The right items of my meal are present – I have chips, fish, and mushy peas – but it's an average portion, and I'm not an average guy. I'm being mugged off in my own patch. At least, it was mine until today.

I suppose I've always known this moment was inevitable. There have been harder, younger men around before, who flexed their muscles and paid the price, but these lads look organised. I've been living off my legend, but today I will need to step up. I'm ready, always prepared, but I'm not the man I once was.

I twist my wrist and frisbee the half-full plate towards the servery worker's face. He's ready for it and slips to the side, leaving it to splatter against the far wall. He twists to gaze at the dripping mess but doesn't turn back. I hammer my fist into the Plexiglas, causing it to crack. The queuing men on my right keep their eyes on the floor.

A screw comes out of his office and looks around. Nobody moves. He's another one of the kids they seem to employ nowadays. Not a bad lad, but ill-suited to deal with a situation like this. He knows that and returns to his office. I walk back to my cell as the four men descend the stairs one by one.

The other officer working the wing is older, thirty-five maybe. He's busy at the gate with meds, but his help isn't expected or needed, unless they plan to kill me. He looks a flabby, unfit type, so I may not receive his assistance even then. His name is Peter Green, and pea green is the colour he turns when prisoners get in his face.

He usually works on the nonce wing because those old fuckers aren't physical so it's a mistake that they've put him here today. With what's about to occur, if the staff aren't on the ball, people might die. That's just the way it is.

Prison violence is unique. There are no rules. Anything can happen when big men put everything on the line, but I have no choice but to fight. Even though the chance of me winning is slim, when you're behind bars, the key to survival is to be in the fight.

# 4

## THE COLD KILLER

When I reach my cell, I hustle in and shut the door. There is a button that locks it from the inside. Officers' keys override it, but the other inmates can't just barge in. It buys me some time to prepare, but there's no point in delaying the inevitable. They'll only come for me tomorrow, perhaps when my back is turned. My padmate, Spenny, sits up on his elbows. He wears the prison grey tracksuit even though he's been here so long he doesn't have to.

'That was quick, or wasn't the food ready?' he asks.

'Neither. You remember the big lad that arrived last week?'

'The heavy bloke with the long hair who you threw a comb at yesterday?'

'That's the one. Well, he's outside, with three of his mates.'

Spenny jumps down off the top bunk, steps to the door, and looks through the observation panel.

'What are they doing?' I ask.

'Just sitting on the pool table.'

'Weapons?'

'Doesn't look like it. I would say with four of them that size, they won't need 'em.'

Spenny is a big lad, but not the sharpest. He reminds me of a young Herman Munster but with rosy cheeks.

'Are you with me?' I ask him.

Spenny looks at the ceiling while he thinks. He's an unusual, joyless type, lacking a sense of humour, but with a similar history to mine. Except he nearly killed three people. He said it was a gang fight, and I suppose he had his reasons, but it's ruined the rest of his life and he's still only twenty-four.

I always wanted a son, but it's too late for any of that, so I've tried to help Spenny in a fatherly way. Talk some sense into him. Sadly, Spenny is too far gone to accept any kindness; his emotions are blocked from being in prison for so long at such an early age.

He rarely sleeps, although few do in here, not properly anyway, we just exist. When Spenny gets out, he will be a stick of dynamite waiting for the smallest spark, as I was. I've told him that spending your youth locked up is a waste, but it took me until I was no longer young to realise that. It's only now, as my power fades, that I understand there was another way.

With my criminal record, I could easily request a single cell, but I prefer to share. Having someone else to talk to is the surest way to stop this place driving you mad. He has been reliable and useful in the past when I've needed backup, but this time is different. These men will cause real damage.

Spenny takes his time with his decision. The way he squints his eyes while he thinks drags me back decades to a connection that Spenny doesn't know about, which is probably for the best. It's a big choice for him, but he understands this life. He went to a secure centre at fifteen for armed robbery. I met him briefly in this jail when he was being transferred to a young offenders' jail, having reached eighteen years old. That was six years ago. He still has at least two more years to do, and then he'll be on licence until he dies. He's so firmly stuck in the system that only death will free him of it.

Spenny agreed to share my cell because I was the top dog on the wing. Drugs, coercion, bribery, whatever, it's all on me – I'm in control of the racket, or I was. Of late, I've become exhausted and bored with everything. Tired of life. And Spenny realises things are shifting. The men outside understand that, too, which is why they are here. It's a shame, seeing as I'm out in a few weeks.

If Spenny stands by my side and we fall, he loses big. Prison management wouldn't return us to main location and he's got years to serve. Standing there in front of me, in his baggy tracksuit and with his thick hair sticking up, he reminds me so much of his dad. Poor Spenny, he didn't stand a chance being raised by that wanker.

Spenny pulls himself back up to the top bunk and shrugs at me.

'Sorry, mate. You're on your own for this one.'

# 5

## THE COLD KILLER

I was expecting him to say that, but it's still a blow. Perhaps, like Prison Officer Peter Green, I'm losing my bottle. Or maybe I'm just getting old. I've spent my entire life fighting, and the tear-up that got me this six-year stretch only stopped because my hamstring went. It was a lucky escape for those who I was educating on the error of their ways.

I suppose it was to be expected that the judge would believe them, but I was surprised Barton did. Him and me go way back. I thought Barton was sound, and he understood me. He'll understand my displeasure when I get out of here. It's true, I'm a man who likes a scrap, and often I'm to blame, but when I'm guilty, I plead guilty. The trial was a stitch-up.

It's been a long three years this time. I've not had a single visitor in all that stir, nor received a single letter that wasn't official.

As for the judge and jury, I don't hold a grudge against them. They merely took the Crown's view. Even so, the judge's statement when it came to sentencing went straight through me. I brushed the words off at the time, but I've had over one thousand long nights to consider them. The summing up is still vivid in my mind:

'I see you before me again, as I have many times over the years. Unrepentant, unforgiving, unashamed, and a danger to others. Yet, this time you forced a full trial, despite damning evidence of your guilt. That will cost you. Not only have you wasted your own life, but you've also ruined other people's. Do you have anything to say before I sentence you?'

For once, I lost my temper. With my teeth bared, I snarled my reply.

'I was born to fight, but the system took that from me. You stole my future when I was barely an adult, and still you misjudge me. If I was responsible for the injuries to these idiots, I would have admitted it. They brought it on themselves. But they are rich, like you, and so you choose their side. They needed to learn a lesson and pay the price.'

'So, you're the judge now?'

'Better me than you.'

The judge stared down at me without anger, which gave his words much more power. He gently pushed his glasses back up his nose.

'Only you can change your ways,' he said with a sad smile. 'If nothing else, consider your legacy. How will you be remembered? Who will remember you? Choose to end this cycle. With that in mind, I'm giving you six years to think about it. If you come before this court again for something similar, you risk losing your freedom forever.'

The bloody judge was right. I chose this life. Only I can decide to be something different. I reckon that's what made this stir the hardest. Perhaps it's the truth that has weakened me, not the years. The conclusion I've reached, though, is that it's too late for me to change, so I'll go out on my shield.

I take my shoes, jeans and buttoned shirt off and pull on track-suit bottoms, a tight T-shirt and my trainers. It's the modern warrior's uniform. I drag out the huge plastic bag with HMP Peterborough on it from under my bunk and place my belongings in it. There's not much, but, win or lose, I won't be sleeping here tonight. If I pack it now, it'll save the staff a job, and they'll just bring it down to the block without breaking anything.

The four lads are still outside. I won't have to really deal with all four though. One or more of them will be along for the ride and when the scrapping starts, they will be straining a muscle while loitering at the rear. In fact, I know the Asian fellow is due on the next open-prison ship out. He won't want to blow that cushy number. And the black guy only has one eye. I suspect he won't be too keen to get that near my fingers.

The mixed-race lad looks as if he's involved under sufferance. In fact, there's something eerily familiar about him, but I can't quite put my finger on it. That only leaves the ringleader. Now, he reminds me of myself when I was his age. He's cocksure. His right hand has formed a fist, and it swings loose next to his body, as though he's brandishing a heavy mace. I suspect it would do similar damage.

These kids are young, but they know about my reign of terror here, so they'll be expecting me to come out all guns blazing. They would have presumed Spenny would stand beside me, hence the numbers. The big guy looks confident and will think he can easily take me, so he'll expect me to go for one of the others first.

They'll be overconfident, being mob-handed, but this is prison. Nobody fights fair, so you can be as dirty or ruthless as you feel is necessary. It's the end result that's remembered, not the method of victory. I will attack the strongest man, because I don't want him behind me having a free pop. When's he's down, maybe I'll have a chance.

I undo the lock and edge outside. It's like musical statues on the rest of the wing and the record has ended. The four who are here for business step forward. I spot Officer Green alone at the wing gates. Our eyes meet and he strides towards me, but then he ducks inside the office and closes the door.

I glance from left to right. The white and mixed-race pair have reps already here. The white guy is sometimes referred to as K or special K and the other is G. They are sometimes referred to as the KGB, but I don't know who or what the B is for. The black guy has his head tilted to one side like a one-eyed meerkat, subconsciously protecting that eye. He and the Asian kid, who has an amazing moustache for someone so young, look composed. A shimmer of doubt flickers through my mind. And then we're on.

I thrust forward two paces towards Meerkat, with my fingers pointed towards his face. They all lean in, and that's their first mistake. When my right foot lands, I push off hard to the left and explode.

I've thrown some quality punches in my time. You know as soon as they land if you've timed it correctly. This one is perfect. It lands plumb on the spot between K's top lip and nose, and a jarring thud shudders down the length of my arm. My back spasms as I'm sprayed in blood.

He slumps to the floor. I'm just a little too slow to lift my guard in place as Meerkat hurls himself at me, Kung Fu style. My ribs crack under the impact of the kick, while G shuts my eye with a jabbing strike. My final thought before the lights go out is that I was wrong about these men, because they all get stuck in. Moustache walks forward as I double over and his knee fires up towards my chin.

* * *

I wake up with the feeling of being in motion. I'm in a bright white vehicle with a woman in a green uniform standing over me. I have a handcuff on my wrist, which I assume is attached to the prison officer sitting on the seat opposite me. That's the least of my problems. My right eye is shut, and has the sensation of someone rapidly inflating a bouncy castle in my head. Darkness descends once more.

## 6

### DI BARTON

Zander and Barton both retreated from the spinning saw blade, but after a few seconds Archie dropped the chainsaw and silence fell. A pigeon cooed from a nearby tree.

'I was just about to tell you to stand back, and that I'd sort it,' said Zander to Barton as they laid the injured man on the grass. Barton smiled as he kept the grip from his huge hand iron-tight around the mangled arm stump. The blood had, at least, stopped squirting out and this man would survive, even if his life would be harder. Barton suspected, for him to be here in this situation, his life had already been damaged beyond repair.

Archie looked shocked now the adrenalin had left him. His wife, Evie, walked up to her husband, stared hard at his face, then burst out laughing.

'I'm arresting you for attempted murder,' said Zander to Archie as he got out his handcuffs, even though Barton knew that it would never stick. Evie strode towards Zander, who'd finished cautioning Archie.

'It was self-defence,' she screamed at him.

'Shut it, Evie,' ordered Archie. 'We don't talk to the police.'

Zander pulled his phone out and rang Control.

'Situation safe. Send the ambulance straight in, amputated limb, and instruct uniform from outside the property to enter as well. This is a crime scene.' He stood and approached Evie.

'You are also under arrest as an accessory to attempted murder.'

'I've done nothing,' she spat.

'Enough, Evie. Keep your mouth shut,' growled Archie. 'We'll be home by dinnertime.'

Barton still couldn't quite believe what had happened. He took a deep breath and remembered who he was.

'Are you both okay?' he asked the husband and wife.

Archie nodded.

'Get them out of my sight,' said Barton to Zander.

Barton's nose wrinkled at the terrible smell coming from the victim, who appeared to have lost consciousness. At least his chest was still rising. The ambulance crew were there in seconds and the patient was soon on his way to hospital. Somehow, Barton and Zander remained free of blood. It felt like one of those scenes where a crazed gunman fires an Uzi from a couple of metres away and yet no one gets hit.

Once the scene was under control, Barton returned to the station and prepared his team to interview Archie. His lawyer arrived within the hour, which was impressive and meant there wouldn't be much delay. Barton had left Zander back at the house to process the scene. The old man was easy to identify because he had his wallet in his pocket. Barton half recognised the surname, and the computer soon told him that the injured man was the father of a known criminal who'd gone missing around the same time as Archie's ex-girlfriend.

Barton preferred to let others do the interview if he knew the suspect well, so he could watch from another room. DS Kelly Strange, who was his best interviewer, took DC Leicester into the interview room with her and went through the formalities. He'd expected Archie to look smug, but the gravity of the situation had affected him. Barton suspected he'd not been personally involved in anything so violent and gruesome for a long time. Barton knew Archie's solicitor well. The man always exuded confidence, despite the calibre of his clients.

'My client has prepared a statement,' he said, pushing a piece of paper over. 'It's what happened in his own words. I'm happy to read it out loud for the benefit of the tape so we can have this matter resolved and have Mr Spencer back home after what has been a shocking experience for him.'

Strange nodded.

'I was out trimming some trees,' said the solicitor.

'Don't you have a gardener?' Strange asked Archie, to see if she could interrupt or provoke Archie from what no doubt would be a well-rehearsed tale.

'I do, but I enjoy keeping my hand in,' replied Archie.

Strange gave him a hard look, then nodded at the solicitor, who continued.

'I'd opened the front gates for Evie to go shopping, and gone back to trimming my trees. Then, this old guy walks down my path and starts shouting at me. I can't hear him over the sound of the machinery. He gets really close and then the hammer drops out of his sleeve. I tell him to fuck off. He shouts this name at me, reckons I know where his son is, whose name I don't recognise, and this makes him madder.'

'You never knew his son?' interrupted Strange.

'I can barely remember my own kids' names nowadays, and I've pretty much retired from any involvement in my businesses now. They run themselves, I'm just a figurehead. Strictly legal, naturally.'

'Carry on.'

'I'll read it,' said Archie, brushing away his brief's concerns with a wave of his hand. 'I pointed the saw at him and told him to stay back. He got his mobile out and tried to give it to me. I cut the engine, so I could hear. He shouted that there was a picture of his son on it. I made him put the phone down and back away, so I could safely look at it. As it happened, I did know the boy. He was a mate of my son's, who you pinned three attempted murders on, even though that was also self-defence. Funny how the world turns in circles, ain't it?'

'Do you know the whereabouts of his son now?' asked Strange.

'Of course not. I told the fella that, and he went bonkers. I fired the saw up to keep him away. He kept ranting and ranting. That's more or less when you turned up. He attacked me. What could I do? I repeatedly warned him.'

Barton massaged the sides of his temples as he listened to the story. Archie's son had almost killed three teenagers without provocation and had been given a life sentence despite being only eighteen. Self-defence never came into it. Unfortunately, Archie's explanation of today's events seemed reasonable from what Barton had seen.

'You didn't have to use the chainsaw. You could have gone back inside,' said Strange.

'I regret that. I do. There's been too much violence over the years. I want a quiet time now, with my Evie. I feel like an old man.'

'You'll need to remain in our custody suite while we finish our inquiries,' said Strange.

'There's one more thing, Sergeant Strange,' said the solicitor. 'There's CCTV down the entire length of the drive and at the front of the house. State-of-the-art, including sound. I'll have it to you in less than an hour.'

Barton almost smiled. Archie was right. There would be hours of questioning, but he might well be home for dinner.

# 7

## THE COLD KILLER – SUNDAY 10TH NOVEMBER

I've been in the prison healthcare department for two days now, slipping in and out of deep sleep, and daydreaming about my distant past. For some reason, I keep rerunning my first real fight. It's as if my brain can't handle anything else until I've processed what happened back then. It was a day that changed me forever.

The enemy had been stalking us and they had double our numbers. It was inevitable they would catch us at some point. I was with Frank Zanthos and Archie Spencer. My mum used to shout, 'Ooh! Frank Spencer's here,' whenever they both knocked at our door for me when we were kids. It was by far the funniest thing she ever said. Strangely, *Some Mothers Do Ave 'Em* is one of the few things that I can recall watching as a family.

Frank used to call my mum Betty in reply. She liked Frank as much as I did. There wasn't anything about him to dislike. Maybe he is the only person I've ever loved. My dad was a wanker who shacked up with an Avon lady a few streets up from us. Every now and again, he'd come around, ignore me, shag my mum and slip her a few quid. The arrangement suited us all.

Frank was unlike anyone I'd met. He was kind and gentle by nature, and handsome to the point of beautiful. Yet, despite being much more intelligent than me and Archie, he was happy to get his hands dirty when there was trouble. We'd played as boys and we were becoming men together. It was his idea to attack first.

Spencer, on the other hand, was less noble. Some children are like that, and growing up they just get worse. He scared even me a little. He possessed a ruthless edge that meant he could hurt without fear, and guilt was an emotion he didn't feel. He made a brilliant soldier.

We waited for the enemy hidden in some bushes atop a rise. We expected them to come up the hill to search for us, but when they appeared, they just stood around and lit cigarettes. They were about fifty metres down the slope. We looked at each other, drew our knives, and I hefted the axe I'd made specially. We ran at them. It was beautiful. Even now, half conscious, I can remember the pure joy and vitality I felt. There were no nerves, only my drumming heart and the blood pounding in my ears. Frank and I even had time to exchange a smile.

To our foes' credit, they recovered fast and were ready for hand-to-hand combat. I threw my axe, and it went sailing past their heads. I slipped past the blade shoved towards my face, and, like a cold killer, plunged my knife into his stomach. The fight ended up as a free-for-all, with people jabbing and slashing in all directions. We took significant blows, but they eventually retreated, leaving us battered and bloody on the grass but victorious.

Despite my injuries, the feeling of belonging and brotherhood erased any feelings of pain. I knew then that I was born to be a warrior. We pulled ourselves to our feet and, with arms around shoulders, trudged back to our homes as the sun set.

I understood down to my very bones that to always win you

must leave nothing out there. Fear must be pushed aside. It was better to die in glory than live in shame. We were only eleven and the weapons were wood. Our enemy was just two years ahead of us at school, but our futures were set. Tragedy was already in the wind, and betrayal was close behind.

# 8

## THE COLD KILLER – MONDAY 11TH NOVEMBER

I'm pleased when I wake the next day, because both my eyes open. The vision is a bit blurred through the swollen one, but I feel more normal. My ribs are tender, but apparently only one has a very small hairline crack. It's my jaw that hurts the most. The doctor at the hospital said I was lucky it didn't shatter.

The prison hospital ward has six beds in it, but only one other is occupied. It's more or less a large prison cell. The metal grey door is locked at night, and the windows are permanently barred. I've heard the other patient groaning and farting throughout the twilight hours and I suspect he's listened to me doing the same. Last time I was in this part of the jail, they gave me one of the eight single cells because of my record. I expect it will be a while before I'm a danger to anyone.

My stomach rumbles, which is another good sign. I press the emergency alarm and a minute later an older officer strolls in. He looks familiar, but his hair is flecked with grey now – the staff must age as fast as we do.

'What took so long? I could have been having a heart attack.'

'I was watching you on the monitor.'

I look to where his finger points and note a camera in the corner of the room. Many like it are spotted all over the prison. In fact, Peterborough is a purpose-built jail, so there are very few blind spots. Big brother is watching.

'My arse needs wiping.'

'Nasty for you. My coffee's getting cold, anything else?'

'Just the breakfast menu, please.'

The officer's eyes narrow in annoyance, then he shrugs it off and sits on the bed next to mine.

'Okay, you have a choice of cornflakes, and, uh, that's it.'

'Perfect, and tea, please.'

There's little to be gained by pissing the staff off, especially in my condition. The man in the far corner of the ward lets out a groan of agony, followed by a whimper. All I can see sticking out of the covers is a shock of pure white hair on the back of his head.

'What's wrong with him?'

'He's dying. Been here for months.' The officer raises his voice. 'It's God torturing him for the things he's done.'

With that, he stands to leave. At the ward door, he stops and looks over at me.

'I'll send the orderly in when he arrives. One of the managers is coming over to chat to you in twenty minutes.'

He leaves the door open, so it must be at least seven-fifteen and, apart from the sobbing opposite me, it's peaceful. Some prisoners try to blag their way into healthcare as you can't be bullied on here, even though it's often full of nutters. Most inmates in general are a little bit mental, and this place gets the cream of them.

I can't get to sleep again with the whining from the other occupant of the ward. I manage to swing my legs out of the bed and, with a shuffling technique that gives me a terrible warning of things to come, I make it to the toilet. My piss is light pink, which is an improvement on the Chianti I was doing in the urine bottle yesterday.

At eight o'clock, just as I'm dropping off, someone clears her throat beside me. It's a woman in a crisp black suit. Everything about her is sharp, including her gaze. She pulls up a seat and sits down next to my bed, putting our eyes on the same level, which surprises me. I've no idea how old she is, but judging by her creamy complexion and lack of lines, not very. Her long blonde hair looks advert-fresh. She is pretty and poised, making me feel old and broken. With luck, I could have had a child her age.

'I'm Jenny Clearwater, Head of Male Residence. I've come to talk to you about your assault,' she says. 'This type of thing isn't acceptable in our establishment. We aim to throw the book at those responsible.'

'You do what you have to do.'

She shifts in her seat slightly and breaks eye contact. Then she gets a notebook out.

'What happened that day?'

'Why don't you tell me what you think happened?'

'Well, that's the thing, we don't know. There was a camera malfunction.'

'By that, you mean it was tampered with.'

'Yes. Someone put hair gel or something similar on the lens. We know the identity of one of the men involved, although he was injured too. Unfortunately, the staff on the wing were in the office. I can guess who the other attackers were, but I need a statement.'

'You must know I'm not going to grass. Why waste your time?'

She reaches over and pats me on the hand.

'I had to try. So, just to confirm, you have no comment.'

I glance from one perfectly made-up eye to the other. My non-compliance is good for the prison management. This way, the incident won't affect their official statistics.

'Can I put a complaint in?' I ask.

Her face alters a few millimetres into a frown, and I instantly recognise what got her promoted so young. I like a steel core and if I was ten years younger, I'd fancy a bit. The thought makes me laugh, which tests my ribs.

'What do you have to complain about?' she says with a raised eyebrow.

'The old guy over there is ruining the atmosphere in here. Can't he go and die somewhere else?'

'Ah, you mean Mr Battersby. We keep him in this ward because it's easier to tend to his needs. The other single cells are all full, so we need you out of here now that you seem better.'

'Better is pushing it. Am I going back to the wings?'

'Security has word that if you return to normal residence, you *will* be killed. So, no. We have a single cell on the VP wing with your name on it.'

'You want me to go with the nonces? No way. I'll take my chances.'

'It's a wing for vulnerable persons, hence the name, not just sex offenders, which in your present condition is you. You wouldn't last five minutes in your state on main residence with a bounty on your head.'

'I thought you said I was better. Bollocks to that. Put me in the block. I've got less than five weeks. I'll do it cold.'

Her smile is ice.

'Obviously, that's your call. However, we have little space in Separation and Care, either. And there will be no TV in your cell. Five weeks will feel like a hundred. Think about that, then tell one of the officers here what your answer is and he'll arrange it. In the meantime, I'll let Birch and Crane know that you might be staying with them in the near future.'

I can't help laughing as she leaves. I'm really starting to like this woman. Birch and Crane are two block officers who've been here since the jail first opened. Time has not mellowed them. I had a right row with the pair of them when I came in three years ago. Birch got a nasty elbow and Crane a low blow. My returning welcome over there would leave me limping or worse.

I lie back and close my eyes. They reckon I have to stay in a bail hostel when I finish this sentence, which is exactly what I don't need. People like me, living with other people like me, only leads to trouble. But I have no choice. And I don't want to be injured when I arrive there, which is likely if Birch and Crane get their chance for revenge.

Doing your porridge without a TV is bad as well. I haven't been right mentally on this stretch as it is. Hours on end with nothing to do might turn me into one of the ones I pity. Battersby makes another moaning sound.

'Can't you be quiet?'

He startles me by slowly sitting up, like Dracula rising from his coffin. He's surprisingly lucid and well spoken, but his eyes are yellow and the skin hangs from his face like a basset hound's.

'I'm dying, show some respect.'

'Like you showed your wife all those years ago?'

He frowns for a moment, then decides he doesn't care.

'My reputation precedes me.'

'I'll say. How long ago was it, twenty years? *The Sun* called it one of the coldest murders in history. Why do that to her? Why not just kill her?'

'I didn't really have a good answer to that during my trial, which is why I was told that I would die in prison. I've spent a long time thinking about it all since. The truth of the matter is I had come to despise her, because she'd become an evil woman. It seems strange now, because we used to quite like each other.'

Battersby had walked into the local police station to tell them he was murdering his wife. When they asked when, he said one word – currently. Officers raced to his house where they found her submerged in the bath. He'd knocked her out, gagged her, tied her to a wooden chair, then left her on her back in the bath. Before he departed to confess at the cop shop, he'd turned the tap on half a twist.

'I don't understand. Didn't you want to get away with it?'

'I'd had enough. I hated my job, my wife obviously, and we had no children. I'd been meeting youngsters through escort sites and attacking them. Mentally, I had unravelled. The net was closing in. There was zip to look forward to. Anyway, the chances of getting away with that kind of thing nowadays is remote. I planned to end it all afterwards, so it didn't matter much.' He stops talking, grits his teeth and arches his back, as though an alien is about to burst from his chest. His hands become claws. Tears pour down his cheeks, but he remains silent.

'I suspect you regret not following through with that,' I shout over at him.

After around ten seconds, he relaxes and flops backwards onto the bed.

'Yes, dying in prison is no fun, but is it ever? To my surprise, I have a strong will to live. Even now, I resist the inevitable. The thought of my wife's last few moments gives me strength. This agony is almost worth it, but there is one thing that's difficult to bear.'

'What's that?'

'The knowledge that I won't ever touch young flesh again.'

I can hardly believe what he's saying, and it takes a lot to surprise me. He gasps, then convulses, and I hear a bubbling mixture of water and air. The smell hits me a few seconds later. I press the call button to let the officer know that I'll be happy to move to the VP wing after all.

# 9

## DI BARTON

Barton had spent the day on his first aid refresher course. He usually looked forward to them because it was an opportunity to catch up with people he'd worked with for decades. This time, though, the instructor was new. When Barton asked after Larry, who'd run the sessions since Barton first joined the force, the woman who'd replaced him shook her head sadly. Larry had cancer. He wouldn't be coming back.

That set the theme for the day and Barton felt quite maudlin when he returned to his desk to check his emails before he left for home. He rapidly deleted the first, which was trying to sell him crypto currencies. How in the hell had they got his police email address? Next he'd be getting stuff about winning the Spanish lottery and penis enlargement potions.

He had an email from his dentist cancelling his appointment again, and there was one from Holly reminding him to confirm that Zander and Strange were coming to theirs for lunch soon. Barton paused and thought of his mother. It was her idea for the meal, but Barton wondered what version of his mother would be present. Dementia was so cruel.

The next email was titled in capital letters. DANGER. It was from his boss, DCI Cox. Work had been a little boring of late. Not that Barton longed for terrible crimes, but what they'd had lately had been bitty stuff, which stopped everyone getting stuck in and working as a team. He pulled his chair forward and opened the email.

Cox had forwarded the message to him after one of her MAPPA meetings. MAPPA stood for Multi-Agency Public Protection Arrangements. It was the process through which various agencies such as the police, the prison service and probation worked together to protect the public by managing the risks posed by violent and sexual offenders living in the community. The email had initially been titled Coming Soon – someone clearly had a dark sense of humour. It was a list of sex offenders who were coming to the end of their sentences and may be released into the local area within the next twelve months.

Barton's eyes scanned down the list of names. He knew them all. Some, he'd arrested and charged himself, others had been dealt with by the other detective team or by Child Protection, but everyone in the building would know their names. A few were notorious, with their faces gracing the national papers at the time of their court cases.

Barton rubbed his chin. Cox was right. This was danger. Barton had been doing the job long enough to know that when he saw a list like this, their workload always went up.

It was a feature of the British legal system. Unlike other places around the world, such as America, where over a hundred thousand convicts were unlikely to ever see the light of day again, there were only around seventy-five men and a handful of women in the UK who had been given whole of life orders. That meant that around fifteen thousand prisoners were set free each year back into the community. Most would not have been adequately rehabilitated.

The first two on the list were actually deported that morning. Sanches and Ramos were career burglars who also raped old people in retirement communities. Real scum of the earth, but at least they were now Portugal's problem. Some of the other names on the list had done things that were even tougher to contemplate.

Many people thought that child rapists should be sent to jail for the rest of their lives, but Barton guessed the average sentence they received would be around fifteen years. Down the list were Zanthos, Ballanchine and Pfeiffer. Barton shook his head in amazement. Was it already twelve years since they were caught?

Barton believed in the police and in the legal system. Few mistakes were made, but he was also aware that when people went into the prison system, there simply wasn't the money to effectively work with all of them so they were less likely to reoffend when they were released. In his view, violent men and sex offenders rarely changed their spots.

Savage men often grew up in angry households and played in streets of violence. The most violent and ruthless survived and prospered. It was learned behaviour. Prison only reinforced that way of thinking. When these men were released, they were already on the back foot. They had no money, poor job prospects, and sparse support. The only thing they'd have an excess of was anger. They felt they had little to lose.

The sex offenders were in some ways worse because their behaviour was usually innate. If you looked at a toddler and became sexually excited, there was little hope for you. And twenty years in prison weren't going to change that. Until very old age arrived, men and women who thought like that were as dangerous on the morning they were released from prison as the day they had arrived in prison.

Barton could understand not wanting to give too many people a sentence without hope, but what was common among paedophiles was their lack of remorse. Sure, they felt regret, but people like that never considered their victims. As the song went, they were only sorry they got caught.

Zander was walking past, so Barton grabbed his attention.

'Hey, look who's leaving Her Majesty's Hotel Peterborough.'

Barton edged away from his screen, so Zander could read the email.

'Ballanchine, Pfeiffer and Zanthos, Crannock, Thompson, great!' said Zander. 'Was Khan the one who was dumped by his girlfriend, then deliberately crashed his car into a field as he drove her home, which ended with her being decapitated?'

Barton nodded.

'I despise Thompson,' said Zander.

Barton agreed. Thompson was a horrible, violent little bully, both physically and literally. He applied that behaviour to everyone he met in life, including his young children.

'What a foul bunch,' said Zander. 'God, even Charles Celestine looks like he'll be out later this year.'

'Yep. What was that stat the super quoted at his big meeting last week?'

Zander put on a newsreader voice to mimic the superintendent's delivery style.

'In England and Wales, around 45 per cent of all prisoners will reoffend within a year of release.'

Barton chuckled but he soon stopped. The reality wasn't a laughing matter. Trouble was coming.

## 10

### THE COLD KILLER

An officer arrives to collect me at lunch and walks me over to the houseblocks when the rest of the prisoners are locked up. It's Officer Green, the one who hid in his office when the shit hit the fan, and I can see he's wary of me.

I lift up the plastic bag containing my things, but it's an effort with my injuries. Green doesn't offer to help. Battersby has fallen asleep or passed out. What a creature. Twenty years in jail with no visitors, no hope of getting out, dying, and only murderous memories for company. It's hard to believe people such as him exist; that they live like that.

Then I realise I've had no visitors, either. Before he curled up in pain again, Battersby asked if I had a knife so he could 'take charge' of his illness. Prison has even taken that option from him, but I agree with the screw who said he deserves to suffer.

When we reach the VP wing, my new cell is on the lower landing. I can immediately tell that it's unlike any wing I've been on before. It's lunchtime and there's no thoughtlessly loud music for a start, and even I can tell there is a level of cleanliness unknown on every other landing. But it still smells of sweat and fear. It still feels, despite its warehouse size, as though there isn't enough air in here.

The cells we walk past contain people who want to fuck children. I want to fuck with them.

'Boss,' I ask the screw, even though he's a dick. 'What's it like on here?'

'Are you asking about the inmates?' replies Green.

'Yeah, is there trouble? Who runs the show?'

'At the moment, there's nobody laying down the law. We had a large, angry rapist terrorising everyone, but he was transferred a week ago. The wing is mostly dirty old men and sick young boys. There are about five on here who are unhinged, so watch your step.'

'Isn't there anyone normal on here?'

'Like you, you mean?'

I subconsciously tense a fist and my eyes narrow.

'Sorry,' he says. 'I detest working here. It's as though what they've done is written on their faces when they talk to me. I have to make comments on their records, read what they've done, and their crimes are horrific.'

'Why don't you just leave, then? From what I've seen, this isn't the career for you.'

'I want to, but it's getting another job that's the struggle. I'm applying all over and often get interviews, but no offers so far. Hopefully, some time soon, I'll never have to set foot in one of these places again.'

I shake my head at his weak attitude. There's something a little unstable about him, that's for sure. I wouldn't employ him either. He shuts the door on me with shaking fingers. I can't tell if he's scared, angry or annoyed. What's happened to him happens to a lot of people in prison, on both sides of the doors. It's not a place to lose your bottle or your calm.

At least he can just quit if it gets too bad. He's not locked in like the rest of us. For some, it feels like drowning. There'll be many prowling their tiny cells at this very moment, with their minds teetering near the brink.

I haven't lost my bottle, but I've lost my aura of invincibility. I saw a documentary on chimps a few months back. The alpha male was hard as nails, but aging. The adolescent chimps kept having a pop, testing his strength, but not wholeheartedly. Then they grouped together and took him out in the middle of the night. Left him permanently damaged. There was an air of inevitability about the alpha's fate. It's Darwin's law: survival of the fittest. Once beaten, the old alpha had to accept a lesser role in the troop, while the ringleader assumed control, took his women and ate the best fruit.

That's more or less what's happened to me, but I won't live like that. I thought that being in prison before meant I was with the dregs of society, but I was wrong because now I am in the darkest of pits. That judge was spot on. I've skirted through life, neither putting down roots nor owning anything except rusting cars. My prospects are poor. I've only got a few grand in the bank and looking for labouring work at the start of winter is a waste of time, even if my knees could tolerate it.

Green leaves and locks me in. It's a cell much like all the others, yet it feels different today. I sit on the blue mattress and bump my arse on the metal bed. The pillow is even thinner and sweat-stained. It's cold in here. The vent is broken on the window, so I can't shut it. For the first time in maybe forever, I contemplate my life. How has it come to this? How is this my normal? Why would I choose a life where I repeatedly return to this?

I pull a jumper on and make the bed. Shivering, I climb under the lumpy duvet, which at least smells clean. An anger rises in my chest, but soon dies as I realise any rage should be directed within. I force myself to focus on my situation. Is this the moment the lesson finally sinks in, or merely proof that I've had enough?

I can't nod off, so I turn on the TV and watch the end of a programme about vets. It's a regret that I've never had my own dog, but you can't take them to prison with you. At 1:30 p.m., they begin to unlock the workers for the afternoon. There won't be work for me, but I rap my knuckles on my door as they open the cell next to mine. Green opens me up and peers in.

'You're not on the list,' he says.

'No, guv. Can I quickly get some hot water, please?'

He wants to say no, but he's a spineless weasel, so he leaves my door open. I filter through the gathering prisoners to the near-boiling urn and fill my flask. They are a strange bunch for sure. There's none of the bravado, the jokes, or the puffed-up chests that you see on mainstream wings. Nobody looks me in the eye, but some are aloof.

I'm on my way back when I see him. I know who it is straight away even after all the years, because he's still tall and noble like his oldest son was, despite the vulture shoulders that occur when you are way on the wrong side of eighty. I'm stunned. Green ushers me back into my cell and I slump onto my plastic seat, where I recall the day it all went wrong.

Frank Zanthos, Archie Spencer and I had cycled over to Ferry Meadows, a local area of woods and lakes, to mess around and look for trouble. We were at that tricky age of fourteen where you're too young for exciting stuff like drink, fags and fireworks, but too old for toys and soldiers. Frank had been quiet all day and I asked him what was wrong.

'It's home. I hate it. I can't bear for my dad to be in the same room as me. My mum is almost as bad. They disgust me.'

Archie and I looked at each other in confusion. Our dads were so worthless, we practically didn't have an opinion of them. They weren't worth the bother. The hairs on my neck came up, but

Archie just shrugged, and Frank pushed his bike on. I wasn't sure what to say, but I wheeled my bike after him and tried.

'You can tell me, Frank.'

'I can't.'

I stopped pushing my bike. That comment hurt. Archie passed me.

'Being young is shit,' he said.

We got to the pedestrian bridge where Archie had once tried to pour paint through someone's sunroof as they drove underneath us on the dual carriageway. This time, Frank looked into the distance. He turned to us, but the traffic dragged his words away. I think he said sorry. He then stood up on the railing and plummeted in front of a National Express coach. I never forgot the sound of its blaring horns.

# 11

## THE COLD KILLER

I find myself pacing the cell. We were only young, so it wasn't our fault that we hadn't noticed what Frank had been putting up with.

Yet the shock of such an abrupt end to our friend's life numbed us, to our lives and everyone else's. If death could come so easily, then who gave a shit for rules? Archie Spencer became the only friend I had, and we ran riot. It was only a matter of time before something serious happened.

Green unlocks me at 5 p.m. for evening association and dinner. I try to act cool, but I'm not. There's a furnace raging inside me. The same one that blackened my soul years ago. Green's right. Looking around, I can see the men on this wing carry something extra compared to mainstream prisoners. For some it's the burden of shame for what they've done. For others, it's pride for who they are. After all, they're among like-minded inmates here. Incredibly, some think they are better than me.

It's hard to stop myself going ballistic and wading into everyone like the night I lost hope, exactly one year after Frank died. I'm not ready to relive that though, and my injuries prevent me from hurting anyone except myself. I grab my plate and join the back of the queue. It's strange. There's no pushing in, and I hear pleases and thank yous. Normally I'd stare people down, but I only want to return to the relative sanctuary of my cell and shut out the past.

The servery worker is as camp as you like. He gives me a big portion of vegetable risotto, which is one of my favourite meals.

'Welcome to the wing, darling,' he sings.

The elderly man handing out the bananas has creepy, soft lips. He smiles at me and I wave the fruit away. When I turn, I'm gritting my teeth so hard that I get a searing stab from the tender underside of my jaw. I almost bump into Frank's father, who is too close behind me. He's so near, I can see the veins in his eyes. Ricardo Zanthos is more decrepit than I thought. He reminds me of the Emperor from *Star Wars*. Too-white teeth, which must be false, flash at me.

'Do I know you, son? I think I do.'

His eyes are an empty brown, with visible cataracts. He looms towards me, blinking uselessly, but I can't look at him so I limp down the wing. When I get back to my cell, I rest my food on the little eating ledge. Years ago, I'd have thrown it at the wall, but I'll be starving later and I've learnt it's not worth wasting anything behind bars.

Ricardo Zanthos got a nasty surprise after his oldest son's suicide. Frank had written a very detailed letter to the police and posted it that day. It listed a fair amount of his old man's pervings on him when he was little. What had brought it to a head was when his charming father had started on Frank's much younger brother. I don't know how Frank found out, but I suppose he recognised the signs.

My mum was fascinated by the whole case, the gossipy cow. Mr Zanthos senior denied everything, but five-year-olds can't make up the stories Frank's brother had told. Frank's dad received eighteen years, which seemed fair enough at the time, and I've never given him a moment's thought since. It's a real shock to see him. He would have been released long ago for the crimes against his family, so he must have carried on being a nonce after he was released to have been imprisoned again. It's not a surprise. Men like him don't change.

My stomach twists and I lie back on my bed and accept the return of the memory of that night. It was the one-year anniversary of Frank's death. Archie and I had cycled to Stamford, a wealthy town about fifteen miles away. Archie had grown into a huge, meaty lad with a temper to match. He'd fight anyone over anything, and I stood next to him.

We were lobbed out of one bar for being drunk and refused entry based on our age at another, but we got served in the Daniel Lambert pub, which was full of teenagers. I wonder if I've ever known my limits with alcohol, but I certainly wasn't aware of them then. For once, we were just celebrating and remembering our friend, but a group of lads started taking the piss out of Archie's clothes. We'd nicked jackets from town, but our jeans were hand-me-downs and dirty from the roads. Archie called them posh twats, and they pushed him over a chair. The fight spilled into a gloomy courtyard. There were five of them, kids much older than us, who were tipsy and over-confident. Archie passed me a knife as they ran towards us.

It was all over in a few seconds. I hacked and slashed and drove my knife into the advancing pack, snarling under my breath as they dropped like flies. The two boys at the rear sank to their knees, pleading and sobbing that I show them mercy. I peered at the writhing bodies surrounding me on the ground, weeping for help, then back at Archie, who just stared at me with profound respect, but he didn't move.

I suppose I was lucky the only thing to die that night were my hopes of getting in the army. Instead, I wore a prisoner's uniform until I was nineteen, and my childhood and innocence were long forgotten. As the police arrived, Archie told me not to say that it was him who brought the knife. He said it wouldn't help, but it would drag him down with me. It was obvious I would get sent down. He promised he'd visit me in jail and send in money and clothes if I kept quiet.

I spoke to a time-served con soon after I was sentenced to eight years for section eighteen, wounding with intent, who reckoned that if I'd mentioned the knife was passed to me in the heat of battle, I might have received a lesser charge. I may have been able to fulfil my dreams of fighting in a glorious war. Instead, I found myself in daily skirmishes without honour, but I learned fast. As Johnny Cash sang, my fists got hard and my wits got keen.

Juvenile prison is difficult to explain. At their simplest, they are places where children lose hope. I never heard from Archie again. By the time my sentence was over, his family had moved and so had my mum. I've not seen her since either. My dad died shortly before I was released but no one thought to tell me. If I wanted a military career, then the only option was the French Foreign Legion. I signed up. Fighting for them, I learned not to feel. Like Archie, I lived a ruthless life, and I did my duty. The years have raced by, even after I tired of that existence and was discharged.

It's only now that I understand that if you create nothing, merely destroy, then you are nothing. To all intents and purposes, I might as well not have been born.

# 12

## DI BARTON

Barton turned off his computer after a long, busy day. He'd had confirmation that there would be no charges against Archie Spencer, who'd been released hours before. The CCTV from his garden had been HD quality, and a microphone had even picked up most of the argument. Barton knew that if the evidence had been damning *against* Archie as opposed to aiding his case, they'd never have seen the recording. Still, it had put the case to bed without any doubt. Whatever Archie was guilty of, it wasn't attempted murder on this occasion.

The elderly gentleman had turned up with violence on his mind, and that was what he'd received. Barton had read the missing person's file for his son, and it had been investigated thoroughly. The truth was, sometimes youngsters became drifters. And if they didn't have jobs, nor claim benefits, then chances were they were living on the proceeds of crime. Many of them vanished, especially after the police started poking their noses into their bosses' businesses. Some resurfaced years later, others never appeared again. A few would be in unmarked graves.

Barton understood the illusion of glamour a gangster lifestyle offered. Watching the movies, it was all girls and guns and high jinks, but the reality wasn't like that in the UK. It was knives and drugs. The people involved lived chaotic, violent, boring existences, interspersed with occasional bouts of terror. Careers were short.

Barton thought back to Archie's comments about his son being framed. From what Barton had seen over the years, to his credit, Archie had tried to keep his boy out of his way of life, but Gilbert 'Spenny' Spencer was born a wrong'un. People like Spenny and his father, Archie, didn't care about the rules because they were a law unto themselves. Only prison stopped criminals like that from offending in the community.

Archie himself had been an angry youth by all accounts, but then he'd disappeared in his teens. When he came back to the city many years later, he'd become a calculating businessman with a ruthless manner. That was when Barton, as a young copper, then detective, had repeatedly come across him. Zander reckoned Archie was like the Grinch: superficially bad, but with good deep inside. Barton was less forgiving. They both agreed his wife's nickname was appropriate.

Poison Evie was attractive in a hard way, but Barton couldn't think of another word to describe her other than psychotic. He supposed it saved on paying for guard dogs if you had her prowling around inside your house.

Barton felt a sliver of sympathy for their child, Spenny, even though it wouldn't be the biggest surprise if in the future he succeeded in killing someone. Spenny was firmly embedded in the court system before he was a teenager, never mind an adult. It was just the way he was. If your nature was violent, from vicious and crazed parents, and you grew up in a dangerous world, prison was inevitable. As were early deaths, yours or others'.

Many so-called gangsters finally grew up and lived a quieter life, but they were often old and past it by then. While they were young and impulsive, the public only slept easily while they were behind bars.

Barton decided to break the news to Archie that he would not be charged personally. If he could, Barton liked to show his face to the few men who seemed untouchable. At some point, they usually made a mistake or got taken out. Barton didn't like to think of the possibility of Archie's son taking over when he got out, but that was a problem to deal with further down the line. Maybe Archie would send him to Spain to assist with whatever Archie was up to over there.

Barton left the police station and was at Archie's big house in a few minutes. Not surprisingly, the gates were closed. Barton pulled up alongside the intercom and pressed the button. He was expecting Evie to tell him where to go, but Archie answered and told him to come in. The gates swung open. Barton drove up the drive and parked and Archie came out in his dressing gown, despite the hour. He stuck out a hand, which Barton didn't really feel like taking, but did. There was still real strength in the grip.

'It's okay,' said Archie. 'I've washed it since. Wait in the kitchen while I get changed. I was going to have an early night after all the excitement.'

Barton followed him into the house and couldn't help admiring the kitchen. Holly would kill for a room so big to cook in. Still, he wasn't there for compliments, so he gave Archie the news a minute later when he returned.

'The charges are dropped.'

Archie stared dispassionately at him.

'Fair play,' he said. 'That's the right call. I know he was only interested in his lad, but he more or less tried to commit suicide. He should have known how kids are these days. First sign of trouble and they melt away.'

'Like your boy?' said Barton.

Archie's large, florid face went red. The danger was evident in his expression, but then he smiled.

'Coffee? I've got a new machine. Have a cup and I'll tell you the truth about my lad.'

Barton pulled out a kitchen stool and warily perched on it.

'Careful, Inspector. I've snapped two of them meself.'

Barton got off and sat in a chair near the huge oak table. After five minutes of faffing around, Archie put two steaming cups of coffee between them and slumped opposite him.

'No, not like my boy,' said Archie. 'Spenny ran from nothing. He had the devil in him from the day he was born.'

'How long until he's out?'

'At least two years.'

'What happens then? Will he be moving back in?'

Archie shook his head as he laughed. 'No chance. He's my flesh, but it'd be World War Three round 'ere. I'd happily pay for a spell in the nuthouse for him, but he wouldn't take it. He can stay in my penthouse at Fletton Quays. My children have been my biggest regret. Well, I let a friend down once too, but hey ho.'

'It's never too late to change or apologise,' said Barton.

Archie sat next to him. He lit a cigarette and blew smoke up at the high ceiling. His once lustrous hair was now grey and thinning. The casual white shirt and black chinos that he wore strained at the waist and chest.

'I'm not so sure I agree. I've been trying to quit smoking for twenty years. There comes a time when you might as well give up giving up.'

Barton shook his head.

'Don't you think it's better to keep trying to be a better person?'

Archie chuckled, but the laugh dwindled.

'Is your daughter living here?' asked Barton.

'A mate of mine in the big smoke told me they saw her escorting a sheikh in a fancy casino. That was very distressing to hear, especially for Evie. Mind you, I don't suppose it was that unlikely that I'd end up producing a hooker and a jailbird. You have kids?'

'Three. They aren't hooking or killing just yet, but there's still time.'

Archie chuckled again. 'See. Another day, another life, we'd have been mates. Instead, you got my boy a minimum eight years and life on parole.'

'I gave him that? He nearly killed three people. There were thirty witnesses saying he started that fight. He entered the pub with a machete.'

'Yeah, well. You need to be tooled up nowadays.'

'Why don't you employ him out in the sunshine? It might calm him down.'

'You'd love that, wouldn't ya? Out of sight. But no, there's too much charlie out there, and that's the last thing someone like him needs. He'd explode in a few days. He's my blood, so I have to look after him. I speak to him most days on the phone, but he won't let me visit. Says everyone will think he's a daddy's boy.'

Barton finished his coffee with an appreciative nod.

'Get him some help, then, because one day he'll pick on the wrong man.'

'I tried all that, but he reckons he's unstoppable. You can't tell kids nothing nowadays. You know what's the truly scary part of it?'

Barton shook his head.

'Spenny thinks he's normal.'

Barton felt weary at the state of the world. It seemed to be becoming a darker place. He heard a beep from a monitor on the wall, which made Archie leap from his seat.

'You better jog on. That's Evie back, and she won't have had a G & T yet.'

Barton couldn't stop himself from grinning at that. He wanted to ask Archie how come he'd married such an unstable, angry person, but wasn't sure how to phrase it.

'You two have been together a long time,' he said.

Archie put his arm around Barton's shoulder as he escorted him to the front door with a big smile.

'See, you're funny. We'd have been pals. I'm certain of it. I know she's crazy, but she is the only link I have to my past. To my youth. I made plenty of mistakes when I was young and let a lot of people down. Mates and family. They're all gone now. I won't do it to her. Anyway, she's good in the sack.'

Barton laughed and walked to his car. Evie had parked next to it and stared hard at him through her windscreen. Archie waved him off.

'See you at my funeral,' he shouted.

Barton had a feeling that he'd be seeing him sooner than that.

# 13

## THE COLD KILLER – MONDAY 25TH NOVEMBER

I finally feel relatively normal. The bruises on my face will be completely gone in a few days and I sneezed this morning without wincing at a terrible stab in my ribs or chin. That's progress.

It's been a strange time being on this wing. Imagine putting sixty sex offenders in one place. They are pally with each other but cagey. On normal residence, there is a hierarchy of crimes. White-collar stuff against big corporations is hardly seen as an offence, whereas crimes against women and children are generally frowned upon. Although, nowadays, a lot of the cons don't seem too bothered about who the victims are.

If you'd smacked a woman or kid in my day, you got a harder smack in return, whoever you were. They were the type of prisoner I liked to have a quiet word with when I found out what they'd done. I used to go in their cells and tell them they'd been hitting a friend of mine. Some wept, others begged, none fought back.

On this wing, crimes are also ranked. Internet filth isn't as bad as actual kiddy fiddling, and the rape of a woman isn't seen as bad as the rape of a child or baby. What a glorious world to live in. Yet, the inmates on this wing aren't youths with rampant testosterone, which is what causes the animal savagery in the rest of the jail. Here, it's just an undercurrent of disgust that permeates the air. I hate it, yet I have to admit that I've enjoyed not worrying about someone putting a blade in me while my back is turned. There are some pyschos on here, though, but they know they have nothing to gain by challenging someone like me. Don't confuse crazy with stupid.

The prisoners talk to me, probe me to find out my crimes. They want to know if I'm like them. I've managed to hide my hatred, but now I'm stronger, I feel compelled to impose my rules. They should understand that what they've done is not okay. This wing isn't justice for their victims. I watch the rapists chat over the pool table and the paedos wandering in and out of each other's cells, all exchanging tips, laughs, schemes and dreams. I need to leave.

Surprisingly, Officer Green has proven the only normal one on here other than me. We actually have a bit of a laugh. He is scared of the few fighters on here, but he doesn't care about data protection and readily tells me what people are in for.

We had a really lengthy chat on Sunday and I found myself telling him Frank Zanthos's story and that it's his dad in cell thirteen. Green was quiet for the rest of the day, shocked even. He later said Zanthos's crimes were some of the worst on the wing, and he'd heard terrible things in his time here. I hint at the urge to avenge what caused my friend to take his life all these years past. Perhaps it was something I should have done long ago.

Green says that Zanthos and his co-defendants are being chucked out on the same morning as me. My eyes widen when he tells me what they're in for this time. More foulness. The truly shocking part is that, having been rearrested after they were released at the halfway point of their sentence, they've now served their entire tariff, so all three of them will be completely free when they leave the prison. They won't have to meet with Probation. They will be able to continue their ways.

I hover near the gate when I'm unlocked. It's nearly dinner time, and I've been waiting all afternoon. I'm finding out the details of my bail hostel today so I breathe a sigh of relief as I spot my resettlement officer, Ella Brannigan, opening the houseblock door. She's a short woman with a long brown ponytail, which swishes behind her as I follow her to the library where we can talk. It smells nice in her slipstream, like strolling through a summer meadow.

Men stand in the doorways of their cells as we pass by. If probing stares were bullets, she'd resemble a colander by the time we are seated and out of sight. She leaves the library door open. A male officer would normally just do this in my cell, but women officers rarely work on this wing.

'You're due to leave soon,' she said.

'That's right.'

'Do you have somewhere to stay?'

'You said that I had to go to a bail hostel.'

'That was the plan, but it wasn't confirmed. There isn't space at this moment in time, so you will be under strict probation in the community.'

'You're kidding me.'

'I thought that would be good news. You will have much less onerous conditions this way.'

'It isn't great news if I don't have anywhere to live.'

'You can present to the council on your release and they'll help.'

'They won't have anything for someone like me.'

'Go straight there and explain you are homeless.'

'It's humiliating.'

'It's your predicament.'

'They gave me a tent and a sleeping bag last time I did that.'

'Perhaps they'll find something this time. Probation are still trying to get something. Maybe they'll have a place by the time you leave.'

I'm surprised but not angry. At least she came to tell me to my face. I've done my fair share of camping, but the recent news has been full of reports about this being the coldest week for a decade. I tell her as much.

'They open the churches for the homeless to sleep in if it gets below freezing,' she replies.

'Peachy.'

'It's better than outside. I've spoken to our benefits liaison officer and he can get you a £100 grant.'

'For warm clothing and a thick blanket, or two bottles of whisky and some strong rope?'

She gives me a tight smile and stands.

'The former, hopefully. You can use the day centre as a postal address for your Universal Credit claim, which I understand you've set up.'

She pushes her seat back, starts to hold her hand out, then thinks better of it. She walks through the doorway and is quickly down the stairs. I follow her out of the library. There's always a mountain to climb when you get out of prison: jobs, housing, money, getting your head around being free, etc., especially if you haven't got any support. I have neither the time nor the inclination to climb mine. I've had enough. She opens the wing gate, steps through, closes it, turns and stares at me while I walk towards her.

'Good luck,' she says. 'Let's hope this is the last occasion we see you.'

I feel like grabbing her fucking ponytail and pulling it through the bars. Then it really will be the final time she sees me. The blood begins to pound through my veins – always a bad sign – when the mixed-race prisoner who assaulted me, G, leaves the next wing to mine and walks towards me. He stops a good three metres away.

'Back from the gates, please,' says Green, who has appeared at my shoulder.

My visitor doesn't look like trouble. 'Let him speak,' I tell Green, who looks at me as though it's a dangerous idea, but then he strolls down the landing and out of sight.

'Do you remember me? My name is Grayson. For a while, I was your son.'

# 14

## THE COLD KILLER

It's hard to credit it, but the sinking feeling in my stomach immediately tells me it's the truth. I can picture the two-year-old boy who I used to pass a football to in the back garden. Small for his age, but he had a nice little foot on him. Grayson Reed. What do I say after all this time?

'You look well.'

He gives me a warm smile, which makes me think he's still a good kid, but he must be well into his twenties, and he's in jail.

'I wanted to say sorry for the kicking you got. Not my idea.'

'It's okay. It wasn't my first. I take it the big guy was to blame.'

'Yeah, my brother, Kevin. That's the thing. When he found out you were here, he planned to confront you after what you did to our mum.'

'What? I didn't do anything to her. She was better off without me.'

'She tells it different. You vanished when she was pregnant leaving her to bring us up alone.'

'She wasn't pregnant when I left. I just thought moving on was best for both of us.'

His casual expression fades for a moment, then he recovers.

'Yeah, she said not to bother looking for you. Don't sweat it. Kevin would have got into trouble even if he'd been born into the royal family. Mum raised us fine.'

I rattle the bars and shake my head.

'That's not how it was.'

'Anyway,' he says, 'I hear you're out in a few days. I just wanted to say there are a couple of photos of you in the house. I think I can recall being in the garden with you, but I can also remember waiting for you to come back to us.'

'I told you. I stayed away because you all deserved better.'

The Senior Officer, a big no-nonsense officer called Dalton, appears around the corner.

'Reed, away from the gate.'

'Yes, sir.' Grayson smiles at the SO and backs away while staring at me.

'Wait,' I shout. 'Is Brenda still in Peterborough?'

He waits for the SO to move out of sight, then edges back towards the gate.

'No, she hooked up with a guy and moved up north. He left not long after, she stayed. That was five years ago.'

'How come you're still in Peterborough?'

'Kevin wanted to search for you. I came to keep him out of trouble.'

'Why?'

'It's a long story.'

'Did you know I was in prison?'

'Yes, we asked around in a load of local pubs if anyone knew you. Turns out you have a heavy rep. Must be killing you, living on that wing. Kevin won't admit it, but I wouldn't be surprised if he didn't cause the fight that got us sent down deliberately, just so he could get in here. He can be mad like that. Won't let nothing stop him.'

'Stupid thing to get a record for.'

'It was already too late for that.'

I want to talk to him some more. He was such a cute little kid. How come it's only now that I understand that it wasn't only Brenda that I left? He gives me a rueful half-wave.

'Why did Kevin want to find me so much? What does KGB stand for?' I ask.

'Think about it. See ya around.'

'Wait. How can Kevin be your brother? You're different colours.'

'You really need to speak to my mum.'

'I don't get it.'

'My dad was a black guy from one of the aircraft bases. You're Kevin's father.'

## 15

### THE COLD KILLER

I watch him leave with an expression that must look as if I've got Bell's palsy. Just before he's out of sight, he stops, turns, and gives me a single firm nod. He's not lying. I lurch back to my cell, trying to process everything. The moment I open the door, I kneel and empty my breakfast into the toilet, eventually slumping beside it after dry-retching. No wonder they both looked familiar, and it's not surprising a much younger version of myself fancied his odds. Strangely, I don't feel so bad about what happened now, but it makes me feel worse about being stuck on this wing.

God, I haven't thought about Brenda in years. She was a nightmare, but great fun. If she wasn't drunk, she was angry. Although I suppose we all were back then. That boy was always fed and clean though, and that wasn't a given where she lived and grew up. What the hell do I do now? She had been putting on weight just before I vanished, but she said it was my fault for buying takeaways, which seemed reasonable at the time. Our volatile relationship meant that I regularly threatened to walk out. She said that if I left, I'd never be with her again. Perhaps we'll see about that.

KGB. Kevin, Grayson and Brenda. Jesus. I'd given up, but now I feel intrigued. I had lost interest in everything, even revenge. I pace my cell with my mind whirring, but, unlike almost everyone else in here, I'm getting out soon. It's time to settle some scores and revisit the past but, just maybe, I have something to live for. I was going to hurt Ricardo Zanthos and not worry about the consequences, but now I think I should be cautious. Too much of a beating and he might squawk, unless I can find an angle, which means he'll take whatever I dish out. Besides, after what Green told me about him and his co-defendants, it makes me wonder if all three of them were involved all those years ago. That's what these men do. They share their trophies. There's some digging to be done.

I'm going to have to work on Green too. The computer system will contain addresses, next of kins, all that jazz. I might be able to get out of here with a shopping list of things to do.

One of the few men who think they're tough on here, MacPherson, had Green pushed against the wall in the laundry yesterday for commenting on the messy state it was in. I wasn't there, but I heard about it. Apparently, Green shat himself. That might be my angle there. Not to put the frighteners on him, but to offer him protection instead.

At evening meal time, I wait near the servery as Zanthos dodders out of his cell, and step in behind him. He tentatively looks over his shoulder but stares back ahead before he makes eye contact. I guess you do that a lot when you've committed the crimes he has. He stops at the back of the queue and I tap his elbow.

'I hear you're out next week. What's the plan? Nice steak and a couple of kids, or straight back on the Internet?'

He only half turns and talks with his usual mocking tone.

'I'll be going home to my wife, who will cook me a marvellous meal. A trip to the beach for some fresh air would be most welcome. She could drive me, and then perhaps lunch at a secluded little pub I know near Old Hunstanton. Do you have anywhere to go back to?'

'No, I don't. Can I stay with you?'

'My wife would faint if I brought a beast like you home.'

'Interesting choice of words. Why the hell did she stick with you after the evil things you did?'

'Guilty by association. Bless her, but she didn't need to move house. All she did was get interviewed by the police, then disappear until I confessed to everything. We have a flat elsewhere in the city under a company name. The authorities don't look for you forever, especially if you haven't done anything wrong. Of course, she went back to our home in the end. All she has is me. I might be a little twisted, but I'm a very successful businessman. She enjoys the perks enough to tolerate the rest.'

The queue moves and he shuffles forward. I peel off before I reach the front and amble to the bottom of the wing, past Green's colleague, Raja, who is unnecessarily supervising the line of men. I still haven't seen any real aggro over here. Green is at the bottom of the wing, staring out of the window at a woman walking the sniffer dog around the perimeter. I rap my knuckles on the glass next to him. I expected him to jump, but he turns to me slowly.

'What is it?'

'How do you feel about Zanthos?'

'I despise him and the two creatures that got sent down with him.'

'What exactly did they do? You said abduction.'

Green stands up straight and takes a step towards me. Up close, he's a big, wide-shouldered man. It's a shame he has no spine.

'Why do you want to know?'

'They seem to be having too easy a time of it on this wing. It's not supposed to be a social club for sexual deviants.'

Green looks down the landing, perhaps to confirm that we're on our own.

'Nobody knows for sure what they did. One of them distracted a mother with a toddler at a park. When she looked back, her daughter was gone.'

'Jesus Christ. They took a kid that age?'

'Yes, it gets worse. There was no sign of the child for twenty-four hours, but then a member of the public rang the police to say they'd found a little girl walking around a playing field on her own, crying. Don't you remember? It was on the news?'

'No, I only watch that shite in here when I've got nothing better to do. The child was okay?'

'Well, kind of. The police gently questioned her. She said she lost her mummy and some people took her to a small caravan and then a warm house for the night. She was scared, but they said she would be back with her mum and dad in the morning. They gave her cakes and sweets, and a bath. She said there were lots of bright light flashes.'

Green leaves the last statement hanging in the air and walks away down the landing. I stare out as he did at the grey metal walls topped with razor wire. For much of my life, this place, and others similar, have been my home. Somewhere along life's path, I have become as happy behind bars as anywhere else. There is comfort in familiarity. On the outside, I feel compelled to live, whereas here I'm only expected to survive.

These last few months, I've had a sense of my life drawing to an end. It seemed there was nothing left for me. I had no purpose and I couldn't find pleasure from anything, but perhaps there is some good I can do. Being involved somehow with my children is probably a pipe dream but I let Frank down. I tried to forget him after he died, but he's always been there.

Maybe if I'd taken note of when his father was first released and made sure there was some real justice, I'd have been able to move on. People like old man Zanthos deserve a proper punishment. If he even looks at a child, I want my face to appear in his mind. That goes for all of them. But for my plan to work, I need their release addresses.

I walk to the office and see the unhinged prisoner, MacPherson, the one who scared Green recently, leave just before I get there. He spits on the floor in front of me but I ignore it. Green looks flustered sitting behind his desk. I stand in the doorway.

'Having a good day?' I ask him.

'Nothing a gun and sixty bullets couldn't sort out.'

'I like your thinking. Say, I'm considering giving Zanthos an experience he'll never forget.'

'There's too much CCTV to get away with anything here.'

'Cameras aren't as reliable as you might think.'

I reveal the trick to him. We talk for over half an hour. I've misjudged him somewhere along the line. In some ways, he's as damaged as the vulnerable people he is here to control. The lunatics really are running the asylum.

'What can I offer you in return?' I ask him.

'I need that idiot off my case. He won't do a thing I tell him and he's making me look stupid.'

'MacPherson?'

'Yes, and Thompson's doing my head in.'

'Thompson is a little prick. You need to man up yourself and sort him out. I can educate MacPherson for you. It's up to you how much. Is that all you want? You're taking a big risk. If we're rumbled, it will be bad news for both of us, but I've got little to lose.'

'Just have a word with MacPherson. You're a persuasive guy, and I'm sure he'll stop if you ask him. Nothing too brutal. If you get sent to the block, you'll probably never return to this wing. I'll get the addresses off the system for all three of them. Zanthos, Pfeiffer and Ballanchine.'

'Okay. It's a deal. MacPherson will remember our conversation even when I'm long gone. I understand fear. It controls people better than anything. I will be on MacPherson's and those old men's minds for the rest of their days.'

I stride back to my cell past Zanthos lying on his bed watching TV, clearly sleepy after his meal. I need to be careful. My plan calls for cold efficiency, but my rage is red hot.

# 16

## RICARDO ZANTHOS – TARGET ONE – 2ND DECEMBER

The elderly man shuffled back to his cell with his meagre dinner. It was common for the servery workers to give the geriatrics less because they knew they wouldn't complain. Zanthos didn't mind, because he often couldn't eat it all. His appetite for food had dwindled, even if his other urges hadn't. He rested his plastic plate on the table and tried the toilet again, managing only a few squirts. It was getting much worse, and that must only mean one thing.

There was no sense in seeing the prison doctors. He was out in less than two weeks and he had private healthcare. The cost was almost ruinous at his age, but he could afford it. What was the point of money if not to spend it? There were no children to leave it to anyway, and more than his wife could fritter away, even though she'd probably have a good go when he was gone.

It had been a shock, but not the terrible surprise most people would feel, when his oldest son, Frank, had killed himself. There was only one important thing in Zanthos's life and everything else paled in comparison. Zanthos's perversions had surfaced during puberty sixty-odd years ago even though there was no abuse in his own past; it was just the way he was made. He didn't see it as a weakness or a sickness. He liked looking at naked young children. That was it. Learning to keeping secrets had made him strong and ruthless, especially in business, and he'd earned millions before it all went wrong. The jury had found him guilty of making indecent images and the rape of a child, and he'd thought his life was over, but now he realised it was only time he'd lost.

God alone knew where his youngest lived now. The authorities had taken him away from them, which was probably for the best, because Zanthos's perverse cravings had grown as the years passed. Instead of the urges dwindling as his testosterone diminished, they became all-consuming. It was as though nothing else mattered in his life apart from where he was going to get his next hit.

Certainly not his wife. She'd been an absolute looker in her early twenties when they married, but he'd still struggled to be with her sexually. At the start, he could manage the gruesome deed, but he'd had to think about other things that interested him. They got on well in every other respect and he often wondered if she'd known or suspected. Then he'd found out that she'd been going through the motions too. They did say you ended up with the partner you deserved.

Zanthos was always exhausted now, though. He knew there was something not right in his body because he kept feeling incredibly faint. He had collapsed on the wing a month back. They said his blood pressure was low, but it had been that way for years. They took him to A & E, but those idiots had just confirmed a load of conditions all old people had. The private docs would take a much more thorough look at everything, but he didn't much care.

Zanthos wanted to sit in his back garden in a sturdy deckchair sipping a daiquiri and spending his time looking at the birds and insects in silence. He hoped he'd last a while yet, so he could grow his own vegetables next spring and pick his own fruit in the autumn in their lovely small orchard. He smiled at the thought of buying a brand-new hardback bestseller and smelling the pages. The prison library books made him sick with the filth that must have touched them before him.

It was a good feeling to know you were leaving prison, just like when he was a child, and his birthday and a much-wanted present were taking their time to arrive. There was truth to the wisdom that to experience the highs, you had to experience the lows first. Once he was free, the rest of his life would be a complete contrast to this smelly, noisy place and, of course, he still had the bunker to retreat to. That really was the pot of gold at the end of the rainbow.

It was hard to say exactly what the thrill of it was. Memories, he supposed. The computer in it was the pot of gold, but if Zanthos was Santa, that was his grotto.

Zanthos popped his head out of the cell doorway and looked along the landing. There was a big group of young men playing pool – killer, by the looks of it – and he strained to see beyond them to spot if they were queueing for medication yet. A wave of dizziness came over him. The officers would shout soon, but he'd need to leave his door open to hear it. He lay down on his bed, took his glasses off and his top dental plate out, and closed his eyes. He rested but concentrated on staying awake because he needed his meds.

The sounds of the wing retreated into the distance, which was odd because he didn't think he was drifting off. He looked up and there was someone standing at the end of his bed. The bright cell light made it hard for him to focus. Bloody fools. Why did the inmates think they could just wander into his cell without knocking? As he reached for his glasses, he saw that his door had been closed. A rumble of fear flickered in his stomach.

'What do you want?' he asked.

The man sat on the bed and calmly explained and Zanthos frantically tried to think of any answer that might help. The determined expression on the face of the man in front of him gave him no doubt of his intentions.

'I've paid my price,' he gasped as his mouth dried out. 'That's the law. I deserve to go home to die.'

Strong hands reached over his head and slipped one of the pillows out from behind him. Thick forearms rested across his body and over his puny biceps, and the pillow was pressed over his face. The man held it firmly in place and Zanthos immediately panicked, as his breathing was shallow at the best of times. He tried to buck and twist, but there was simply not enough strength left to fight the assailant off. To think he'd spoken politely to this person a few hours ago. Zanthos's head was squashed further into the mattress as he felt warm breath on his neck. The man spoke slowly and clearly as Zanthos's brain protested. Then a sharp pain struck through Zanthos's chest. Even in his last moments, he only felt sorry for himself.

# 17

## DI BARTON

Barton glanced at his watch and grimaced. It was time for him to leave work, and he wasn't looking forward to going home. There was no escaping from it, though. If he was late this evening, he'd only have to do it tomorrow night.

Zander and Strange entered the office simultaneously, even though they'd been busy doing different things. Barton had noticed they were a little off with each other since they went out for drinks together after the conclusion of The Ice Killer case, but Barton couldn't put his finger on what had changed. Strange sat down at a desk on his left and Zander at one on his right.

'Why are you scowling at me?' asked Zander.

'Was I?'

'Yes.'

'Sorry, unfortunately it's bath night tonight.'

'About time, too.' Strange smiled sweetly.

'Not mine, cheeky. I haven't been able to fit in a bath since 1994. It's my mum's.'

Barton's mother had come to live with him and his family since developing dementia. It had been easy so far, good even. She had been like a child enjoying a holiday to begin with, but now she was deteriorating rapidly, both physically and mentally. She might be fine for a whole day, then wake up the next morning screaming, not knowing where she was or who he was. Barton's wife, Holly, now woke her with a cup of tea in a beaker because Holly's size made her less threatening.

'Do you have to bathe your mum, then?' asked Zander with a frown.

'No, but I have to help cajole her into it. She's even less enthusiastic about baths than Luke, and he's seven. My wife does the actual bathing, but Holly couldn't get her out last time, so I had to help.'

Zander gave a little cringe. 'Can't be easy.'

'You should be proud that you're man enough to be there for her,' said Strange, pointedly.

'It isn't that,' replied Barton. 'Although obviously it's not ideal, but my mum cried when I last helped her out. She kept saying, "No, Dad, no," which was how she often referred to my father. It's a terrible disease. I keep thinking she was such a proud, stubborn woman that she would rather be dead than suffer the indignity.'

All three of them were staring grimly at each other as they considered that possibility when their boss, DCI Cox, strode into the office. Since returning from maternity leave, she had real focus. Her suit looked as though it cost more than Barton's car. She peered around the room at the sea of glum faces and smiled.

'Looks like I'm just in time with my interesting news,' she said.

'Pay rise?' asked Strange.

'Extra holiday?' asked Zander.

'Consider it an early Christmas present,' replied Cox. 'Do you remember Ricardo Zanthos?'

Barton closed his eyes for a moment as he dredged his memory.

'Oh, yes. How could I forget? The newspapers called them The Three Paedos like The Three Amigos.'

'The very same,' said Cox.

'Thank the Lord that we weren't involved in that case. I'd have struggled to be nice,' said Zander, while playfully punching his palm.

'There's only two of them now,' said Cox. 'Zanthos is dead.'

'That is good news. Did God send down a bolt of lightning?' asked Zander.

'No, and it might not be natural causes.'

'Really? Wait a minute,' said Barton. 'I'm sure I got an email a little while back to warn us that him and his cronies were coming to the end of their sentences and that they would be released without being under probation. Wasn't he still inside?'

'That's right,' said Cox. 'He died in prison.'

# 18

## DI BARTON – WEDNESDAY 4TH DECEMBER

Barton's suspicious nature kicked in. He knew hard work when it landed in front of him. Strange, on the other hand, beamed.

'His crimes were obviously before my time up here, but I've always wanted to investigate in a prison,' she said with enthusiasm.

'Before you get too excited, I'm betting this won't be simple,' said Barton. He raised an eyebrow in Cox's direction; she smiled.

'Why's that?' asked Strange.

'Prison murder victims are usually killed by their cellmate over what to watch on TV, or if one of them is too messy. Inmates live their lives on the edge, and it's often something small that escalates. But our boss here only said "might" not be natural causes. She didn't name a person who killed Zanthos this morning.'

'On the ball as always, John,' said Cox.

'Did it happen today?' asked Barton.

'No, he died two days ago,' replied Cox. 'The prison staff didn't notice until lock-up around seven on Monday night. Zanthos was lying on his bed and failed to respond when the officer asked if he was okay. He wasn't breathing and was cold. At his age, they assumed that he'd peacefully passed away. There was no sign of a disturbance and no visible injuries. The prison doctor knew he was ill, and he'd been to the hospital for tests, which confirmed he didn't have long to go without help, but when you get near eighty, the operations are likely to kill you faster than any underlying illness, so they just upped his meds instead.'

'Why are we involved, then?' asked Zander.

'The prison has to investigate all deaths in custody, like we do, but they get a lot more than us, and they have a different system to follow. Even though it was probable that he died naturally, they still put a file together for the coroner. The security staff know what they're doing and everything seemed normal, but last night they realised that when they checked the security cameras on the wing, one of them had something sprayed on it a few hours before lock-up that evening.'

Barton steepled his fingers for a moment and considered that titbit.

'That means if someone went into his cell after that, they wouldn't be seen,' he said. 'Sneaky. Is there anything else pointing to foul play?'

Cox shrugged and placed a piece of paper on Barton's desk.

'They said they finished the investigation this afternoon. Here's the contact at the prison. I mentioned you'd pop in on your way home. He didn't sound desperate, so it might be inconclusive.'

Barton's mind caught up with the situation.

'Has a PM been ordered? Please tell me the cell hasn't been cleared.'

'Of course. The post-mortem is due tomorrow morning. As I said, they have everything in hand, but they've called us in as a precaution. See how you get on.'

And with that Cox exited the room leaving Barton staring from one sergeant to the other.

'I'll take Kelly with me,' he said.

Zander nodded his head, as though he was happy to stay, and Barton and Strange left and went down to the car park. Barton had cycled in to work that morning as a gesture to staying healthy, even though he only lived a mile away, so they took Strange's car. Barton smiled because it looked like rain and he could ask her to drop him off at home afterwards.

'What's the plan when we reach the prison?' asked Strange.

'Just chat to whoever's in charge. Cox knows that the PM results will direct the investigation at this point, so there's no huge rush, but we need to have shown an interest. The prison and us are on the same team. It's gone six now, so by the time we get into the jail the inmates will be locked away and we'll be able to easily visit the landing and look inside the cell without any grief.'

'Ah, yes. We don't want to run the risk of being lynched, seeing as we're responsible for a lot of them being in there.'

Barton laughed. 'To be honest, it's not that bad in there. Remember, Peterborough is a local jail, so most of the prisoners are short-termers or they're on remand. The serious felons are usually moved on quickly when they're sentenced. There might be the odd nutter, but we can cope with that. Although it's true, if the inmates recognise us, they'll still take the piss given half the chance. The death happened on the sex offenders' wing, though. It's a different vibe from the main wings.'

Strange parked up outside the prison, and they'd only been waiting at the gatehouse for five minutes when their contact from security arrived. She was a middle-aged woman in a loose suit.

'All right? I'm Jessie Quick,' she said with a smile, in a thick Liverpudlian accent. 'I'll take you through to the security suite and you can see the footage. I'm not as suspicious as I was earlier because I've double-checked the CCTV going back over the previous week and haven't spotted anything interesting.'

They wandered through the admin area of the prison, where

the desks were empty. The security office was on the second floor. Quick gestured to two seats, which were in front of a desk and facing a huge screen. She went around the other side of the desk and, after a few presses on the keyboard, brought up a recording on the big TV. It was like staring through a windscreen without wipers in heavy rain.

'As you can see,' she said. 'Not very helpful.'

'But obviously, it's suspicious,' replied Barton.

'Yes, but it's the only questionable aspect of the whole case. I've been and checked back and there are other cameras on the wing that have been messed with over the past few months.'

'Is that usual?'

'Yes, of course. Inmates can sneak under the camera and smudge it without being identified. Even if you could tell who they are, they may well have done it to cover for someone else, or they could be playing silly buggers and doing it to mess with our heads.'

Barton nodded. He knew that if you gave criminals nothing to do in a cell all day, they'd just think of ways to annoy and irritate, if not to break the law.

'There were no incidents on these other occasions of camera smudging?' asked Strange.

'No, although we wouldn't always hear. If you get a kicking in here and you live to tell the tale, it's usually best to suck it up, especially on that wing. No one likes a paedophile. Being a grass as well isn't helpful. Do you want to see the cell?'

'Definitely,' said Barton.

It was dark and gloomy when they stepped outside to walk to the houseblocks. A gentle, misty rain had arrived, which gave the place an almost fog-like glow under the bright lights around the prison. It was eerily quiet; the clang of metal locks the only sound. Quick had unlocked and closed about twenty doors by the time they reached the wing they were heading for. You'd need to be Spiderman to get out of here, thought Barton.

Barton occasionally wondered if those he had caught and prosecuted sat in their cells cursing his name after they'd been sent down, or if they took it on the chin seeing as they were guilty anyway. When they opened the houseblock door, he saw five wings stretching off a central observing area. A woman's head popped up in a window of the room in the middle. Quick gave her a thumbs-up.

'That's the night staff,' said Quick.

Barton could hear music and shouting from the wings. He shook his head at Quick.

'How long does this go on for?' he asked.

'A couple of hours. The night staff will ask them to turn it down around nine. If they don't, we cut the power to their cells.'

The VP wing, though, was quiet. Barton stared along the expanse of cell doors and scowled at the thought of most of the county's sex offenders watching TV behind them. Meanwhile, on the outside in the community, people's lives had been ruined or ended. Quick spoke as she walked, seemingly as if she could read his mind.

'The sex offenders get the longest sentences, but they're the hardest for our prison to move on. To have their risk downgraded and move to a C-Category jail, they need to confess to their crimes first to show there's a prospect of rehabilitation. Many of them won't, despite the damning evidence against them, so they rot in B-Cat jails for years where there aren't many courses or education. The man who died had never given any details of his crimes, although he admitted his guilt at court to get the third off for a guilty plea. He was actually due to leave shortly. Such a crying shame he'll never get out.'

'I take it he won't be missed,' asked Barton.

'Truthfully, he was no trouble. He never came up on our radar in security. Few of the men on here are a concern if they don't have access to women or children. The main issue is them swapping photos or catalogues, or having pictures sent in.'

'People send in child porn for them?' asked Strange with disgust.

'No, family photos, which aren't allowed. Remember, these men usually say they were set up or just plain innocent. Sometimes, for their wives and relatives, it's easier to believe them.'

She stopped outside cell number thirteen. It was the only cell with a padlock on the front.

'Unlucky for some,' she said without smiling. She unlocked the padlock. 'This lock is to stop the staff going in here.'

'Why would the staff want to go in there?' asked Strange.

'We're always short on equipment. I doubt any of the officers would shed a tear for this guy, so there may be a few who wouldn't care about this investigation, or maybe they'd just need the TV or the mattress for another cell. I assume you'll want CSI in here.'

'Yes, we'll get it sorted tomorrow and then you can have the cell back,' said Barton.

He stared through the doorway after she had opened the door, but didn't enter. This would be the only chance to retrieve any meaningful evidence from the room before the next resident moved in. The cell was clean and tidy. Funny to think this had been a man's home for years. Barton's eyes scanned the little luxuries: soaps, shampoos, a tube of mints. His gaze dropped to the carefully folded underwear and paired socks on the shelves.

The bed was made with the imprint of a body on the thin-looking duvet. The pillow had a deep head-shaped dint in it.

'No signs of struggle. No attempts at resuscitation,' he stated.

'No, he was stone cold.'

There wasn't any point in entering the cell, so Quick locked up.

'I'll nip to the mortuary tomorrow lunchtime,' said Barton. 'I haven't seen a friend of mine in there for a while. I'll give CSI your name, assuming you're in tomorrow.'

'Yes, I'll be here. We'll see what both bring up, but I doubt it'll be much.'

Barton looked around the wing. Each cell had a door card next to it with the name of the occupant and a picture. He walked slowly down the line of doors and read each one. He knew most of the names, if not the faces. The Child Abuse Investigation Team would have nicked most of them as opposed to CID. Many admitted their guilt at court. Not to save their victims the trauma of a trial, but to save themselves having to argue against the glaring, sickening facts in front of their own families.

Zanthos had been an ill man. Barton didn't care that he was dead. After what he'd done, it was hard to feel any sympathy, although he might have family who'd be upset, despite his crimes. Yet, Barton didn't fancy investigating his death either. Offences against children were sometimes the simplest to investigate because the teams were so motivated, but not many would give a shit about a pervert who might have met an early end.

The law was the law, though, and good police placed their feelings aside. Barton always put everything into every case because investigations had a habit of snowballing. Cases involving children had a habit of leading down paths where nobody wanted to go. Barton had a feeling that this case was just the beginning of something terrible.

# 19

## DI BARTON

Barton and Strange left the prison and returned to the car park. Barton looked back at the barred windows and smiled, grateful that he got to return to his family and a cold beer.

'That was weird,' said Strange. 'I've been in a jail before but not on male wings, so I've never really had a feel for it. It's a relief to get outside. It's also nice to think I can go home and do whatever I like.'

'Yes, I agree wholeheartedly.'

Strange shivered and zipped up her coat.

'It's a shame that most criminals don't consider that side of things when they're planning their crimes,' she said. 'I suppose they reckon they'll get away with it.'

'Correct, although I wonder sometimes with the sex offenders. They tend to be a brighter bunch, from all walks of life. I think they know they might end up behind bars, but they do it anyway because they don't have a choice, it's a compulsion.'

'Bunch of sickos,' replied Strange.

'I agree with that too, as would most, which makes our job here difficult. The list of people who'd want to hurt a man like Zanthos is usually a mile long. At least in this case, if it was murder, the killer had to be on the wing, so we've narrowed it down to sixty or so.'

'I guess Mortis could find an injection point or bruises on the corpse,' said Strange.

'Exactly, or more likely a big tumour or a disease-riddled heart, which would make it conundrum solved.'

They got in Strange's car and were soon driving down the village road to Barton's house. She swung the vehicle into Barton's street but didn't park up.

'Fancy a coffee, or something stronger? We haven't spoken much lately,' he said.

'No, it's okay. I keep saying I'm going to get into running again, but never do. I really feel like some fresh air right now.'

'No worries. Before you go, how are you and Zander getting along?'

Strange ran her fingers through her blonde hair and laughed.

'That obvious, is it?'

'No, I'm just a very perceptive person.'

Strange didn't laugh at that, so Barton kept quiet.

'Right. I'll tell you, because I don't have many people to talk to about this sort of thing, but do not breathe a word to anyone, especially not to him.'

'Scouts' honour.'

'After the Ice Killer got sentenced, you left Zander and me to have a few drinks to celebrate the result. To cut a long story short, we were on the tequilas well before it was dark. I woke up in his bed, partially clothed, with very little recollection of what the hell happened before then. It was seven o'clock and I had a doctor's appointment at nine, so I quietly dressed, left a note, and sneaked out.'

'And the problem is?'

'Neither of us have mentioned it since, and it was over a month ago.'

'Why don't you ask him if he remembers what happened?'

Strange shook her head at him.

'Do you know nothing about women? Get out of my car, you crazy man.'

Barton left the vehicle, chuckling. Then he realised he'd forgotten to ring Holly to say he was going to be a bit late. The front door was unlocked, so he edged inside and stealthily tiptoed towards the kitchen door, which was half open. He could hear Holly's voice.

'A camping holiday isn't a vacation. For mothers, it's just looking after your children in a less convenient location.'

'Exactly,' said another voice. Barton recognised his wife's friend, Emma, who hated all men after her husband had moved to France without telling her.

'They expect us to go to work but still do the majority of the domestic chores,' replied Holly.

'When we said we wanted it all, we didn't realise that meant doing it all,' said Emma.

Barton detected a slurring of words and the cackling was a warning too. Even though the fridge was Barton's closest friend, entering the kitchen at this moment would be as suicidal as blundering into a lion's den with a freshly slaughtered goat over his shoulder. He stepped back a few paces.

'We heard you, John,' shouted Holly. 'Come in, let's have your lame reason for being late.'

Barton poked his head around the door.

'I was in prison,' he said.

Holly giggled. 'That's better than your usual excuses. Bath time's over, you'll be pleased to hear. Emma helped me. We pretended it was a spa, and she was in and out no bother.'

'Where is Mum now?'

'Watching cartoons with Luke.'

'Going to join them, are you?' said Emma, with a smile. 'Holly was just saying how helpful you are around the house.'

'Hey, I do my bit. You don't see Holly under the car when there's a problem with it, and who carries all the cases on holiday?'

Barton realised Holly had definitely been drinking as she snorted.

'Oh, John.' She laughed. 'Good try. His idea of sorting our car out is to make the AA guy a coffee when he arrives, and only a man would think picking four suitcases off a carousel once a year is the same as a year's worth of hoovering and dusting.'

The women laughed their heads off as Emma topped up Holly's glass. There were no wins for Barton here, only further punishment, so he walked out of the room. As he closed the door, he heard a final comment from Emma.

'In some countries they have donkeys to carry their bags for them. They're sweeter and more reliable.'

'They probably smell better, too.' Holly laughed.

Grumbling, Barton went into the lounge and said hello to his mum and Luke, but they both ignored him. *Masha and the Bear* were on the TV and Luke and his mum each clutched a big fluffy toy. Luke had a Porg figure from a recent *Star Wars* film, and his mum had Bugs Bunny. It was sad. His mother had shrunk and regressed so much that she and Luke appeared almost the same size. Barton had seen a lot of dementia in his career but it didn't make it less shocking. After wandering over, he kissed them both on the top of their heads. His mother shooed him out of the way so he plonked himself next to them on the sofa and tried not to think of the next stage.

# 20

## DI BARTON – THURSDAY 5TH DECEMBER

It was still dark when Barton heard the floorboards creak towards his bedroom. He opened his eyes, expecting to see Luke standing over him, but instead it was his mother who hovered millimetres above him.

'I had a scary dream,' she said.

Barton considered a quip that it was him who'd had the shock, but he held his tongue and got out of bed. He guided his mum down the stairs to the kitchen and turned the oven on. There were three packs of bacon in the fridge, so he opened them, filled two oven trays and slid them in to cook. It was another coping method. Life was never as bad with a bacon or sausage sarnie in your hand. He smiled when he realised all his coping methods involved food.

Barton hadn't noticed that his mum had put the kettle on and was making three cups of tea. He watched her to make sure she was safe while thinking that dementia was such a strange disease. When she'd finished, she handed him a mug with a skeletal shaking hand and placed another on the kitchen table.

'That's for your dad when he gets up.'

Barton thought that really would be a nightmare if his long-deceased father turned up to drink it.

After fifteen minutes, Layla, Luke and Holly had been drawn downstairs by the smell. Lawrence needed earth diggers to get him up nowadays. After constructing their sandwiches, they all sat around the table and tucked in. It wasn't until they'd nearly finished that Barton noticed his mum had only taken a few small bites of hers.

'What did you used to say to me when I was little, Mum? Big belly bust before good food be lost.'

'Sorry, John. It doesn't seem to be going down easily.'

'That's okay. Go in the lounge with Luke if you're finished, and I'll bring you another cup of tea.'

After she'd gone, Barton started doing the washing up and he gave Holly a meaningful look so she could see what a good boy he was being. Holly put her arms around him.

'I meant to tell you yesterday. When we bathed her, she was much thinner than last week. And the day before, I found her dinner in the bin. She's deteriorating fast. I'll get her another appointment with the doctor.'

'I'll come with you. Work owe me enough hours.'

Barton spent the next hour attempting to put a flatpack wardrobe together and was in a foul mood by the time he needed to leave for the mortuary. He could have rung Mortis for the results, but sometimes it helped to look at the body. Different questions often arose when the harsh truth was staring you in the face. The pathologist, Mortis, whose real name was Menteith, was a silver-haired Scotsman who had a wide breadth of knowledge. He was an important part of the team.

Luke had his cap gun out and had been irritating everyone just before he went to school and while Barton was getting ready to leave. Barton nipped into the lounge to say goodbye to his mum, who was still on the sofa. Luke was leaping around, shouting, 'Yee-hah,' and shooting his mum's fluffy bunny from close range.

His mum's gaze dropped from the TV, which had been turned off, and she spoke in a slow, loud, sinister voice to Luke.

'It's a very bad habit to shoot at a rabbit,
Although you may think it fun,
But it wouldn't be so funny, if you were the bunny,
Or he was holding the gun.'

The corners of Luke's mouth slowly drooped, then he burst into tears and ran out of the room. Barton remembered his mum saying that rhyme to him as a child and, despite Luke's upset, it was nice to see she was on form today. He stepped from the house, hearing Holly talking to Luke.

'She said what about the rabbit?'

'Nanny said it was going to shoot me.'

* * *

Zander only lived in the next village along, so Barton picked him up and they drove to the hospital, parked up and strolled to the mortuary on the ground floor.

'We're not here to watch it, are we?' asked Zander.

'No, just to weigh the organs,' replied Barton.

'Very funny.'

Mortis was drinking a coffee in the post-mortem room when they arrived.

'Can I get you one?' he asked.

They both shook their heads. The bodies were kept in cooler drawers, so, unless the staff had been examining an old corpse, the room rarely smelled different from anywhere else in the hospital.

But Zander reckoned there were particles in the air, and neither he nor Barton wanted to open their mouths unnecessarily.

'Nice of you to pop in. You shouldn't have bothered. We have a telephone,' said Mortis, with his usual deadpan tone.

'We missed you,' said Barton. 'How's your wife?'

Mortis's wife had just got over a cancer scare.

'Back to normal, and her results are imminent to see if they've found it all. She's great. Demands sex every day.'

'Nice. With anyone we know?' asked Zander.

Mortis cracked a small smile.

'Who says this kind of work isn't fun?' he said. 'Right. Mr Zanthos. You want to hear if his death was suspicious or not. The facts are, he was an old man on plenty of medication with many problems. The Grim Reaper would have had him in his diary. It seems he died of coronary atherosclerosis, very normal.'

'Heart attack through furred arteries?' said Zander.

'Well done. Very furred in this instance.'

'Not murder, then? Case closed?' asked Barton.

This time, Mortis's smile was wide.

'Not so fast. There are a few suspicious clues. He could have been attacked, which then caused the heart attack. Were there signs of assault in the cell?'

'No,' replied Barton. He took a deep breath. 'Go on, what is it?'

'If you wanted to kill someone old like this and not leave a sign, suffocation is by far the best method. This man's muscles had atrophied, so he'd have struggled to fight off a determined baby. Even in healthy people, we sometimes can't tell if someone's been suffocated. There are a few signs to look out for. Often people bite the inside of their mouth as they panic, which might not show in this case due to the absence of teeth on the top row. There are some bruised cells around the mouth, not many, but noticeable under a microscope.'

'So, he could have had his face smothered, but, due to being weak and having bad circulation, he couldn't struggle much, and the stress brought on a heart attack?' asked Zander.

'Correct.'

'Bollocks,' said Barton. 'Is that likely?'

'No, I'd guess he just checked out. Ill-fitting dentures easily damage the mouth at his age and any bruising could have occurred as he ate.'

'But you're saying it's inconclusive.'

'That's right.'

'Brilliant,' replied Barton.

'That's what I like. Another happy customer. Bring biscuits next time.'

Zander and Barton said their goodbyes and returned to the car park. Barton drove them back towards the police station.

'Investigation time?' asked Zander.

'Yes and no. What have we got?'

'A dead body and an inconclusive PM.'

'If he had died at home, this case would be filed away, but it happened in custody, so the coroner will want us to probe deeper. We'll need to return to the prison tomorrow and talk to everyone who was on the wing that day. If we do it now, then we might find something, even if we don't realise it at the time. If we leave it, even for a week, quite a few will have left or been transferred.'

'Right. Who are you planning on taking?'

'Strange.'

'It's okay, I'll do it.'

'You hated it last time we did it, what, five years ago? Said you had to hit the pads for an hour afterwards to disperse the rage.'

'Exactly. I want to save Kelly from that.'

'She wants the experience. Shall I tell her you said not to let her do it?'

'Very amusing. The people on that wing get in your mind, though.'

'Talking of Kelly, how are you two getting on?'

Zander shifted in his seat. 'What did she say to you?'

'Nothing.'

'Good.' Zander paused and Barton could see he was waging an internal struggle. 'Between you and me, she slept over at mine after we went out a while back.'

Barton merely nodded. He thought he could see where this was going, but he was wrong.

'But,' said Zander, 'she left, all sneaky like, and I can't remember what happened.'

'Why don't you ask her?'

Zander stared at him as though he was bonkers and turned the radio on.

# 21

## DI BARTON – FRIDAY 6TH DECEMBER

Barton arose early the next morning and left the house before anyone else got up. The previous afternoon, he'd spoken to the manager who was running the prison this week, who had agreed that he would lock down the VP wing until Barton was finished. It would be a long day, but it was the only way to do it.

Strange picked Barton up and they arrived outside the jail at 8 a.m. She was dressed as though she was going to a funeral and Barton wondered if this was deliberate, considering where they were spending the day.

'Zanthos's crimes were before my time,' she said. 'Do you remember them clearly?'

'I can just about remember the earlier case because of the horror of the son killing himself before exposing his father. The little girl's abduction was pretty shocking, but it never quite caught national attention because the child turned up the next day and said she wasn't abused, even though we knew she was. They admitted abduction because the evidence gave them no choice. Luckily, there was no trial and cross-questioning, because the girl thought she was well treated and there was nothing to be gained from making her think otherwise. The perpetrators probably thought they'd get a soft sentence because of that, but the judge slammed them for twelve years.'

'Were you part of the investigation?'

'No, I was away on a course, but DCI Cox was involved initially, until specialists took over. I read the case file last night. It was gutting reading, because the kid who was abducted said she wasn't touched in a bad way. But your mind starts imagining things. I've always hated child cases since having my own, but we have a job to do.'

'Yes, I'm not looking forward to interviewing sixty sex offenders, to be honest. It sounds like a lot of effort for an elderly man who probably just died, especially considering what he did.'

'Correct, but the prison needs to show that it looks after all its residents, as they like to refer to them now, whatever they've done, especially if they're old and infirm. Due process has to be followed because all of us are under such scrutiny. If someone else dies in the prison next week in similar circumstances, we'd be deeply in the shit for not having investigated the earlier death.'

'Do you reckon we'll get anything from the inmates?'

'You watch. You'll learn a lot about the type of men on this sort of wing, and they won't all be sex offenders. Some will be on there for an easier life, perhaps for their own protection because they've stolen or borrowed on other wings. There are regular prisoners who look like paedophiles, but aren't. Of course, there will be rapists, and others who committed crimes thirty years ago and DNA advances have caught up with.'

'Will the inmates be out of their cells?'

'Normally, yes, but don't worry. They'll keep them locked up until we've finished, just letting them out individually for appointments. We might get some banter from the other wings as we walk in, but that's all part of the experience. The VP wing won't complain about being shut in as a mainstream wing would do. They will know someone has died on their landing and an investigation is imminent.'

'Won't they clam up?'

'Some will, but others won't be able to stop themselves from blabbing. As you know, human nature can be a wonderful thing for detectives. I'll have a shortlist of possible candidates at the end of this, I bet. We'll then put it on file in the hope that we'll never look at it again. On the other hand, there might be a killer about who now has a taste for it.'

Strange took a deep breath at the gatehouse and followed Barton in. Barton knew the man who met them. His call sign was Victor One, and he ran the prison until the men were locked away when a night manager arrived.

'Monty,' said Barton. 'Long time.'

'John, good to see you. You look well.'

Barton introduced Bill Montgomery to Strange, and they walked up some stairs to Montgomery's office. He passed Barton a box full of files.

'I'll get you both a coffee,' he said.

Barton looked through the records. He had every prisoner's details, from their crime, sentence, start and release date, but also their pre-convictions, which gave him their entire record. He flicked through Zanthos's file, which was on the top. It was proof of a lifetime of criminality that was hard to understand. Montgomery returned with their drinks.

'We have a small library on the VP wing where you can do your interviews. If you spend five minutes for each one, it will take you around five hours. We'll serve their lunches straight to their cells so they won't come out and discuss anything. The wing officers are Green and Raja. They were both on the night Zanthos was found. There were fifty-eight prisoners on the wing that evening. You'll need to interview all remaining fifty-seven. Luckily, no one has been transferred or left since, although we have quite a few leaving next week, both releases and transfers.'

'And you've cleared this with the prison intelligence officer?'

'Yes, some of the inmates are under investigation by other agencies. Those agencies have been notified and confirmed receipt. These are voluntary interviews, so if we go to compulsory, we'll notify them again. There'll obviously be forms to fill if you want to remove any of them from the prison for interviewing at a later date. This wing contains some of our most dangerous men.'

'Do you have any theories on what happened?' asked Barton.

'I'd say he died of natural causes. Green's a weak officer, but Raja knows the score and would have an idea if there was any disquiet on the wing.'

'Any intel after the event from listening in to their phone calls or reading their post?'

'No, nothing really. A few commented on it, but they all think he passed from natural causes. It's a fear for some here, dying alone.'

They needed to wait until the inmates had been given breakfast before they went over, so Montgomery took them on a tour of the jail. He showed them the gym, healthcare, the block, and visits, including the new video suite where court hearings took place without the inmate leaving the prison. They even sneaked a sausage sandwich each from the kitchens.

At 9 a.m., exact details of their recording devices, power cables and laptops were taken. Then they walked over to the male houseblocks. Barton hung back and watched Strange's face as the big metal doors were opened and the unique aroma raced out to greet them.

'God,' she said. 'Does it always smell like that?'

'It's worse in the mornings because nobody's showered yet and the windows have been closed all night,' said Monty. 'But after a few minutes, you won't even notice it.'

They walked in and strolled towards Y-wing, where it appeared the officers had locked down the wing. A few mainstream prisoners were still queueing at the med hatch just outside. One of them spotted Strange and he turned round with a 'how you doing?' expression on his face, but withered under her glare. Montgomery opened the gates for them. They entered and the two wing officers walked over and Monty introduced them all.

'I'll leave you with Raja and Green. Have them ring me if you need anything. Do you want lunch? I can take you to the staff canteen or get some sandwiches sent over.'

'Sandwiches would be great,' said Barton. 'We'll be as fast as possible so hopefully your residents won't be locked up all day.'

Montgomery was the same age as Barton and smiled at his use of the term 'residents'. Even the prisoners thought calling them that was ridiculous. Yet Barton knew it made sense. Being called a prisoner or a junkie stripped away that person's identity. If you wanted people to change, they needed to have some self-respect, and some pride, so they could try to forge a new path. People who considered themselves worthless easily quit and returned to old ways, or just gave up completely. And if that happened, society, and therefore the innocent, suffered in the long run.

Raja and Green shook hands with the detectives. Raja had a firm grip, but Green's was weak. Green left to check everyone was behind their doors, while Raja beckoned them up the stairs to the library.

Calling it a library was a stretch, thought Barton. It was a room with three bookcases crammed with ageing paperbacks and a plain metre-long desk with three tired-looking plastic chairs. Weak sunlight lit up the swirling dust, which showed it wasn't a popular place. Strange sat down and placed the box of files on the floor behind her. Barton eyed the other chair suspiciously, but it held as he sat on it gingerly. Raja handed them a piece of A4 paper, then stood at the door.

'Fifty-six cells, mostly singles, a few are empty. That's the list from that night. How do you want to play it?'

'We'd like to talk to you and Green about the prisoners, but I'll do it after I've interviewed everyone, so I can judge their reactions without any bias. If you could unlock the first man and send him in, then get the next one to wait on a chair outside. It'll be quicker that way. Anything I need to know beforehand?'

'Some of these men are violent, but I doubt they'd do anything stupid. Some will need to pass parole boards to be released, so their behaviour over the years is important. Zanthos, Pfeiffer and Ballanchine's release date is in a few days.'

Raja widened his eyes slightly at that. Barton nodded respectfully at Raja and began to suspect his understated style made him good at his job.

'Do you think Pfeiffer and Ballanchine might have had anything to do with it?' he asked.

Raja shook his head and chuckled. 'No, they were thick as thieves, and you'll see they aren't the type. Who would you like first?'

'Let's start with cell one.'

'Um, that's the special double with the wide door.'

'And?'

'The inmate is in a wheelchair. Paralysed down his right-hand side after a stroke.'

'Okay,' said Barton with a smile. 'I'll speak to him briefly at the end, but we can probably rule him out.'

'Cell two, then. Mr Balchunas.'

'He's also disabled, but I'll send him up.'

Raja left with a grin. Strange looked at Barton as she opened her notebook.

'This might be easier than we thought,' she said.

Barton and Strange set the recorders up. He would need to tell the men they shouldn't say anything if they thought it might incriminate themselves, but that was fine. If they clammed up, which was likely, they would go on the list. But Barton knew many of them would have a natural inclination to help, especially if they weren't involved. Maybe it was just a human urge to be useful. Balchunas walked in, bowed, and stood to attention behind the chair as though he'd turned up for a firing squad. His right arm was missing from the elbow down.

# 22

## DI BARTON – PRISONER INTERVIEWS – CELL 2

Balchunas eyed them suspiciously after entering. Barton introduced Strange and himself, cautioned him, and explained that the conversation was being recorded. He also informed the inmate of his right to free legal advice.

'Sit down, please. This is an information-gathering exercise,' said Barton. 'Are you happy to continue?'

Balchunas nodded cautiously.

'You're serving a sentence of six months for indecent exposure.'

'Yes, but I'm innocent.'

Barton had already looked at the man's crimes.

'You exposed yourself outside the rowing club.'

'I went pee. Tricky one arm.'

'Wouldn't that make it more necessary to urinate in a toilet as opposed to in public?'

'I homeless, sleep rough.'

'Did you know the person who died on here four days ago?'

'Someone dead?'

'Yes. Tell me what you think might have happened.'

'How die?'

'That will be all, Mr Balchunas.'

* * *

*Cell 3*

The next man confirmed he was happy to talk. It was Zander's nemesis, Thompson. He was short, thin and menacing-looking with a thick boxer's nose. Barton saw he was fifty-five.

'Mr Thompson. Did you know the man who died?'

'Yes, he was a pervert. Good riddance.'

'Do you know if anyone wanted to punish him?'

'We all wanted to hurt him. He was a smug prick and a sex offender.'

'You got convicted of raping your first wife twenty years ago. Doesn't that make you a sex offender?'

'We were married. How can that be rape?'

'You also have a history of violence against others, including children. Did you have anything to do with Mr Zanthos's demise?'

'If I'd done it, they'd still be mopping up the blood.'

* * *

*Cell 4*

Mr Smith, twenty-two, sexual assault of eight girls in a school playground, who, apart from wearing stone-washed double denim, closely resembled Tony Blair, took the seat. He sounded remarkably normal.

'Yes, I knew Mr Zanthos very well.'

'You were his friend.'

'We were lovers.'

'Right.' Barton rubbed his eyes. 'Did you murder him?'

'No, we were due to be married.'

'You don't say.'

'Not really, he was my father. Madonna is the one for me.'

'That's it for now, thank you,' said Barton.

*Cell 9*

Mr Drummond, mid-forties, walked in with a scowl. After the formalities, he crossed his arms. 'No comment.'

'We haven't asked you anything yet,' said Strange. 'We just want to know if you saw Mr Zanthos arguing with anyone.'

Drummond leaned forward with real malevolence in his eyes. He put his hands under his chin and smiled sweetly, then crashed his hands onto the table and roared, 'No comment.'

'That will be all, Mr Drummond,' said Barton.

'Fuck you.'

*Cell 12*

Mr Platt, mid-sixties, investment fraud, good shape, strode in and did a double take.

'Mr Barton,' he said. 'They finally caught you, eh? I knew you were crooked. Welcome to the wing. I only have a single cell, but I'm happy to share.'

'Tempting, Mr Platt. I'm just here to ask some questions.'

'Yes, I killed that dirty old man. He was rude to me.'

'How did you kill him?'

'Prison beans give me deadly farts. I straddled him and gave him a full load.'

Barton heard a brief titter come from Strange before she nipped it in the bud.

'Will you admit to that in a court of law?' asked Barton.

'I'm prepared to demonstrate how I did it.'

'We'll be in touch.'

'I could show you now.'

'Out!'

* * *

*Cell 14*

Mr Celestine, forty-five, but he looked much younger with a rosy complexion and an odd basin haircut. His size and the way he walked in reminded Barton of John Wayne, but his voice was boyish. He held out his hand to Strange, who stared at it as though it were an enormous tarantula. She shook it anyway.

'Charles Celestine. Friends call me Chuck.'

'Please take a seat, Mr Celestine,' replied Strange, with an arched eyebrow.

Celestine took a seat, crossed his legs, and peered at them over his small spectacles as if he'd spotted a rare deer in the distance.

'Do you know why we're here?'

'Mr Zanthos's death, I assume.'

Barton had met enough unstable people to identify one fast.

'That's right. Are you aware of a reason why someone would want to harm him?'

'Of course.'

Barton flicked through Celestine's record with distaste while he waited for further enlightenment. He vaguely remembered Celestine's case because it was so shocking, even though he'd had no professional involvement in it. Celestine merely grinned at him.

'Why would anyone want to kill him?' asked Barton.

'He was a conceited pervert. It's a deadly combination.' Celestine laughed much too loudly at that, leaned forward, and whispered, 'And he was irritating.'

Barton exhaled and counted to five.

'You killed your neighbour twenty-five years ago,' he said. 'Why did you do that?'

'*She* was irritating.'

'She was a grandmother, and you mutilated her.'

'Grandmothers aren't all good.'

Celestine chuckled and clapped his hands.

'Do you think this is funny?' asked Strange. 'Get out of here.'

Celestine stood up and his clown mask slipped for a moment. Equally fast, Barton recognised a very dangerous man.

'I think it's entertaining,' said Celestine. 'Living normally was hard for me. I often heard voices, which distracted me. All the bills, and things like insurance, and money management, and shopping. Not to mention trying to hold down a job. It was all very stressful, and I lost my mind. That's why I attacked her. Her being irritating just made it easier. But I wouldn't do anything to jeopardise my current life. I love it here on this wing. Everything's done for us, even your dinner is cooked for you.' He winked slowly at them and his lazy smile reappeared. 'I don't know how I'll cope when I get out.'

With a swish, he waltzed out of the room. When he'd gone, Strange exhaled deeply.

'Please tell me that scary psychopath isn't getting out any time soon?'

'I'm afraid he might be.'

Barton shouted for Raja to come into the room.

'Is Celestine still leaving later this year?' asked Barton.

'Chuck? Yeah, he passed his parole nearly a year ago. He's been in a D-Cat for a year, no bother there, and he returned here for a course. Did he wind you up? He's a bit of a joker. In fact, I'd say he's the happiest man in here.'

'When is he out?' asked Barton.

Raja scratched his head while he thought.

'I'm his personal officer. If lifers like him pass the parole board, they usually get eighteen months in an open prison to see if they can cope with the loosening of their conditions. They might get day release near their discharge date to attend job interviews or do volunteer work. I'd say he'll be out in about six months. In fact, he said to me a few days ago he'd be out in time to play at Wimbledon, so early summer.'

'Isn't he still dangerous?' asked Strange.

'I'd say so. He's served a long sentence, though. Life with a minimum of twenty years, and he's done nearly twenty-six. Maybe he's changed. He's a pussycat in here.'

'Do you think it's likely he'd have killed Zanthos?'

'No,' replied Raja immediately. 'Not like that. He's content here and his record is for reckless violence.' Raja paused for a second. 'You know, I've come into contact with thousands of volatile prisoners in my time here. Even though some of them pretended they were, I wasn't convinced a single one was a psychopath. But then the powers that be moved me to this wing, and I met Chuck Celestine.'

* * *

*Cell 22*

Mr Khan, nineteen, approximately seven stone, sentenced for death by dangerous driving, cried during the formalities, and had to be helped back to his cell. Barton crossed him off the list.

* * *

*Cell 27*

Mr Pfeiffer arrived as though dressed for Sunday lunch. He wore a sensible buttoned-up shirt and cream jumper above grey, sharply creased trousers. Barton couldn't help thinking of a bank manager who only felt comfortable smartly attired.

The man appeared sprightly for his advanced years.

'You, Ballanchine and Zanthos committed the same crime,' said Barton.

'We were found guilty of it, yes.'

'Weren't you guilty?' interjected Strange.

'I've spent the best part of twelve years thinking about what happened. I don't wish to keep reliving it. I assume you're here because of Zanthos's death.'

'Yes. Do you believe it was suspicious?'

'It was a shame, that's what it was. He only had a few days to go.'

'Did he have enemies on here?'

'Not as such. There are many unpleasant men on here. Also, the tough conditions make people act out. But committing a crime like killing him would mean spending the rest of your life here. Only someone who was completely crazy would do that.'

'Or a person with nothing to lose?' asked Barton.

'Everyone here has their freedom to lose.'

* * *

*Cell 36*

Mr Grace seemed to think he was in a fast-food restaurant. Barton told him he would bring his meal to his room when it was ready.

*Cell 37*

Mr MacPherson, a twenty-seven-year-old, smiled at them both and gave them each the finger. His record was filled with violence, some of it against a group of women in a nightclub. He merely laughed at them and pushed the chair over when he left.

*Cell 42*

Mr Sampson, sixty, a violent sex-offender, smiled and nodded until he heard the introductions.

'I thought you were here about my appeal.'

'Unlikely, seeing as I arrested you.'

'You stitched me up. I didn't know that girl was fifteen.'

'Sticking your hand up a skirt in a busy pub is an offence whatever their age.'

'I was drunk and slipped over.'

'Did you ever have an argument with Mr Zanthos?'

Sampson's top lip curled into a snarl.

'I don't talk to the fucking paedos, and I definitely don't talk to the Old Bill.'

* * *

*Cell 48*

Mr Ballanchine had a face that Barton felt like putting his fist through before he even spoke. Despite his being only a few years from eighty, there was a keen, smug look on his face and he had intelligent, taunting eyes. His still-full head of grey hair and beard were trimmed to perfection, but there was a tinge of yellow to the man's skin.

'Terrible shame, but not a terrible shock,' said Ballanchine. 'That's what happens to old people when they don't stay fit like I do. I'm still on the top landing, you know. Those stairs are my friend. Otherwise, you die in your sleep.'

He stopped talking to cough. It went on and on.

'Why is it a terrible shame, then?' asked Barton when Ballanchine had recovered.

'I really liked him. Decent chap. Strong constitution. Never wavered under questioning. I hoped to spend more time with him after we were released. We had similar interests and goals, but I wanted to open his mind to new experiences.'

'Wasn't it your shared interests that put you here in the first place?' asked Strange.

'Allegedly,' replied Ballanchine, who leaned back in his chair and put his hands behind his head.

'You were recalled to prison for being at a location you were all specifically barred from, namely a playground. Then, after you were released on licence again, you were caught with indecent images. Don't you care about coming back to jail?'

'There are a few things I want to do one more time, then after that, I care not. I don't mind dying here if that's where I end up. Zanthos's death only proves that you need to take your pleasures when you can.'

* * *

*Cell 52*

Mr Asher MacDuff, thirty-one, serving five years for rape. Barton remembered him well because he had a striking resemblance to Zander. He was a firefighter who'd maintained his innocence all the way through the trial, but the jury had found against him. Prison was beating him. He gave them brief eye contact and a sad smile.

'Hi, John. Here to tell me it's been a mistake?'

'Sadly not, Asher. Do you know anything about what happened to Mr Zanthos?'

'No, he was a polite man, who I liked. We didn't talk about our crimes. I'm innocent, and I'm in here, so everyone gets a fair shout from me.'

* * *

*Cell 56*

Barton warned Strange to be wary of their next customer. Mr Crannock, slim, tall, with incredibly muscled arms, forty-five years old, and long, nicely combed hair like in a women's shampoo advert. He stared hard at them as he took the seat.

'Inspector Barton, you must be here to apologise for lying in court. I see you've brought this bitch for my in-cell entertainment as way of apology. Thanks, even though I prefer brunettes with more meat, but times are tough.'

'Keep it civil, Mr Crannock.'

Crannock leaned forward and placed his hand on the table next to Strange's pen. She went to pick it up and Crannock grabbed her wrist and pulled it towards him over the table. He grabbed Strange's shoulder with his other hand, but Barton was ready. His huge left paw was around Crannock's throat, squeezing hard, lifting him up onto his tiptoes. Crannock let Strange go and held his hands up. Barton shoved him towards the exit. He staggered but managed to find his feet.

'See you next time, Barton,' he said, blowing Strange a kiss.

He slammed the door on his way out. They could hear him arguing with Green as he went down the stairs. Barton looked down at the table.

'Hey, where's my pen gone?' he said.

Luckily, that was the last one. Barton let the pen thing go. He knew the inmates were given pens to write home, so they weren't considered dangerous items. Strange flexed her wrist after Crannock had left. The majority of the other men they'd questioned had been shifty, delicate individuals who had been caught accessing child porn or old fellows who'd touched children in the seventies and eighties. Strange had been expecting just that, but wings like this also contained angry, strong men who had been moved off mainstream wings purely because the other inmates had ganged up on them. One on one, they were incredibly dangerous.

Raja popped his head in. 'You said you wanted a chat with us as well, so I'm just going to help unlock everyone and then I'll be back.'

'Christ. To think I volunteered for this,' said Strange when he'd gone.

'Eye-opening, isn't it?'

'Yes. That was a good lesson I just learnt with Crannock. I'm interested to hear what the wing officers have to say. What kind of person would want to work surrounded by this lot all day?'

# 23

## THE COLD KILLER

It's interesting that the police came in. They clearly suspect that Zanthos's death might not have been natural. They've interviewed every single con on the wing, though, which means they obviously have no idea who's responsible. But Barton is a clever git. He may well have a clue and today was smoke and mirrors, perhaps trying to identify witnesses or find those willing to grass.

If so, that would be typically clever of my old nemesis, Barton. No one was ever going to confess, but that man has a remarkable ability to judge someone by merely talking to them, even just watching their mannerisms. He won't find this case easy, though. His career will be on the line, even if he doesn't know that yet.

When Barton leaves, it's time for the evening meal, although today it's just a ham sandwich and a packet of crisps at 4 p.m. I stand and watch Green supervise the queue. The other officer is nowhere to be seen, so now is as good a moment as any.

I wait for MacPherson to collect his dinner, then follow him back to his cell. It's funny how people drop their guard at mealtimes. Everyone does it, though. The way to survive prison with your sanity relatively intact is to get into a simple routine. Look forward to little pleasures like the fact they have Walkers crisps as opposed to a cheap brand.

MacPherson is fit, but he's no fighter. If he was hard, and he isn't, I'd jab him in the back first, break a rib maybe, to make sure I won. But that isn't necessary with this weasel. He enters his cell and sits in front of *Friends*. It's one of the episodes with Bruce Willis in. I step in too, closing the door for him with me on the inside. MacPherson looks to his right but doesn't meet my gaze.

This is the part I loved the most. The terror on my victims' faces versus the power I feel. MacPherson understands what's about to happen now, and he knows he can't win, because he has to live with men like me. I smile, but it doesn't feel right. MacPherson puts his food under the table, so it won't get ruined.

Some people fight anyway, which I admire, but he sits back on the edge of his bed and stares ahead.

'Why?' he asks.

'You've been giving someone I like a hard time.'

He briefly looks up at my expression, which is unforgiving.

'I've seen you chatting to him. He's a fucking screw, and you've got to be a snitch. It's us against them, that's the way it is.'

'You've watched too many movies. These are kids with jobs to do. I didn't see you messing with that big officer who was on here yesterday. The one who looked like he chewed marbles. People who pick on the weak are just bullies.'

'Isn't that what you're doing?'

'I'm in the lesson-giving business. I'm all about control.'

'That screw is weird. There's something off kilter. Weirdos like that don't tell me what to do.'

'Maybe not, but I can order you what to do. Leave him alone.'

A flash of the rage that sent him here appears on his face. He stifles it.

'Who do you think you are? You're nothing more than an old man on the paedo wing now. Get over yourself.'

I flex my fingers and roll my shoulders, then stride towards him.

'For some reason, what I was about to do wasn't sitting quite right. Thanks for making this easy for me.'

# 24

## DI BARTON

While they waited for the wing officers to return, Strange went through each file one by one while Barton made a list. Afterwards, he had six names, which he passed to her.

'If this was murder, I'd be reasonably confident that one of these men did it,' he said.

Strange read out the list.

'Thompson, Drummond, Celestine, MacPherson, Sampson and Crannock.'

'All six have a history of extreme violence against men, women or children.'

'Don't you think it could be any of the others? There were a lot of weirdos, or can't I use that term any more?'

'No, person first, remember. People with unusual behaviour. But no, if the man was killed, and it's still more likely that he wasn't, the person responsible would probably have violence on his record already. To take a life requires a certain rage or lack of empathy. That kind of behaviour has usually revealed itself in a lesser form by the time they come to kill.'

'What about women killing their partners after years of abuse?'

'Good exception, but hardly relevant in this case.'

Strange pondered the list.

'Crannock would be my favourite.'

Before Barton could reply, Green came back in and sat in front of them in the same seat the prisoners had used.

'Do I need to hold the Bible?' he asked.

Barton smiled. Perhaps he'd got this guy wrong. Green was overweight, but in a similar way to Barton. There was definite strength within him, but you needed more than that to gain respect from the prisoners.

'We'll be out of your hair soon. I just have some questions regarding Mr Zanthos.'

'Fire away. I've been on this wing for three months, more or less solidly. I know who's pally and who isn't.'

'Mr Zanthos,' said Strange. 'What was he like?'

'Stereotypical dirty-old-man sex offender. They keep themselves to themselves or stick with other similar inmates. A few will admit to having made mistakes, but they water down their offences. Others whimper and apologise, but whether they're sorry for their victims or themselves is difficult to decipher.'

'And Zanthos?'

'Nothing. No remorse or regret. Do you know what he said to the laundry worker after he lost Zanthos's duvet cover?'

Barton shook his head.

'I'm going to screw your kids when I get out because that's what I do.'

Strange blanched. 'Did he get battered?'

Now it was Green who shook his head.

'Nope. I had my eye on him afterwards because I thought he might be done in, but he was left alone. As disgusting as he is, you could almost respect his bravery to taunt a man like that when he's twice his age.'

Barton nodded. Green knew his stuff. Sex offenders were often clever. If they were charged with abusing a boy in a toilet, they'd tell the courts they were just helping him. They would accept that they should not have been in there, and shouldn't have touched him, but they would swear it wasn't sexual. Zanthos was probably used to power. He might well have been a successful businessman when he was younger and all these years later he had still been bright enough to use his age to his advantage. That had almost certainly made him more likely to have been killed too.

'Did he have enemies?' asked Barton.

'Not so much. He was aloof, which is grating, but his offending was not as evil as some on here. There's a hierarchy of crimes, where those who've committed the worst offences are considered scum.'

'So they do treat each other according to their crimes?' asked Strange.

'Yes. People who watch child or snuff porn on the Internet would not consider themselves as bad as those who touch actual children. Adult rapists believe they are better than child molesters.'

'And child killers are the lowest of the low,' stated Strange.

'Correct,' he replied.

'How do you feel about Zanthos dying?' asked Barton, throwing a curveball.

'It couldn't have happened to a nicer man.'

Barton read out their list of six men and handed it to Green.

'Do you think one of these people could have murdered him?' asked Strange.

Green ran his eyes down the names.

'I suppose it's possible. Celestine is virtually insane. Sampson often pushes the weak around. Thompson failed his parole board and won't be getting released, so he's been in a foul mood, but he's a bully not a killer. I never saw the other three talk to Zanthos.'

'Okay, thank you. Can you send in Mr Raja?'

In just a moment, Raja walked in. He was the opposite of Green. Thin and upbeat with thick, bushy hair that would have looked like a microphone if it were a little longer. Barton got a good vibe from him. Despite that, Raja gave them a lot of vague answers.

'You seem very relaxed. Do you enjoy working on here, Mr Raja?' asked Barton.

'Yes, as you can see, I'm not physically imposing like many officers so it's easier than working the other wings.'

'Some of these men are prone to real rage,' said Strange.

'Yes, but they act alone. I do kickboxing as a hobby, so I could keep a single man off until help arrives, but I can't cope with more than one. To fight like that you need to have control of your fear.'

Barton considered his answer. He would not want to work here.

'And what they're all in for doesn't bother you?'

'I don't think about their crimes. If you do that, it gets to you. Then you'd be tempted to kill them yourself.'

Barton could understand that thought process, but punishment was for the courts, and those courts took a dim view of anyone who took justice into their own hands. He shrugged. He could always come back and grill the officers again, it was the prisoners who would move on sooner or later.

'I'll walk you out if you're finished,' said Raja.

Barton and Strange collected up their things, left the library and stood on the landing. Strange's eyes widened at the sight of nearly sixty men milling around, many of whom were looking up at them. Raja gestured for them to follow him down the steps. Barton didn't feel scared. The inmates were the ones at risk. The irritation inside him was growing and getting close to fury after speaking to these lowlifes. He couldn't wait to get outside.

At the bottom of the stairs, there was a load of gasps as a tall inmate staggered out of one of the cells. He was clutching his nose.

'It's MacPherson,' said Strange.

MacPherson lurched to the pool table and sprayed a large stream of snotty blood all over the cloth. He looked across at the detectives and spat a gob of spit in their direction. Green came out of the office, locking the door behind him.

'I'll sort this,' he said to Raja.

Barton noticed Green didn't seem to be in any hurry, merely watching as Raja unlocked the wing gates. Raja escorted them all the way to the gatehouse. When they got back in the car, Barton had a light-bulb moment.

'Do you know something incredible? I might have been wrong.'

'And you're admitting it?'

'I only said might. Consider what just happened to MacPherson.'

'I suppose he could have been assaulted as revenge for killing Zanthos.'

'No, think about what kind of person did that. Does that make him more or less likely to have murdered Zanthos?'

'I don't know what you mean. Are you saying whoever attacked Zanthos, also assaulted MacPherson, and is on a rampage where they take out everyone they deem worthy of their wrath?'

Barton smiled.

'Sometimes even I'm surprised by my genius.'

'Go on. Spit it out.'

'Our list of six are all violent men, not known for having limits. I doubt they'd have had the restraint to kill anyone and not leave a mark. Didn't some of them say they'd have beaten him to a pulp? None of them seemed to know that he might have been suffocated. Maybe it was someone else.'

'You mean a person with a bit more control.'

'Yes. If a man like the person who just assaulted MacPherson had gone to kill Zanthos, they'd have needed to wipe the blood off the ceiling afterwards.'

'Right, so instead of six potential murderers, we now have over fifty.'

Barton chuckled.

'We didn't get a confession, but today has been a good day's work. Unfortunately, unless CSI come back with something, it's a waiting game.'

'Waiting for someone else to die?'

'Correct. One murder can be hard to solve, but if it becomes two, then it's generally only a matter of time.'

'Let's hope this is the last we hear about it,' said Strange, without conviction.

They drove the rest of the way to Barton's house in silence. After he'd got out, Strange leaned over.

'Are you okay, John? You don't seem the full ticket.'

He looked up and down the street as though he was ready to explain, then just gave her a grim smile. How did you explain what it was like to see your mother fade away before your eyes? He couldn't help feeling selfish for complaining, when surely it was his mum who was struggling.

'I just need a good night's sleep.'

'I just need a shower,' she replied. 'Although I doubt a tidal wave could wash today's experience away.'

# 25

## THE COLD KILLER – THURSDAY 12TH DECEMBER – LAST DAY IN PRISON

I've been awake since four and packed my stuff. It didn't take long. I gave my toiletries away to Khan, who is one of the strange young lads on the wing even though he's probably a festering pervert. I don't know what's wrong with me, but I have a bit of sympathy for some of the younger men on here. Green told me there are quite a few with learning difficulties who have been prosecuted for inappropriate relationships with kids, but developmentally they are still children themselves. Their lives are as good as over anyway if they're already here. Who the hell will want to help them now?

To my horror, I've been getting respect from everyone off the wing. Raja told me there's been no trouble from anyone after what I did to MacPherson. They were all expecting me to start going around the cells taking stuff seeing that I was the daddy. Thank God I'm leaving.

My cell is unlocked at 6:30 a.m. There are five of us being released today, and when we reach reception they stick us in a small holding cell. There's a quiet bloke with one arm who I've never spoken to, Crannock, who is a nasty career criminal and sits in the corner not looking at anyone, and Pfeiffer and Ballanchine. I'm too close to the two horrible old men. They are smug and friendly with each other. I wonder if they've been plotting to ruin another child's life while they've been inside.

Our crimes are different, but in some ways we are the same. Once you get a name and a reputation for pub violence, when there's a tear-up in a boozer, the police know exactly who to go and see. Same for burglars. And it's the same for sex offenders. If a kid goes missing, the police visit all the sickos who aren't currently behind bars. We're all stupid to continue doing what we do but it's who we are. It's hard to stop, but when the slate is clean once and for all, that's precisely what I'm going to do. I don't want to spend the rest of my life rotting in jail.

Ricardo Zanthos is already dead. He's been terminated. I feel that Frank has been avenged in some way, so it's time to talk to his mother. I try to concentrate on what I'm planning to say to her, but Pfeiffer and Ballanchine keep intruding on my thoughts. Pfeiffer and Ballanchine laugh loudly at a shared joke. I feel my body turning to rock. Who will put an end to these two's offending?

Despite their advanced years, they're acting like children on a school trip. Their confidence and enthusiasm annoy me when they should live in fear, after what they've done. They both chuckle in their whispered conversations to each other, but they must be deaf because the room is small and I can hear most of it. It's obvious they have something very exciting planned. Some kind of trip or visit. Crannock clears his throat.

'If you two don't shut the fuck up, I will take great pleasure in snapping every bone in your arthritic bodies with my teeth.'

After that we sit in silence for two hours. Finally, at 8:45, it's as if they can't process us fast enough. My bank cards and ID are returned to me and I'm relieved to see my debit card still has a few months to run. Soon we're heading towards the gatehouse and the big prison gates. I've been looking forward to this moment – first they'll herd us leaving cons into the dark of the vehicle lock. Then there'll be a grumbling sound and the huge metal gate slowly edging open, letting in sunlight and fresh air. And finally we'll see a world without bars where we can pick up the reins to our old lives. But this time I have no interest in going back to who I was before. What would be the point?

So I'm disappointed to discover that the prison chucking-out routine has changed. Instead of being shepherded through the vehicle lock, we are led down a corridor and past some scanners into a room with a small café where there is a group of nervous-looking women, obviously waiting for their husbands and partners to be released. Nobody seems interested in us.

I watch Pfeiffer and Ballanchine shake hands and walk outside. The other idiots have already vanished. Two men who were sitting discreetly in the corner rise and follow the old fellows and I suspect they're the vice squad, or whatever they call themselves these days. Those two being released without any licence conditions will be a nightmare for them, even if they know where they live.

Pfeiffer and Ballanchine will have signed the Sex Offenders Register, where all the details of their current lives will be kept: addresses, bank accounts, passports, you name it, and it needs to be 100 per cent up to date. But they won't be expecting much trouble from those decrepit old men. Unlike me, they don't have to visit Probation. I've got three years of that.

My last offender manager was an older guy called Jock and we understood each other pretty well. He gave me a break a few times, so I never messed him around after that. Every meeting and arrangement was kept. Jock was only sixty when he dropped down dead at work just before I came back in.

My new offender manager is young. June Agyepong visited the prison two months ago and explained that she would meet me the morning I got out to take me to my secure accommodation. Obviously, that situation has now changed. She has a firm, dry handshake and is tall enough to look me in the eye.

'Am I in The Continental or The Ritz tonight?' I ask.

'I've managed to get a room for you at the Holiday Inn.'

'The council paying for it?'

She nods.

'How long for?'

'Follow me.'

I accompany her to a line of doors, one of which leads to a small office. She steps inside but doesn't take a seat. I edge in and push the door to, but don't shut it.

'Just a night,' she says. 'You need to go to the council tomorrow morning and declare yourself homeless. They'll try to help.'

'They'll try to help?'

'I'm sorry. It's the time of year when they really struggle. We're constantly losing social housing and the families need to be rehoused, so there's very little in the city. There might be something elsewhere. Grantham maybe. It's getting chilly, so the churches will open soon. At least you can sleep somewhere warm and dry.'

'I've just spent years sleeping near a load of strange men. It's not tempting to spend any more time with them, even if the Lord is watching. When do I have to report to you?'

'Monday.'

'Good. You know what the queues are like, and it will take a while to choose the colour.'

She frowns at me.

'What colour?

'Of the tent.'

Her expression softens. She searches her brain for any other kind of resolution, but it's clear she's done her best.

'As I said, I'm sorry. Something will turn up. Isn't there a sofa somewhere you can crash on if they can't get you a bed for a few nights?'

'You said you'd find me a place to stay. Homeless people drink, and that's bad news for me.'

'We had you a room at the approved premises, but they have staffing issues.'

'Do they need a minimum number of staff per resident?'

'Yes, so they lost five rooms. There was only one space free for the prisoners who left this week. We gave it to someone more needy.'

'You mean more dangerous than me.'

She gives me a tight smile. I don't blame her. Shit happens. It'll be pointless to go to the council, apart from the free tent, but it's not their fault either.

'I found a place for you in a private house, but they asked for your record and declined.'

This time, it's me giving her a little grin. I suppose it is my fault. Never mind.

'I'll pass on the hotel.'

This unsettles her. 'Why?'

'It's one night. A waste of time. I need to find a camping spot. Buy a stove, warm clothes, all the rest. I might as well get to it. There's no help for me at the council. Let homeless women with kids have my room. I'll see you Monday – 10:00 okay?'

'Fine. Can I give you a lift?'

We walk towards the door together. I'm about to say no, but someone arriving leaves the door open and a cruel wind races in. There's stubborn and then there's daft.

'Sure.'

At the door, she lets me exit first. You have to admire these probation workers. They spend a lot of time with the worst of us, often on their own. She's taking a calculated risk, driving me. My record is for violence against men and, obviously, I won't hurt her, but she's still pretty brave.

We step outside and I stroll into gently drifting snowflakes. The horizon is top to bottom with light-grey clouds as far as the eye can see. I overheard the old men in the holding cell comment that there's going to be two days of extremely heavy snow. That's perfect and gives me plenty of time to do what I have to, but am I still ruthless enough to do it?

# 26

## THE COLD KILLER

I'm surprised by June's car when we reach it. She must love speed. Although, a low two-door Honda isn't the best choice for the weather. The roads are foul, all water and piles of slush. Still, the car handles it well. I relax in my seat and enjoy the ride after so long without experiencing one, even though cars were never really my thing. I drove bangers and fixed them until there was no point. I guess I didn't like having anything I couldn't leave behind.

'Nice wheels. Didn't realise the job paid so well,' I comment as we arrive at the council offices.

'It doesn't! The money's rubbish. It's a private plate, so the car looks newer than it is. I won't even be getting mileage for this.'

'Why bother coming to the prison, then? You could have made me come to the office this morning first thing.'

She pulls up near the building and turns the engine off. I was wrong about her being young. Up close, she has laughter lines and the beginnings of crow's feet, but there's a peacefulness about her, which makes me think nothing much would shock her any more. She's going to get a nasty surprise.

'I feel we've let you down with your accommodation, and it's only an hour out of my time. Go inside and sign on for your benefits, then get on with sorting your life out. When I asked my boss about you, he replied that he was surprised by the length of the sentence that the judge gave you. Apparently, there was a lot of provocation from the other side. He said you weren't an unreasonable man as long as you didn't believe you were being taken advantage of.'

'Nice to hear, I think. I do appreciate it, but this doesn't make us friends.'

A twitch of her cheek indicates her amusement, but that's all there is.

'No, it doesn't. If you don't arrive as agreed on Monday, I'll have you recalled to custody so fast, you'll still be in your sleeping bag when they turn the key to lock you in again.'

I sign her form before turning to get out of the car.

'Thanks for the ride.'

'We're here to work with you nowadays, but it's a two-way street. You will need to see me regularly to start with. I want to see commitment. Eventually, I'll give you as much rope as you need and then it'll be up to you what you do with it.'

I get out of the car. Holding my prison bag in one hand, I wave with the other. Should I feel guilty? Probation is going to shoulder some of the blame for what I'm going to do. They'll think it was due to my lack of accommodation or ask why June couldn't see I was out of control.

She drives down Broadway and disappears into the swirling snowflakes. Peterborough almost looks picturesque from here with the cathedral dominating the skyline, but I can see numerous piles of clothes on top of flattened cardboard boxes in closed shop doorways. If the forecast is right, some of them will soon be death beds. I guess there are worse ways to go.

The wind howls around me as I stand in front of the entrance to the council building. There are Christmas decorations up, although it's clear whoever put them up did so half-heartedly. The place is rammed. There are queues next to queues. The people in them shiver each time the automatic door opens. It's a day for warm pubs and hot pies with loved ones, but it's been decades since I did that.

I spin on my heel and walk towards the town centre. I'll not give them the satisfaction of begging for help that isn't there.

It feels Christmassy in Cathedral Square. The huge tree in the centre takes my mind away from my current life for a few moments, as will the Whopper and large fries I've been dreaming about for months. After the bland diet I've had for the last three years, for a few minutes I'll experience heaven on earth. Then I'll visit Mountain Warehouse and the charity shops.

I soon find Burger King is now a fancy restaurant selling gourmet burgers, but the Wimpy is still open. It's early, but I can still get a burger and fries. When I leave thirty minutes later, I have a griping stomach ache from the rich food, and a sense of disappointment that the burger didn't quite hit the spot as I was expecting. They do say the real pleasure is the anticipation. Even so, the toilets in the Wimpy were a vast improvement on what I'm used to and a treat to use.

There are charity shops everywhere, which I don't recall from before either. That can't be a good sign. The woman in Oxfam gives me everything in my basket for five pounds, which is nice of her. I must have *just-released inmate* written on my forehead.

Next I head to Mountain Warehouse. I need some very specific things if I'm going to survive. Most important is a thick dark-blue parka with a large furry hood. The other essentials are an okay tent, a top-of-the-range sleeping bag, sunglasses, a warm beanie, a metal spade, a sharp outdoor knife, some long nails, a torch, and a comfy airbed. I'll be sleeping in the woods, not living in them. For food, I'll only be a twenty-minute walk from a variety of convenience stores and takeaways.

I spot a second-hand rucksack in the window at Barnardo's for three pounds and stick everything in it, except the airbed, which I'll have to carry. I normally wouldn't bother with a mobile phone, but this time I'll need one although it'll be switched off most of the time – they can only track phones when they're turned on. Reading keeps me sane without a TV, so I also nip to The Works and buy some paperbacks, then I pick up bottled water at Tesco. I have everything on my list.

I trudge past Asda and Iceland, then cross the pedestrian bridge over the River Nene, and stroll by Charters Pub and Restaurant. A beer would be good, but I know myself better than that. I carry on walking down the path, stopping occasionally to let cyclists past. I receive a few funny looks wearing sunglasses on such a grey day, but, combined with the beanie, this way my face and head are completely concealed.

I'll nip to Oundle Road and get a takeaway tonight, maybe a few cans of beer, but I need to set my tent up first. I don't want to be doing that in the dark. I'm heading just past Woodston Ponds, which is a nature reserve that few know about, because near there is a small wood where I've camped before. The snow seems to have settled here, away from the cars and houses.

The first part of the wood has a single track to walk along the edge, the rest is overgrown. It's only three hundred metres long and fifty metres wide, but it was well used by the Lithuanians when they joined the EU and were allowed free movement. I've shared a fire with many of them over the years. They're a nation of drinkers, or at least the ones I've met are, but they aren't any trouble. Not to me, anyway.

The best spot already contains a red tent. I edge carefully

towards it, but there's a big rip down the back, probably from a fox, and I can see it's been abandoned. The key to putting up a tent is making sure the ground is solid and not liable to flooding. It's so close to the river here that if the rain was torrential I'd wake up a foot under, but I've seen the weather report and it's just more of the white stuff.

Half an hour later, I'm finished. It's nicer than my prison cell and a damn sight more comfortable than the African jungles where I did most of my fighting. The Legion didn't let you drag a ten kilo inflatable airbed around with you either.

I could stay here for months, and have done for four once, but there are downfalls to this kind of living. In the winter, everything gets damp. I had a mate before, long dead now, who lived near here and let me use his washing machine and tumble dryer. The job centre people also allow you to sign on with a friend's address, so I used his. They don't give you much grief down there when you're sleeping rough. Who wants to employ a homeless person? They can always tell even though I tried to keep clean. With no job and no prospect of one, the biggest problem with this lifestyle is that boredom can lead to mischief.

There are four people that I plan to visit. One will take a whole day and I'm startled by the flare of hope that rises in my chest when I think of it. The other tasks are a couple of hours max. I need to get started immediately. Speed is of the essence. As long as they're all done within a week, it will be fine. Any longer than that and the police will have started to join the dots and I assume it'll be Barton who'll be running towards the invisible spider's web.

I sit on the airbed and open the mobile phone box, remove the phone, insert the sim, and turn it on. This type has a pound credit before you need to pay with your debit card and top-up. I might get five calls out of it if I'm quick. It's got half a charge too, which is plenty.

I take the piece of paper out of my pocket and ring the number. Who knows if he's organised yet? At least he'll understand that I am. A gruff voice answers.

'Yeah, speaking.'

'It's me. I'm all set. I'm seeing the woman first thing, Pfeiffer will need his chat if he's in place, then I'm on the train to wherever the hell Alnmouth is. I'll be in touch after I've completed each of my steps. Ballanchine will be the final play. By then, the police should be on to me. Final decisions can be made at that point about Archie Spencer, but the others remain our focus. I'd get out of town with any money if I were you. Start afresh.'

'It's too late for that. Money means nothing to me. I won't be making old bones.'

'Blow it, then. Live like a king for a while. He'd appreciate that.'

'You reckon? We'll talk after the next step. We're doing the world a favour.'

We agree to communicate by text from now on, so I turn the phone off to save the battery. A shop might let me charge it for a bit if I give them a sob story, but I'd rather not bother. I stare at the phone as the screen goes blank. That man is one damaged critter to be capable of everything he's done, but I can handle him for a week. God only knows what he'll do at the end of all this, but that's his problem.

We have a pact now. At the end of all this, those who need to pay, will pay. Between us, we will put things right.

I once considered myself some kind of Jack Reacher, or perhaps a modern-day Clint Eastwood, come to take out the trash, but that's laughable now. A twinge of embarrassment has me grimacing. All I really did was cause pain. Sure, everyone I taught a lesson to was an arsehole, but I provoked them. Few blokes in their own boozer back down when a stranger walks into their local looking for trouble. I was just concocting a fictitious war to try to give me purpose, whereas now I realise I was wasting my life. Now I'm in the last chance saloon. Now, the story ends.

# 27

## DI BARTON

On the way home from work, Barton stopped at the address where Mr Zanthos would have been released to that morning had he not died. Barton and his team had tried on numerous occasions to get hold of Mrs Zanthos since his demise, but nobody ever answered the door. It was an annoyance. Most people were contactable at any time on their mobile phone, but some elderly people still didn't have one. The Zanthoses didn't even have a landline.

Zelensky had suspected that someone was at home once because it looked as if a light had been turned off, but then again, the light could have been on a timer. No further incidents had come to them from the prison and Barton's team had been busy with a spate of violent muggings in Farcet, a village two miles from Peterborough, so the case wasn't a high priority, but Barton's gut told him to keep popping around. The hospital had released Zanthos's body to the funeral parlour, so Mrs Zanthos was obviously in touch to give them instructions.

Maybe she was in mourning or being comforted by friends, but Barton didn't think so. If all else failed, he would ring the crematorium and find out the date of the service.

Zanthos's co-defendants had been released today. Barton didn't think they'd get up to too much trouble at their age, but you could never tell. He banged his fist on the door one last time in frustration, then returned to his vehicle and drove home.

He pulled up on his drive and got out of the car. As he put his key in the front door he heard riotous laughing coming from the dining room so he poked his head around so he could just see through the window. The three kids, Holly and his mother were sitting at the table chuckling at each other. They spotted Barton and all of them gave an enthusiastic cheer, so he entered the house fully expecting to be about to become the butt of some almighty joke.

When he reached the dining room, though, he saw they had three photo albums spread out. Barton sat down in the chair next to his mum, who had Luke on her lap. She reached over and squeezed Barton's hand; a gesture he couldn't remember her making for a very long time.

'Daddy,' said Luke, 'why are you dressed in those funny trousers?'

Barton looked down at a photo of him and his sisters in a line wearing fashionable flares from the seventies. Unfortunately for his street cred, the picture had been taken in the early eighties when Barton was about ten years old.

'Back then, we got most of our clothes from a hip and happening place called the jumble sale, didn't we, Mum?' he said.

'They were different times. I lived through rationing, so nothing was wasted.'

'How come you and your sisters have the same hairstyles?' asked Layla.

Everyone laughed their heads off again, even his mother, who was responsible for the odd haircuts.

'That's because I used the same bowl to cut around for all of them.' She chuckled through moist eyes.

'What made you get these out?' said Barton, smiling at a picture of him taken during his goth stage around age fourteen. He looked like the love child of John Candy and Alice Cooper.

'Your mum has spent the day going through what she brought with her. We've had a really good time, clearing stuff out, setting things straight, and reminiscing. She made an album from our wedding, which I've never seen. It's brilliant. Look how young we were.'

Holly placed the album in front of him and Barton watched as his mother squeezed his wife's hand as she'd done to him, the pair of them sharing an unspoken moment when their eyes met. He wondered what they'd been talking about all day. Barton looked at the pictures outside the church and marvelled at how thin he looked, when at the time he'd imagined he was heavy. If only he'd known.

Lawrence, whose father had left shortly after his birth, was toddling around at the front of the posed photos. Then there was one of Barton holding him in his big arms as though Lawrence were a little dolly, as proud as any dad. He glanced at Lawrence, and they shared a moment like the one his wife and mother had. Luke looked up at his granny's face.

'Was Dad a good boy, or naughty?' he asked in a solemn voice.

'He was a rowdy child who had outgrown me by the time he started senior school, but his heart was always in the right place.'

Barton almost pinched his leg to make sure he wasn't imagining things. His mother wasn't known for compliments, nor for being tactile. Holly winked at him. He looked back at the photos and he was beaming in every one. There had been no nerves that day. He just felt lucky. Even now, all this time later, Holly proved his decision right, time after time. Holly had said there'd be great days alongside the sad days if his mother moved in, and she had been spot on.

'Mum said we could have a takeaway, and you'd get it,' said Layla.

'Did she, now? Actually, I fancy a curry.'

'No, we all want Chinese.'

'Wait a minute, if I've got to get it, and, I assume, pay for it, shouldn't my vote carry more weight?'

'You're right,' said Layla. 'This is a democratic house. But we voted before you got home. Hey, look at this one. You seem to be going logging in the Canadian woods.'

Barton peered at the photograph.

'That's me on the way to our school-leaving disco. You guys call them proms nowadays. I looked very cool.'

He got to his feet to head out to fetch the Chinese to a volley of jeers. Barton stopped in the doorway and took a sneaky photo of them at the table. He knew that when the end came for his mother, he would remember this moment and be thankful for it. Luke was staring hard in his direction.

'I'm starving, Dad. Why are you still here?'

# 28

## THE COLD KILLER – FRIDAY 13TH DECEMBER

I wake after an amazing night's rest with almost the whole morning gone. The temperature has dipped dramatically, but I'm toasty in the sleeping bag. I dropped off to the sounds of owls and rustling undergrowth. It's a joy not to rise to the smell and noise of hundreds of men. I take a big glug of water, eat a couple of KitKats, then get dressed.

Serving in the forces toughens you up, and it teaches you to carry only what's necessary. All I need is my bank card and warm clothes. What's the worst that can happen? Mrs Zanthos is the only unknown, but this is a job that only I can do. It's a job I must do. The rest of my plan is just a bonus.

I unzip the door, step through it and stretch. My tent is green, a colour I selected for camouflage. The chances of anyone seeing it where I've pitched it are slim, but having someone steal the sleeping bag would be annoying. Mind you, I suspect vengeance warms the soul so after all this I'll probably be able to sleep outside with nothing covering me.

I decide to empty the rucksack into the tent and take it with me as it's big enough to conceal what I need to buy. It's over an hour's walk from my new home in the woods to B&Q, then on to Longthorpe and the address Green gave me for Mrs Zanthos. I wonder if the wing feels different today without us lot on it. Green and Raja had probably filled our cells before we left the jail, and we'd have been instantly forgotten by everyone on there.

I walk along the river with the bitter wind biting into my face. It feels glorious after being stuck in prison for so long. There's the odd icy bit of sleet in the air, but that stinging sensation is welcome. The best bit about this weather is that people are wrapped up, so no one will think twice when I wander into the DIY shop covered up.

By the time I reach Maskew Avenue, I'm sweating from my head to my toes, despite the snow having picked up with enthusiasm. The car park is almost empty, and the snow has begun to settle. I stamp my feet when I get through the entrance.

I take off my scarf but keep my hood up. The heat melts the flakes in it, which drip down my face and cool me down. It's quiet and I don't pass anyone as I head to the garden tools. Now isn't a time for scrimping, so I pick the most expensive item they have, and carry it to the counter. The assistant holds it nervously.

'Bag?'

'No, thanks.'

'Card or cash?'

'Cash.'

'Okay, take care. It's really sharp.'

The young assistant can barely remove his gaze from the tool as he hands it over. I could have been fifteen years old and I doubt he'd have noticed. A minute later, I'm on my way, my purchase fitting perfectly in my rucksack. It's crazy how much the weather has changed in less than fifteen minutes and it's almost a white-out now. I've got good boots and a warm coat, but I don't want to be out for too long in a pair of jeans.

I make good progress, even with the snow settling. The crunch-crunch sound is strangely soothing. I hike down Atherstone Avenue, Audley Gate and Thorpe Road, and I'm soon at Longthorpe Green where it's a real winter wonderland. Rich people don't need to park their cars on the street, so the large stone houses make me feel as if I've stepped back in time.

I find the house I'm looking for, take the weapon out, put my gloves on, then walk up the drive and ring the doorbell. I am already imagining her face will be a picture, but no one answers the door. My ears strain for sounds from inside, but the heavy snow has created a world of silence. There are lights on, so I try the door again but it's locked. I knock loudly. There's a kink in the blinds, which I step towards and peer through. The TV is on.

I check the side of the house where there is a long driveway. The house is huge and goes a long way back. It must have at least five bedrooms, I would have thought. A large car, unrecognisable with the pile of snow on it, blocks a garage at the bottom, but there's a gate next to it, which must lead to the back garden.

I scrape past the car, which has been parked poorly, and rattle the locked gate. It's old wood, so I put my shoulder into it. There's a splintering sound before it gives enough for me to slide through the gap. I find myself on the edge of a picture-postcard garden. A gust of snow takes visibility to only a few metres, but I can make out a wooden picnic table with a patio beyond it, leading to an open back door. I'm about to head towards it when the snow suddenly stops.

I sense rather than see a movement on my left. Now, as the sky clears, I spot footprints down a path into the garden, which are clearly fresh. A person in a red plastic coat appears and walks in my direction with their head down. Grey flannel trousers and orange wellies complete the outfit. The figure strides with purpose, but the steps are slow and measured. It's not until the figure is standing in front of me that it looks up. Cold, light-blue eyes stare into mine.

Even with me holding the handle high, I have the impression I'm more surprised than her.

'What are you doing in my garden?' she snaps.

'Your past has finally caught up with you.'

## 29

### THE COLD KILLER

She's very old. Even older than her husband, at a guess. It's strange how she came out of the snow yet doesn't seem to be covered in it.

'Do I get to know why?' she asks.

'Your husband was killed in prison for what he did. You should also suffer for those crimes.'

'What have I got to do with his offences? I didn't have any involvement with what he was up to. I was visiting my sister the entire time that little girl was taken.'

'I spoke to him inside. He said he was looking forward to getting home, back to the people who understood him.'

There's a flinch from her at that and I know I'm definitely on the right path. Frank blamed both of them at the time, but only Mr Zanthos went down because his father was the only one that the brother mentioned. It was only many years later, while I was on an ambush in a mosquito-infested swamp in Rwanda, that I thought it was unusual that Frank and his brother could be interfered with for so long and their mother wouldn't know anything about it.

I suppose it's not impossible, but she's guilty of something, I can tell just by looking at her.

'Sit at that table.'

She shuffles now and looks unsteady as she puts her legs one by one over the bench and sits down. I stand behind her, holding the axe in both hands.

'I'm only going to ask this once. If you tell me the truth, I promise I won't kill you. If you lie, I will know.'

'I didn't know. He tricked me, and would do it when I was out.'

'Are you trying to say that you didn't notice that your own children were being abused?'

To my surprise, she straightens her shoulders and tips her head back a little.

'Okay, I knew something wasn't right. But he was a monster. He kept me at home with no money, no friends, no way out. I relied on him.'

I take a few deep breaths.

'I'm afraid that's not good enough. Nor convincing enough. Goodbye, Mrs Zanthos. Unless you can tell me why I shouldn't cut you to pieces.'

She places her face in her hands, but there are no cries or sobs. I rest the head of the axe on her shoulder. She tenses, then gabbles.

'I lost both my children to him. Please, you must understand. I've suffered for decades because of my husband's actions. Turning a blind eye isn't a crime worthy of death. And he never interfered with them. He just took pictures.'

I swing the axe behind me in a big arc and grunt slightly as I tense my shoulders. She looks round at me.

'Wait! I'll show you the room.'

I'm well through the backswing and the blade is flashing down, but I was always going to miss. At the last moment, she splays her fingers out on the table to brace herself for impact and the axe thuds into the wood, taking most of her little finger with it. Her face contorts in pain, but she only makes a small gasping sound. Small squirts of blood pulse from the wound. After reaching in a pocket, she puts a handkerchief over the stump and presses on it.

'I'll show you,' she says, rising from the seat.

'Your injury?'

'I was a nurse. This will stop the bleeding for the moment.'

She walks down the path again, holding her hand. At the end of the garden, there's a picket fence and a gate that leads out into a small square of scrubland, which doesn't seem to be the field beyond or part of the garden. Footprints in the snow turn to the left, going into a thicket of bushes. She follows them. There's a little gap that she walks through into a clearing. She bends and lifts a white tarpaulin from a mound of snow. I might have missed it if she hadn't touched it.

Underneath is a tall, thin door built into the grass at a forty-five-degree angle. She pulls on the handle and it opens outwards, then she treads down five steps. There's a plinking sound, and a light comes on, which reveals a room not much bigger than a small shed. Revulsion runs through me as I realise, to a child, it would look like a caravan. Returning up and outside, she gestures for me to go in.

'That's where he keeps his pictures. All over the walls. Far end for the early ones. Near end for the little girl from the park. He doesn't hurt them; he likes to take photos. Honestly, no damage is done.'

I'm still holding the axe. It's not an ideal weapon in an enclosed space, but this is an old woman. It can't be a trap. Even if she shut the door on me, I'd be able to get out.

She steps back, so she is against a snow-covered bush. I stare at her, feeling uneasy. I edge inside, having to crouch a little, but the room is slightly larger than I thought and two people could pass each other. At the far end, I can see a desktop computer and a printer. I look around to see Mrs Zanthos staring at me from outside. The sky has darkened behind her. Night and more snow will soon be with us.

'Wait there,' I order her.

She nods, and I walk a metre inside. The room is around three metres long with decking for flooring. The walls have been painted white and on them there are hundreds of photographs of children in various stages of undress. Many of them look innocent at first glance, but there's a small girl in a bath, and others where the children just have their underwear on playing in a garden. Something about how close up the pictures are is deeply unsettling.

I carry on towards the desk. The photographs are older now, some curled with age. Occasional black and white shots look particularly severe, but most are in colour. As I near the end, I see a vaguely familiar face. Ivan Zanthos, Frank's younger brother, aged about five. Then the last ones are of handsome Frank. In most of them he is clothed, but he is older than the other children, and he stares at the camera with the vacant eyes of the damned. There's a photo that makes me drop the axe. It's him and Archie Spencer playing football in the garden. I'm in goal.

I spot a fading picture on the wall behind the computer. Two grinning men lean against an old Bedford van. Zanthos and Pfeiffer. They'd clearly known each other for years.

I quickly glance back to the door, expecting it to be shut, but it's still open. The grey night and trees look solid in the gap. Mrs Zanthos is out of sight and the only sound is the whistling of the wind through the doorway. I pick up the axe and take a deep breath. They all knew about the room, her included. The floor beneath me has been swept. There are no cobwebs in the corners. This place has been cleaned and painted recently, and the three men who took that child have been in prison for years.

I lurch to the door, feeling entombed. I peer outside; it's clear she's gone. I scramble out and slip and slide back towards the house. The rear door is still open. I race towards it, sliding in the snow, but I soon realise two things. Her severed finger remains on the table, but the car has vanished.

# 30

## THE COLD KILLER

I pick up the finger. It's already cold, but there's a fair amount of blood on the table and the concrete floor underneath. A little idea springs into my mind. Perhaps I should post it to Mr Barton, but no, that would be too much of a cliché. I put it in my pocket anyway. The police will be here soon if she rings them, but maybe she won't dare.

The room, more like a shrine, has chilled me to the bone but I force myself to return to it. Leaning against the computer to see if I can date the Bedford van from its number plate, I move the mouse. The screen comes to life. There's no password or screensaver, or even any icons except Windows Explorer. I click on the saved files and it brings up hundreds of them. There are drop-downs upon drop-downs. I open one of the JPEGs. It's of a young child climbing the ladder for a slide. My skin crawls.

Maybe I was destined to finish up here, to help close the loop. Mrs Zanthos can run, but she won't escape. There's nowhere for her to escape to. You can't evade who you are.

I return to the Zanthos house and walk the rooms. There's real wealth here. I find a set of screwdrivers in a drawer in the kitchen, which will come in handy. The walls and alcoves are covered with huge paintings and I swing my axe through an enormous chandelier, smiling at being covered in sprinkles and flakes for the second time today. The carpet upstairs is so thick and lush that I'm tempted to take my boots off so I can feel my feet in it, but my train is in an hour, so there's no time for that.

Mrs Zanthos won't come back here any time soon and she won't be ringing the police in a hurry either. I find a drawer containing gold and silver jewellery. There's even an A4 envelope stuffed full of cash with barely any attempt to hide it. I'm not even sure I've ever seen this many fifty-pound notes before – there must be at least a hundred. Perfect. Money can't buy everything, but this much will help make my plan easier.

I glance around and frown. There's something about this place that isn't quite right but it's hard to put my finger on what it is. I head back to the lounge and, sitting on the brown leather sofa, staring at the burning logs, I realise. Despite the leaping flames and scorching heat emanating from the fireplace, it feels as cold in here as any post-mortem slab. And why are there no photographs inside the house?

# 31

## DI BARTON

Barton had invited Strange and Zander to his house for lunch on Friday separately and didn't mention that the other was also invited. They'd both looked at him suspiciously when he'd mentioned it, but agreed after he explained it was Holly's idea as she hadn't seen them for a while. If Holly asked you around, you came.

Although it was actually his mother who'd suggested it. She said she wanted a nice lunch with a big cake. It would be her treat, with her insisting she wanted to cook and serve. She'd said to ask that lovely coloured friend of John's to come and anyone else they felt like inviting, which had given Holly the idea to thaw relations between Zander and Strange.

Barton didn't correct her outdated terminology but it was another worrying sign. His mother was usually on the ball with that sort of thing, but it was as if the past forty years were rapidly vanishing.

Barton loved living a five-minute drive from Thorpe Wood Police Station. Although Zander reckoned that was the wrong attitude and that Barton should say he lived a thirty-minute walk from work. When Barton got home, Zander's car was already there and Barton found him in the kitchen laughing with Holly. The kids were at school, so Holly had decided she'd serve up in the dining room. Barton poured them all a glass of iced water from the jug, hiding his smile when Strange turned up a few minutes late. When Holly seated her next to Zander, Barton had to pretend he'd dropped something on the floor to cover his smirk.

'This reminds me of the good old days,' said Zander.

'Was that when you used to get drunk at lunchtime, then do high-speed police chases without seat belts?' asked Strange with a bit too much snap.

'Erm, no. I'm in my forties, not my seventies. I was looking at that photograph of Mr B over there in his uniform after passing his probation. It brought me back to how exciting policing seemed when we were young.'

Zander gestured to a picture on the wall of Barton in his twenties. Barton's mum was at his side, staring up with pride.

'Oh, right,' said Strange. Barton observed her rubbing the sides of her head.

Holly had known Zander for a long time and insisted on mothering him despite them being the same age. She was the only person who called him Shawn. Strange had spent last Christmas with the family and was a regular visitor. When Barton had told Holly that Strange's and Zander's boats had bobbed together at the culmination of The Ice Killer case, but that now they were oceans apart, Holly's eyes had lit up, then narrowed. Barton could see she was hatching a plan.

Barton stood to offer to help dish up, but just then his mother appeared and gave him a stern glance, which made him feel like a little boy itching to get away from the table. He decided to sit down and introduced his colleagues to his mum again, even though she'd met them numerous times before.

A minute later, Holly came in holding two steaming plates of roast chicken and all the trimmings.

'It's a bit like Christmas Day,' said his mother, reappearing with a plate precariously held between two hands. Barton glanced up at the robust woman next to him in the photo, then at the shuffling lady beside him. He rose to help her.

'That one's for Zander,' said Holly.

'Which one was that?' said his mum, looking at Strange.

Zander put a finger up. It wavered as the plate ghosted towards him, the contents sliding menacingly to the edge. Barton grabbed the plate and placed it gently in front of Zander and guided his mum into her seat.

'This is great,' said Strange as they tucked in.

Holly tapped the back of the old lady's hand next to her and Barton couldn't help comparing them.

'All I did was dish up,' said Holly. 'This lady was on a mission.'

Barton focused on his meal and let the conversation wash over him. Holly kept trying to get Strange and Zander chatting, but neither took the bait. If they did get together as a couple, Barton could see both good and bad sides. There were pressures in policing that were hard to comprehend unless you'd done the job yourself so at least they could share their load, but he had already decided it would make sense to put them in different departments if they did become an item. He didn't want to lose either, but change was always coming.

Barton realised he did have a bit of gossip that might get the conversation started. Strange had dated one of the local crime scene managers, Sirena, briefly, and after they'd split up Sirena had returned to Greece to look after her ageing father.

'I have some intel,' said Barton, when it was quiet. 'I heard through the grapevine that Sirena is back in Peterborough.'

'Really?' said Strange. 'I hope her father's okay.'

'DCI Cox saw her. Sirena's dad had made enough of a full recovery to tell her to leave.'

'Oh.' Strange laughed. 'That's great news.'

Barton grinned at Zander, who didn't look quite as happy.

Soon, though, the banter picked up and Barton couldn't help wondering why they didn't do this more often. Barton felt someone's gaze on him. It was his mother. He'd watched her trying to absorb the conversations going on, but then she seemed to relax and look around peacefully. She held eye contact and winked at him.

It was then that it dawned on him that his mother knew exactly what she was doing when she asked for this. It was a last hurrah. She knew the end was coming and she wanted to feel like a mother and a host one last time. Barton felt his eyes begin to fill up.

Holly was taking orders for pudding when his phone rang. Glad of the distraction, he excused himself from the table.

'Barton speaking.'

'Hi, sir, it's Malik. I'm just ringing to let you know there's been a suspected burglary in Longthorpe.'

'Anyone hurt?'

'Not sure at this point, but the back door was wide open.'

'Okay, why are you calling me?'

'Well, the guy who died in the prison, Zanthos, it's his house.'

Barton's brain caught up. 'Ah-ha! I bet the evasive wife wants to speak to us now.'

'That's the thing, sir. Uniform have been through the property and there's no sign of her. Her neighbour called it in because there was a fire in a shelter behind the back garden. Uniform think there might be a body in there.'

# 32

## PFEIFFER – TARGET TWO

Saul Pfeiffer had experienced an uneasy night. After so long inside, he'd got accustomed to sleeping behind a locked prison door. It was the only time that he felt completely safe. Each day was the same in prison, but at least there were no temptations to distract him – the noise silenced his dreams.

He'd been popular at senior school, winning the hundred yards dash each year until he'd started getting attention from girls. He'd thrown the race in his last term because the attention of the women revolted him. In fact, all adults repulsed him. He had never married, and an attraction to children began to surface, the older he became. He met like-minded Zanthos in his twenties, and they'd become friends, eventually bonding over their shared fantasies. By the time they retired, those fantasies had grown into an obsession for both of them.

Saul's proclivities weren't completely sexual for him. They were more of a fascination with youth. Before computers, he'd had to satisfy himself with children's clothes catalogues, but the Internet changed everything. There were secret chat groups for others like him and he made friends with people for the first time since he was a child. For once in his life, he didn't feel alone or a freak. And there was so much great stuff to look at. He was in heaven.

But, as he suspected it might, his desire to look at images progressed to wanting something more. He dreamt of observing that perfect skin in real life, perhaps even touching it.

Saul had excelled in finance during his career and considered himself to be the most intelligent person he knew, so he understood what was happening to him. All the focus on children with others online had started to normalise his behaviour when he understood deep down it was anything but normal. Yet, what did he have to lose? He suspected people like him didn't get into heaven, even if they apologised profusely.

So, Pfeiffer started visiting different parks all over the city where he sat on benches and watched the children. Later, his favourite spot became the play areas on the British Sugar site because it was next to a road. If the weather was bad, he'd stay in the car and observe without fear of being called a paedo, which was an occupational hazard if you forgot what you were doing. He just drove away if anyone got suspicious.

That would have been enough, but he noticed another old man doing the same thing. It took years of nodding and comments in passing about the weather as they sat at separate benches until Mr Ballanchine introduced himself. It was Ballanchine who came up with the plan.

Afterwards, Pfeiffer found it hard to believe he agreed to it. The chance of getting away with what they did was slim, but curiosity had blinded him and, he supposed, lust. That weakness led to a twelve-year sentence. The shame would have been too much for most normal people to bear and suicide a likely conclusion, but Pfeiffer was not a normal man.

After the sheer terror of the first few nights in jail, he got used to it. He was on a wing with his co-conspirators after all, and he'd lived a life blighted by shame. He could easily cope with a bit more.

The scheme had been simple and Pfeiffer played his part in it because he didn't have a criminal record, unlike Ballanchine and Zanthos, so the police might be more likely to accept his protestations of innocence. The plan was for him to distract a mother long enough for Ballanchine to sneak her kid into the untraceable van. Then Zanthos would drive them away. It would have been the perfect crime if it weren't for the police monitoring the chat group.

He blamed Ballanchine. No one was supposed to touch her. And she wasn't supposed to be kept overnight, but she fell asleep. Pfeiffer stayed up all night watching her. It had been wonderful. They'd returned her the next morning, unscathed.

So, despite everything, he didn't regret it. The police had them nailed, but they never found Zanthos's amazing shrine beyond the back of his garden and the thought of returning to that special place kept him focused and strong in jail. And now it was time.

His fingers fumbled with the buttons of his shirt. He pulled his jacket on and perched his trilby at a jaunty angle. His best suit was loose after prison, but he'd soon fill that out again. He stared in the mirror. He didn't resemble a devil and didn't consider himself to be one. God had created him this way. How could it be wrong? It didn't hurt to look at nice things.

'I'm just off out to a friend's house,' he shouted to Norma, his sister, who was doing the washing and was deaf as a post. He had to tap her on the shoulder and shout it in her face.

'Okay, Saul.' She smiled. 'Enjoy yourself. I've got a lovely bit of salmon for tea, so be back by six.'

'I wouldn't miss that for the world,' he replied.

He climbed into his old Jaguar Sovereign and it fired up first thing. Norma was a steadying influence. She had kept his house and car running while he was inside and had been his only visitor.

She'd lived a tough life and was a little odd herself. Her ex-husband had beaten her nearly to death twenty years ago, and Pfeiffer had collected her from the hospital and taken her home. She never ventured out.

The roads had been gritted, but it was slow going to Longthorpe from Alwalton. It'd snowed so hard that even the parkway was down to one lane. Still, he'd waited a long time for today. A few more minutes would only heighten his pleasure. He pulled up outside Zanthos's house with a little skid.

He took a few deep breaths and tried to wipe the huge grin off his face, but it wasn't easy. Zanthos had enjoyed the more risqué stuff on the computer, but Pfeiffer liked to stand in the middle of the room and merely look at all the photographs on the walls. Such youth and innocence, such beauty. Often, he'd find himself drawn to one picture and he'd stare at it for hours, feeling as if he were falling inside it. A trickle of sweat ran down his temple when he stepped from the car.

The sky was laden with clouds, as though it could fall in at any moment. As he knocked on the door, large, heavy snowflakes flurried around him. It felt like being in a snow globe. He wondered for a second if Ballanchine would be there as well. The shrine wasn't Ballanchine's thing, though. Zanthos and Pfeiffer, on the other hand, had spent many happy hours in there. Ballanchine had already told him when they were inside that he would reoffend soon after getting out. Ballanchine was a real paedophile, and Zanthos had said before he died that he planned to steer clear of him. Pfeiffer wanted nothing to do with him either.

Pfeiffer shivered at the prospect of Ballanchine's place in this weather. Imagine the mould and damp. Bedsheets heavy with mildew. Ballanchine would be lucky to survive the night. Without much money and in failing health, Ballanchine might as well commit one last crime and be in prison because his options were so poor. From what they'd heard about care homes, they weren't that different from prison, anyway.

It occurred to Pfeiffer, as he waited at the door, that Mrs Zanthos was single now. She made a good Madeira cake, too. He had just pressed the doorbell again when he noticed the curtain twitch. When the door opened, Pfeiffer struggled to believe his eyes.

'Well, well, Mr Pfeiffer. What are you doing here?'

Pfeiffer recovered fast.

'I could ask you the same question,' he said. 'I've come to pay my respects. What are you doing here?'

'Your respects to Mrs Zanthos, or your little room out the back?'

Pfeiffer knew the game was up when the door swung fully open and he saw the weapon. He smelled burning and feared the worst for Mrs Zanthos. There wasn't any hope of fighting his way out of the situation, so he turned and shuffled through the snow in the hope he'd be allowed to leave. He slipped as he neared the car and went down. A strong arm helped him to his feet and opened the car door for him.

'We're going for a little ride.'

Pfeiffer got in the vehicle and put his seat belt on. The man, who no doubt planned to do something nasty to him, entered and sat behind him.

'Drive to Oundle Road, slowly. Go through town. The roads will be better.'

Pfeiffer's hands and feet had gone numb, but he managed to start the car.

'Okay,' he said under his breath.

Pfeiffer put the engine in gear, started the wipers, and crept forward. It was madness, driving in such heavy snow. Visibility was no more than ten metres, but only a few other people were foolish enough to be out, and they reached their destination intact. Pfeiffer was instructed to turn right and, with a sinking feeling, pulled up next to his favourite playground as directed.

'Now, talk. I need to hear everything from the moment you first met Zanthos. I know it all already, but I want you to confirm it. If you lie, even once, I will know, and I'll set fire to this car with you in it. A fiery hell, in advance of the one where you will no doubt end up.'

Pfeiffer looked at the man's face in the rear-view mirror. He could tell from his expression that this was a man who was on a mission to the end. Pfeiffer thought of his warm house and the nice piece of salmon waiting for him, so he told him everything. From the start to the finish, even his feelings and needs.

After he'd finished, to his surprise, he felt unburdened somehow. As though it was good to admit to what he'd become. The man squeezed his shoulder gently, but then he gripped him hard. There was a slight ripping sound, which he assumed was the upholstery of his seat, before searing pain tore through his chest. He gasped, looked down and pulled his coat open. The knife blade was so long, a good inch poked through the middle of his shirt.

Always a practical man, Pfeiffer knew this was the end. He raised his right hand and wiped the condensation from the window so he could see the swings for the last time, but it was snowing too hard.

# 33

## DI BARTON

Strange, Zander and Barton got into Barton's 4x4 and, thanks to the thick tyres, were soon at the address for the suspected burglary despite the poor driving conditions. Barton didn't turn the engine off straight away. His sergeants seemed a little distracted after the big meal. They were probably sleepy after the wedge of cake they all gulped down before they left. Barton's mother had fallen asleep at the table with her fork still in her hand.

'Focus, guys,' said Barton. 'The fact we are here a few days after her husband's demise for something completely different speaks volumes. We need to be on the ball because this could be anything. I wouldn't be surprised if this didn't turn out to be another murder.'

Both gave him a serious nod and they all got out of the car and stood outside the house. There were two police response vans outside, but there appeared to be little movement until a grey-haired woman in slippers and a light-yellow housecoat appeared, holding an umbrella. The female PC escorting her lifted the cordon tape and the old lady shuffled through. She looked at the three of them and instantly worked out that Barton was in charge.

'I've been telling those kids in there that she's a good person.

Had to put up with terrible accusations. She was always worried someone would come looking for her husband to cause mischief.'

'What kids?' asked Strange, looking puzzled.

'These bloody kids playing at police. They told me to wait out here or go back to my house.'

The PC grimaced, but a flurry of snow quickly concealed her expression.

'DS Zander will escort you to your property and take a statement. We'll need everything you can tell us. You could be really useful to our investigation,' said Barton.

Strange walked away down the path to the Zanthos house without commenting and disappeared into the snow, so the woman peered up at Zander.

'Come on, then, son. I've a nice bottle of sherry on the go.'

Smiling, Barton followed after Strange and the PC, regretting his choice of footwear. It was unusual weather for Peterborough. On the east of the country, it rarely snowed. In fact, this was the first proper fall they'd had since the case of the Snow Killer. The forecast said it would be gone in a few days, but as he opened the gate and saw black smoke rising from a thicket he had a nasty feeling that when it disappeared, bad news would remain behind.

At the rear of the property was an overhanging porch and a picnic table. The wind had swirled the snow up so there was a covering up to the back door. A uniformed constable was stamping his feet there in a vain effort to keep warm.

'Afternoon, sir.'

'Can you give me an update, please?' said Barton.

'It's fairly simple at this point. The neighbour saw the smoke from the back garden and, being nosey, came around to check it out. She found flames bursting out of a sunken shed, and no sign of the owner in the house despite the back door being open. She went inside and looked for her, but the place was empty. You don't need police training to see that the rooms have been ransacked and therefore presumably burgled.'

At that point, another PC whom Barton didn't recognise came out of the house. Barton nodded appreciatively at her covered shoes and the plastic gloves on her hands.

'Definitely empty?' asked Barton.

'Yes, weird though. We rang it in, but I thought I'd have a look around seeing as the neighbour said the occupant was of an advanced age. Nothing much useful, I'm afraid, no mobile phones left behind, no visible blood stains. I did find a half-drunk cup of tea on the table with a half-eaten biscuit on a plate. The heating is on constant, not on the timer. TV's on too, but on silent. From my observations, I'd say the owner heard the doorbell and never came back.'

'What's your name?' asked Barton.

'Nicola Pignatiello. Pigs, for short.'

Barton grinned. Only a confident, attractive person would be happy with such a nickname. When Barton had been in uniform, he'd been called exactly that almost daily.

'Good work. Any other possible explanation?'

'My nan's always leaving her front door open, never mind the back. The occupant could have nipped to the shop, forgotten an appointment at the doctor's, or any number of things.'

'And the fire out the back?'

'An officer is out there guarding the scene, but it's not as sinister as we thought.'

Barton made a mental note to ask about this woman. She looked a little like a young Monica Bellucci, but her nose was more prominent. Naturally talented detectives were hard to come by.

'Where's the fire brigade?' asked Strange.

The sergeant cleared his throat.

'I arrived at the same time as the response vehicle. It's chaos across the city with the roads. Two of the local appliances are out using their cutting equipment on the parkways, and the others are at that electrical warehouse blaze. This fire wasn't at any risk of spreading and seemed to be dwindling.'

'I take it there wasn't a burning body.'

'No. Only piles of newspaper and what looks like a melted old-style computer monitor and printer. The fire has probably burned out now.'

Barton looked from the sergeant to Pigs.

'Well done, you two. Good work.'

Barton smiled at them both. Despite what the media liked to portray, the force was conscientious, experienced and motivated, like these two. Mistakes were rare. If it weren't for the criminals, his job would be easy.

Barton decided to look at the fire first. He asked Strange to put covers on and have another search in the house. His brain was firing off connections left, right and centre. The snow had stopped as suddenly as it had started, so Barton could see the end of the garden. Everything seemed normal. The thicket on the left at the bottom behind a metre-high fence looked well established. The PC down there had taped off a section of the fence, but on close inspection it was a concealed gate. Alarm bells rang.

Barton smiled at the PC but didn't say anything as he walked around to where the last of the tape was and slid through a gap in the branches where he could make out the shape of what could be a secret room. The fire had gone out, and the smoke was clearing. The property backed onto farmland, which was separated by another fence. He thought back to what he'd read of the abduction investigation.

The child said afterwards that she believed the men were taking her to her mum, but they were friendly. They gave her some sweets and a funny-tasting drink, but she was sleepy. She remembered half waking in a warm house, but also mentioned a caravan.

Barton stared at the burned computer, then around the walls. The interior of the room was scorched, but there were square patches, which looked as if they'd had picture frames or posters on. Barton didn't need to be Poirot to guess the purpose of this shelter. Zanthos's wife, who had proclaimed innocence and had been elsewhere during the time of the kidnapping, must have known about this place.

He would need an incident room setting up right away. It was going to be a late night. Something horrific was in motion here and the bad news was that he had a feeling they were playing catch-up already.

# 34

## DI BARTON

Barton and the team were back at the station and he now stood at the front of the incident room next to a whiteboard. Strange, Zander, Malik, Leicester and Zelensky were present and Barton appreciated them being there because 10 p.m. had been and gone. At this point, he wasn't entirely sure what they were dealing with.

'Listen in, please,' said Barton. 'We have the death of Mr Zanthos in prison, but let's put that to one side for the moment and look purely at today. Strange.'

'Right,' said Strange, walking to the front. 'A suspected burglary has occurred. We need to contact the owner, Mrs Zanthos, but she's disappeared, which is either worrying or suspicious. The whole county is looking for her, but we're aware she can be hard to get hold of. We don't yet know what was stolen. The neighbour said she'd not been further into the house than the kitchen, so she was no help on that. The intruder could have just been opportunistic. Normally, we'd leave this with uniform, who would thoroughly investigate in due course.'

They all chuckled at that. Burglaries were rarely investigated nowadays unless expensive goods had gone missing or someone had been injured in the process. Strange waited for quiet.

'It's the fire out the back that is giving us most concern. It's reasonable to conclude that it was a secret room probably connected to Mr Zanthos's offending, which Mrs Zanthos must have known about, and was never discovered in the original investigation into her husband. The fact it was set on fire today is likely to mean one thing. Mrs Zanthos, or someone else, torched the place to dispose of the evidence. Any other views?'

Zander put his hand up.

'Is it feasible that the fire was started by an electrical fault?'

'Possible, but unlikely, according to the firefighters on the scene,' she replied. 'The fire chief said it was highly likely that the newspaper was used as fuel. Paper burns hot, so in a confined space there would be nothing salvageable from the computer.'

'No one leaves their door open in weather like this,' said Barton. 'My money is on foul play against Mrs Zanthos. Who else is in the picture?'

'At this point, it could be anyone,' said Leicester. 'Zanthos's death in the prison wasn't widely reported, and he hasn't been buried yet, but it is possible one of his victims went there thinking he would have got out the day before.'

'Good point,' said Strange. 'It's also conceivable that one of the two remaining perps visited. They're both old, maybe they knew about the room and decided to get rid of it before it was ever found.'

'Surely Mrs Zanthos could have done away with it while they were inside. She must have known about it,' said Malik. 'Why would she wait? I reckon the person who destroyed it did so against her will.'

'Perhaps. We certainly have a lot of avenues to explore,' replied Barton. 'I like the connection to Mr Zanthos. The day after he was due to get out of jail, his house gets ransacked or burgled. We find a secret building in the rear of the garden on fire. I've rung DCI Cox, who has been in Devon with relatives, and given her the heads up. She was involved in the abduction case and remembers the garden because it was so well tended. They didn't search beyond the fence at the property. Why would you? They had the girl back with her parents, relatively unscathed, and three suspects in prison all admitting to the false imprisonment of that child.'

'They admitted guilt straight away?' asked Strange.

'Yes, the evidence was conclusive. Their chatroom messages were already being monitored, so it was a case of joining the big dots after the crime was committed. They had two of them on a traffic camera near the area, crystal clear. That's what fouled them up. They hadn't known there was CCTV and ANPR everywhere, they thought it was only in town centres and on motorways. If you consider that they were looking at a sentence with a starting point of twelve years for abduction, then it's extra for it being a young child, so eighteen years would have been reasonable. An early guilty plea gets that back down to twelve, which is a big difference, and what they received in the end. The van was found not long after, which I'm guessing they suspected it would be. All three men's and the girl's DNA were all over it. Case closed, so pleading innocent would have been a waste of time.'

'And the girl said she wasn't messed with?' asked Zander.

'No, apart from having her face and hair washed, which is weird. She also saw mobile phones.'

'Of course, they took pictures,' said Zander. 'They should be banged up for life, or castrated.'

'Both,' agreed Zelensky.

Barton nodded at Zander, who'd lost his young child to CO poisoning several years ago, and lost his marriage shortly after. Since then, he was very focused on child cases. Strange, too, had been quite fervent earlier as they processed the scene. Barton understood the rage officers felt when they were investigating crimes against the vulnerable, but it could stop people thinking straight. Calm heads were needed.

'Correct me at any point, but the best-case scenario is that Zanthos died of natural causes. His wife is old and forgetful, and has merely gone out or away.'

Zander grinned at him. 'Nope, there's too much going on here.'

'Agreed. This seems personal. Who would want to punish Zanthos?'

'The child or the mother, or one of their relatives,' said Malik.

'Yes, although Cox said the girl's family had moved to live with extended family in California.'

'Maybe whoever murdered Zanthos in prison has been released, and come and abducted, or killed, his wife too,' said Zelensky.

'Yes, but his wife wasn't involved in the case, so why?' said Barton.

'She wasn't proven to be connected in that case. Perhaps they faked her alibi, so she was out of it in case anything went wrong. That way she could make sure no one got hold of their material, which they probably kept in that room.'

'Very good,' said Barton.

Zelensky was a petite blonde, even shorter than Strange, but she had the same determination to progress. She had coped with the trauma of the violent death of her previous boyfriend by throwing herself into the role with all her heart and time. Too much of her time, realised Barton, because she was often at work hours after her shift had officially finished.

'Maybe the room was for her and her husband. Like some kind of shrine for their depraved habits,' she said.

Barton wrote Mrs Zanthos in the middle of the board and put an arrow to Mr Zanthos.

'Yes, that sounds credible,' he said. 'It's doubtful she wouldn't know about it, but all the evidence has been destroyed inside. The CSIs found what they think was a melted keyboard and the monitor for a computer, but no tower. Maybe she's gone to hide it, but why not just fry it with the rest? Who else is likely to be involved?'

'Maybe they were being smart,' said Strange. 'Forensics can get data off almost anything nowadays.'

Barton nodded.

'Seeing as his co-defendants were released yesterday,' said Zander, 'I would normally say they were definitely involved, but you've met them. They're old and frail. I can't imagine them getting up to too much mischief, especially in this weather.'

'Perhaps they got out and picked her up and together they took the tower and burned the remaining evidence,' said Strange.

Zander clicked his fingers.

'That fits with the neighbour's comments. She saw a few cars pulling up over the morning and afternoon, and people arriving, which she said was unusual. Mrs Zanthos rarely had visitors. It could have been either Pfeiffer or Ballanchine coming to give her orders.'

'I'm not sure that makes sense,' said Zelensky. 'They served six years and were released on licence. They could have incinerated the place then. They were recalled to prison, did another eighteen months, and then got released again, but still it remained intact. And again, they were recalled, eventually having to complete the rest of their sentence behind bars. Why do it now? I reckon it would be too important to them. There was probably a life's work in there.'

Barton yawned. It was 11 p.m. The easy thing would be to send them home and crack on tomorrow because the case could explode in the morning. Yet, there was always something they could do right now that might help. The team could cope with little sleep for a few days, but any more than that and mistakes might slip in.

His team were rabbiting to each other as he pondered their next steps. Was there anything obvious that he was missing? Barton suspected the worst. If Mr Zanthos was killed inside, he wouldn't be over-surprised if his wife was now dead somewhere outside. The two men released yesterday both had form for kidnapping, and they might have been worried about the computer. Strange was right, they could pull everything off a hard drive nowadays. The three men could have spent their last few years plotting about what to do when they got out.

He looked out of the window at the clear sky. A gritter trundled past the front of the station. If the forecast was right, that was probably it for the snow, but the temperature was due to drop significantly. Still, tomorrow would be easier. He cleared his throat and prepared to see if the team were on the ball.

'It's late. We'll have an early start in the morning. What needs doing tonight?'

Zelensky put her hand up. She hadn't got comfortable calling him John, like most of the others.

'Sir, we need to pick up Pfeiffer and Ballanchine right away. They're already involved in some way. They could have killed Mr Zanthos in the prison, and they could have taken care of Mrs Zanthos as soon as they were released.'

Barton nodded in agreement, but Zelensky hadn't seen how they were beginning to struggle with old age. Strange smiled at him, and he knew she'd deduced what he had.

'I agree,' she said. 'We need to talk to them, but I have a feeling that instead of them being responsible, I'd worry about them being next.'

Zander looked round at Strange and slowly applauded. They all contemplated that thought in silence for a few moments, then

Barton sent Strange and Malik to bring in Pfeiffer, and Zander and Zelensky to fetch Ballanchine. They had release addresses for both of the men – Pfeiffer was close by in Alwalton, and Ballanchine's property was only in Glinton, a village about ten miles away. They would keep them in overnight and question them tomorrow, unless they gave them something that needed acting on immediately.

The first few days of an investigation like this were always manic. They would need to submit all the information to HOLMES, the police computer. Barton had a whole load of paperwork, authorising and notifying, before he could leave, just to get the ball rolling, so he got to it. He thought of Holly at home, yet again holding the fort.

Uniform had confirmed they would have a revolving team keeping an eye on the Zanthos property tonight and ongoing. There were no further updates there. Thirty minutes later, Strange was the first to ring through from Alwalton.

'Hi, John. The house is locked up and we've knocked loud enough to wake the dead. No evidence of a disturbance. There's a light on in the lounge, but no signs of life. There is a car shaped gap in the snow, but it's been partially filled, so the car must have left some time ago. We've also spotted more recent tracks of footprints leaving and arriving at the property. They disappear at the path, which has been well gritted. Someone left here a little while back on foot and returned.'

'Okay, let's call it a night. That could have been a visitor or just someone delivering leaflets. I'll have uniform look in tomorrow. You go home and get some rest. Meeting at 8:30.'

Zander rang in next.

'Zero going on here. It's a small run-down cottage, and the garden is wild. Nothing dodgy, though. It's really isolated, but there's a light on at a farmhouse a little distance back on the same road. I'll knock there, then head home. I'm due to start at six, so I'll catch up with you then.'

Barton worked for another half-hour, then decided to call it quits as well. Leicester had stayed to help, so Barton sent him on his way. Barton liked to sleep on a case because his brain had a habit of processing all the data overnight, and he often woke up with fresh insight.

Barton was pulling his coat on when his phone rang. It was one of the PCs who was on duty at the station's front desk.

'Sir. I spoke to Sergeant Strange before she left, and she updated me on the burglary and fire. I've also read the email informing us of people of interest in case events escalated this evening. Well, I've just had an old woman walk into the station.'

'Is her name Zanthos?'

'No, she wanted to file a missing person's report, but the person had only been missing since 6 p.m. We've been flat out, so it's taken us a while to get to her.'

'Spit it out, who's she looking for?'

'Saul Pfeiffer.'

# 35

## THE COLD KILLER

The train is less than an hour late as it trundles into Alnmouth station, which is surprising, considering the conditions. I'm guessing that as the snow has been well forecasted, they are better prepared. The big plough on the front of the engine was proof they were on the ball, and I only had to wait ten minutes for the connection at Newcastle. It's bitterly cold this far up north. There are only four other souls getting off, all of them women. We crunch along the wet concourse on thick grit.

There's someone to meet the other passengers, three of whom I now see are teenagers. One receives a kiss from a fatherly figure and the girls shuffle off after him, pulling their coats around them. Outside, there's only one taxi idling in the rank. The other passenger, a woman my age, glances in my direction. I nod to her and she gets in, giving the driver a cheery hello. He pulls away and leaves me alone and frozen. At least it's stopped snowing.

I post Barton his little present in the postbox outside the station, but the animosity I feel towards him is fading. Although, he needs to learn from his mistakes.

I planned to scope out the address, then find a bench or somewhere to sleep on until the morning, but it's too chilly for that, even with my warm clothing. The best thing to do when it's like this is keep moving, or perhaps sit in a twenty-four-hour McDonald's. A village this small probably hasn't got one though.

But, instead, I decide to get a cab to the address I've been given and knock on the door. I'm nervous as I've ever been in my life before. Until now I have never understood the fight-or-flight reflex, even in my first firefight when many new recruits pissed themselves or ran the wrong way. I understand that now because I could do the same.

Brenda was a night owl so I know she'll be up if she's at home. It doesn't really matter. The important part is done. If she rings the police, so be it. I just feel tired and worn down by my existence. Perhaps I'll be more upbeat in the morning.

I was changing from the man I was before I discovered I might have a son, but that new information took my breath away more than the cold. I try to recall my thoughts from back then but it's hard. Part of me, the good bit, if it still exists, knows I should stay out of their business, but I have to know if Brenda really did have my son. I've had a sickness in my stomach ever since Grayson told me, even though I know he could have been lying.

Kevin is clearly a headcase, so it wouldn't be a surprise if he was mine. Headlights blind me as I stare up the road, then a hackney carriage taxi stops alongside me. Decision made, I clamber in woodenly, already stiff from the chill, and give the driver the address.

He glances back at me, shrugs, and puts the blasters on full whack. It's amazing when the heat hits me, but when he pulls up a minute later and tells me the fare's a fiver, I'm tempted to ask him how much to stay seated for another five minutes, so I can feel my feet as well as my hands. But, instead, I pay him and look down the street when I get out.

The cars are lumps of snow and I spot a bin on its side with frozen rubbish spilling into the road. An animal of some kind furtively slips behind a van. The house number I'm after is right in front of me. It's a Victorian terrace with a paved front garden. It looks cared for. In fact, it seems well-to-do at second glance, posh even. Maybe Brenda lives with someone new. Feeling more panicky than when running towards machine-gun fire, I stride up the steps and press the buzzer. I force myself to breathe in and out. A hall light comes on and a figure approaches through the misty glass.

The door opens until there's a little thud as the chain stops its movement. Half a face, no make-up, mousey hair and a kind eye peek out.

'Yes.'

What do I say after all this time, after how I left?

'Brenda?'

'Yes.'

'It's your soldier.'

The eye blinks twice. I remember I have my hood up, so I pull it off. She jumps back in shock and slams the door shut. I stand rigid for at least a minute. What did I expect? I suppose her reaction is fair, even if it's a blow. There's been a fire in me since I heard about our son and as it dwindles, standing in the cold, I realise those flames were hope. Men like me shouldn't have that because we are too violent for this world. I was built for war, not peace.

I turn round and take small light-headed steps back down her path and into the road. When I met Zanthos in the prison, I wanted revenge, but it doesn't seem important now. Nothing does, except to know if I have a son. Pulling my hood up, I trudge in the general direction of the railway station.

'Wait.'

A shrill voice echoes out into the quiet snowy street. I stop and turn. In a small pair of pink slippers and a tight pair of jeans, she treads carefully down the steps into her front garden, yanking her cardigan around her. She's aged, but not as much as I expected. She still has a slim waist with a big bottom – that bottom used to make me grit my teeth.

I often joked that the local evening news had reported that Kelly Clarkson had been seen rooting around in the discount bin at our Kwik Save, but it was actually Brenda.

'Is it really you?' she asks.

I turn and hustle back to stand in front of her but struggle for words while she studies my face. Then she cowers and collapses to her knees. I reach out a hand, which she slaps away. She bows her head for a few moments, then clambers to her feet.

'Hey, I would never hurt you.'

She raises an eyebrow, wipes her nose with one sleeve, then her eyes with the other.

'I suppose you'd better come in before we both freeze to death.'

I follow her inside and close the door behind me. There is a row of women's shoes next to the skirting board, so I unlace my boots and place them there. When I look up, she's shaking her head but doesn't say anything.

The house is long and narrow, but very clean, and there's some nice furniture amongst a few tired items. There are photographs on the walls, but it's too dingy to make out any faces. We walk through a cosy lounge with the TV on quietly, pass through another doorway, then she points to a dining-room table. She fills the kettle in the galley kitchen while I take a seat.

'Coffee?' she asks.

'Anything warm would be great.'

'Irish?'

'If you're having one.'

'I need something strong, what with you showing up. What's it been? Must be well over twenty years.'

I nod and involuntarily shiver. She opens the cabinet under the sink, and removes a bottle of Bell's whisky and puts it on a tray. While the kettle boils, she takes a long glance at me and moves to the thermostat on the wall and twists the dial. She eventually brings over the tray with two mugs of white coffee and the whisky, then sits down opposite me.

'How did you find my address?'

'I bumped into Grayson.'

'In Peterborough?'

'Yes.'

'I told him nothing good would come of looking for you. How did he find you?'

'We were staying at the same hotel.'

Brenda was always on the ball.

'Prison?'

'Prison.'

She gives me a cold emotionless glance, pours a glug of whisky into both of our mugs, then takes a swig from the bottle. She grimaces and screws the lid back on.

'I knew he'd end up there. He's a good kid really, but he blames everyone else for the problems he causes. Was he on his own?'

'No, with another lad.'

She places both hands on the table and rises. There are more pictures on the wall. She reaches up and takes one down.

'I don't have many photos of them. They always hated having their pictures taken. Is this him?'

There's a picture of a smart young man who looks about sixteen. He's in a tuxedo, jaw clenched, staring defiantly into the lens. His hair is different from how mine was until I started getting crew cuts, but he has my forehead, and I spent my youth with the exact same expression. Brenda used to say that the Action Man figure and I had the same face. Hence the nickname of Soldier. The girl on Kevin's arm is beautiful in a cocktail dress. She seems to be whispering into his ear. It's a great shot.

'Yes. That's definitely him.'

'That's Kevin.'

'I didn't recognise Grayson, but he came and told me who he was. Is Kevin my son?'

She looks at me for a few moments before answering.

'Yes, he is. Well, you played a small part.'

I suppose that's fair.

'What's he like?'

'He flew off the rails when he was young. I'm not sure if that's your fault or mine, but he calmed down a bit towards the end of school. He wanted to join the army, but his record got in the way. I explained to him that's what happened to you, too. It must have festered because he decided he was going to find you.'

'Why didn't you tell me about him?'

'Why should I? You'd gone.'

I think of what I've missed out on and a lump forms in my throat, so I change tack.

'I hear you're the KGB. Kevin, Grayson and Brenda.'

Brenda looks at my face with an expression I struggle to decipher. It's kindness with a hint of pity, or perhaps amusement.

'Not quite.'

She points at the two kids in the photograph again. Her finger going from one to the other.

'Who's the girl?' I finally ask.

'Kevin's twin sister, Barbara.'

# 36

## THE COLD KILLER

The mug slips from my hands and drops into my lap, but I'm too stunned to move, even though it's scalding. It feels as though my eyes are going to fall out of their sockets. There's a buzzing in my head as if a train is going through it. Then, for the first time in my life, I weep. It's a shameful, embarrassing sound, all the more pitiful because I'm focusing on my pain, despite knowing deep down that Brenda and the children will have suffered more.

Brenda fetches a tea towel and throws it at my lap.

'I'm glad you've turned up because I was worried about the boys. I fooled myself into thinking that I didn't want to know, but I did. They're not bad lads, they just do stupid, impulsive things. I expect you have a lot of questions, but before that I'm going to tell you my story. All of it, and you're going to listen.'

I wipe my eyes with the tea towel, then rest it on my lap. 'Okay.'

'Grayson can't have been two years old when you started to slip away from me. You were great with the boy, but money was tight and I didn't feel right. You remember we began to row. Our relationship was centred around booze and I feared you'd leave me, although I hoped you wouldn't because your bond with Grayson was strong, despite him being another man's child. You weren't sleeping though. I woke you up one night because I was desperate to talk, but you were in the middle of one of your dreams and grabbed me by the throat.'

'I don't remember. I'm sorry.'

'Shh, just listen. I know it's not simple. I knew you'd been involved in wars and you'd done things that were hard to forget, but you never told me anything about them, even if I asked. There was also something that happened in your childhood that you wouldn't speak about. Often, you woke up drenched in sweat with your fists clenched. Other nights, you'd scream the name Frank in your sleep. Sometimes it felt like you spent the whole day half awake and half asleep. You were a stranger at times, but my best friend at others. Perhaps I should have made you talk to me.'

She takes a big sip of her cup of Irish coffee, then passes it to me.

'We argued but left things unsaid. You even called me fat and lazy during one of our final quarrels. I hadn't noticed the weight gain. It explained my tiredness, too. It wasn't like how I was pregnant with Grayson. The twins were sucking the life out of me, although I didn't realise it at the time. I took a home test, and it was positive, but I didn't know how to break it to you. We had a huge ruckus that last morning because I was stressed about going to the hospital. I threw a cup at you, if you remember, and missed.'

'Yeah.' I grin and she does too. 'You broke the clock.'

Her smile fades.

'We both said some bad things to each other. At the hospital, they did the scan and told me it was twins. I realised I had to tell you that night, but when I got home, you'd packed your stuff and left.'

I put my hands over my face as I recall that evening. I'd been labouring, as usual, on building sites and had been sacked for arguing with the foreman after arriving at the site in a foul mood. When I returned home, I decided that was it. It was time to leave. I grabbed my rucksack, filled it, and twenty minutes later I caught a train to London where a bricklayer had told me they were providing accommodation for work on a new shopping centre.

After I'd calmed down, I missed Brenda and Grayson, but I took the easy way out. I drank until I forgot. I hadn't planned to stay too long in London, but it was a laugh. Sometimes I'd think of them. I liked the fact that maybe I had something to return to, even if I never did actually go back. There was a load of hard-drinking Irish who were happy to exchange blows at the end of a night and shake hands the next day. They were my kind of people. I got into fights with anyone who wanted one. There were two stints inside during that time, both for Actual Bodily Harm. The years flew by and I already knew not to dwell on the past.

I've been staring into the fire and didn't notice Brenda get up, but she returns with a pair of small whisky glasses and pours us each a big glug.

'You know the crazy part? I was sure you'd come back. There was no Facebook or whatever back then. We had no mobile phones. I had no way of chasing you. But I had a blind faith you'd return. Maybe in a few weeks, or perhaps months. Next thing, I had three kids in nappies. I don't know how I survived. The next decade was a blur, but I still had the odd twinge of hope if the doorbell rang unexpectedly, or I saw a familiar face in the crowd. It took a long time to realise how pathetic I was being.'

'It shows your strength that you got through it.'

'Well, for some reason, I called our twins Kevin and Barbara, so I must have been out of my mind to be so unimaginative. Life took over and three kids was a handful. Your son was a bad apple, and I couldn't control him, even from a young age. Boys like that need their fathers. He dragged Grayson down until he was probably worse because he was older. The later school years were tough times, and the police were regular visitors. It wasn't fair on Barbara, so a few years ago we moved up here for a fresh start. The lads weren't supposed to come, but they lost their flat and came for a visit and didn't leave. But it's too quiet for them round here. Barbara's gone to university in Scotland now. I'm not certain if it was because the course she wanted was up there, or to get further away from her brothers. We both knew they'd end up in prison. What did they do?'

'I asked an officer to check their record. They both had previous for a non-domestic aggravated burglary, which basically means they broke into a factory or warehouse with some kind of weapon. They were disturbed by a security guard, who was hurt in the process of them getting away. Grayson said they weren't on the rob, just having a look around.'

Brenda takes another swig of the whisky but doesn't grimace.

'And this sentence?'

'Affray. They went looking for a fight, and their victims got broken bones.'

She frowns. 'I'd like to break their bones.'

'That should have been my job.'

She doesn't smile.

'You know, when you get a knock on the door at night around here, you don't usually answer it. I've been expecting that knock from the police ever since they left. Telling me that one or both are dead.'

We sit in silence for long minutes, both lost in thought. I feel sadness for what I did, but fate took a hand. A small smile creeps onto my face. I've always been able to blame someone or something else for my fuck-ups. Maybe that's what I taught Grayson before I left. It's strange. I was ready to give up, but perhaps I can help in some way.

'What are you grinning at, you idiot?' she asks with a smile.

'I suppose I'd better tell you my tale of woe.'

'Let's go in the lounge. I'll put the hard stuff away and open a bottle of wine or we won't remember anything. Then you can tell me everything.'

And so I do. I leave nothing out. I tell her all about my brawling youth and Frank's death. My time in juvenile detention and later in prison, and even my years in the Legion. I tell her what I was thinking when we were together and how I've drifted through the years. Eventually, I even explain how I punched our son in the jail, and how I ended up on a wing full of sex offenders. She can't help laughing at that, and I do too. We both have the same sick sense of humour and ability to find life's strange ways amusing. The only thing I don't mention is the events that are in motion. I think of them as Frank's revenge. One day, I will tell her about that, too. Most importantly I try to tell her how sorry I am. It feels like I mean it.

'I can see you're a bit different. In the old days you were always ready for a row,' she says.

'I've never hit a woman.'

'No, but you would get so angry that I'd worry about it. Nobody dared cross you.'

'Yeah, and look where it's got me. This is going to sound mental but, now the shock has worn off, I'm pleased that I had them. You know, the kids.'

'You won't be when I give you your backdated maintenance bill.'

We chuckle, then full-on belly laugh. It's over quickly, but it's good to get it out. She tops up my glass, which finishes the bottle.

'Tell me about Barbara, please.'

She runs through our daughter's life in fine detail. Barbara is a success, and my heart bursts with pride despite my not even having met her. It's lovely to think that I could help create someone who sounds so nice and positive.

'Does she ever ask about me?'

Brenda tuts and changes the subject.

'What's your plan now? Little bit of fighting before returning to jail?'

I almost laugh when I remember I said something similar to Zanthos in prison.

'There are a few loose ends need tying up, then I had nothing much planned. But I owe the kids, and I'm in debt to you. Is there any way I can make it up to you?'

She slowly twizzles the stem of her wine glass and I wonder if she's flirting but I push the idea away. She rubs her chin as she thinks, then puts the glass down without having drunk any.

'I don't understand my boys at all. I got by on benefits when they were young, but I had to work two jobs to make ends meet later. They became latch-key kids. I lost them to the rough and tumble of the estate, and there was nothing I could do. Is there a way back for them?'

I'm unsure if it's the wine, the whisky, the warmth, or all three, but I hope that we all have a chance to change. Could I learn to enjoy the simple pleasures in life? Could they?

'They're only young. They need to hear from someone who's made the same mistakes, so they can understand first-hand what that life is really like. But they're little more than teenagers. They might not want to listen.'

'Shame you can't visit them.'

'I've got to tie up some loose ends in Peterborough. There's a man I have to put the past to rest with, then I'll get a message to them in the jail.'

'I'm not sure a prison email will make a lot of difference.'

'There is something else I could do for them.'

'Like what?'

'I feel ridiculous even saying it.'

'Go on.'

'I could be a father. Not that I've had much experience.'

'I would have said you were a natural, until you vanished.'

'Well, I'd like to try. There is a big thing *you* can do to help them.'

'What's that?'

'They'll be out of jail in about nine months. If they leave without somewhere stable to live, they've got little chance of escaping that way of life.'

Her face falls.

'I can't handle them on my own,' she says. 'I don't think I want them back. It's only now I'm getting my life on track. I had my first decent date in a long, long time a few months ago. I've missed out on holidays and so much more. It's quiet and peaceful here. I know I can be happy.'

'I'll help. I'll move up here and be around. I need to get out of Peterborough as well. There's only bad news for me there, too.'

She studies my face and shakes her head, then rises from her chair and yawns.

'I've got work in the morning, luckily only a few hours to help out, but I still better be off to bed.' She stands in front of me. 'You know, I dreamed of you turning up for ages. To start with, I'd have had you back with open arms, then, for the rest of the time, I imagined the swear words I'd use when I told you where to go.'

'And now?' I ask with a raised eyebrow, emboldened by drink.

'Don't push your luck. I wouldn't chuck a mangey dog out in this weather, so you just qualify. I'll fetch you a blanket.'

It's a kindness I don't deserve. I've spent my life trying to be the big man. Even if I was in the wrong, I made sure I won, but I don't want that now. What do I want? Any small part of Brenda's set up sounds good right now. She returns and places a blanket on the sofa next to me.

'I'll see you in the morning. Don't you dare disappear again.'

I grin at her. I won't let her or my kids down this time. I hope that's not the booze talking. Kevin and Grayson will also hear my story in person. I know that for a fact, because in less than a week I'll be back inside.

# 37

## THE COLD KILLER – SATURDAY 14TH DECEMBER

I'm woken by the sounds of cutlery clinking together and the smell of fresh coffee. I check my watch and it's only 6 a.m. My head is tender and my mouth is dry. I close my eyes again.

'Come on, sleeping beauty. Get this down you and I'll walk you to the station. I work nearby. When did you say your train was?'

'Half ten,' I reply through closed lids.

'You'll have plenty of time to look around town, then, see if it appeals for when you make it your home.'

I pop one eye open and smile at her laughter. She beckons me to the table where two plates are set. She pours me a strong coffee. All I can manage is a slice of toast, which has an unusual texture I haven't tried before.

'This tastes funny.'

'It's sourdough.'

'Is that good or bad?'

'It's healthy.'

I cover it in whatever the hell organic marmalade is, and it's okay. After breakfast Brenda gets me a towel and shows me where the upstairs bathroom is. The shower is so good, so hot and powerful, that I gasp and laugh out loud. Afterwards, smelling of lavender and roses from her shower gel, I feel like a new man, until I pull on yesterday's clothes. I chuckle when she asks for my email address, but we exchange phone numbers. Having to get my number off the sim card doesn't look great, but she knows I was in prison.

The freezing night has frozen the snow rock hard, but I detect a slight warming in the air. It's still bloody cold, but the sky is clear. This makes the just-melting paths deadly when we start our walk. She clings onto my arm, and I have to say it feels good.

Brenda is wearing a thick coat, but only a pencil skirt and black loafers underneath it, which I assume is her uniform. She slips and hangs on wildly, nearly dragging me down with her. A passing dog walker smiles at her face, which is full of life. He's the only other person we pass.

Outside the station, she releases her firm grip on me. She gestures to the surrounding area.

'I hope you like it.'

'I like who's in it.'

'Don't overdo it, or I'll assume you've gone mad. When will I next see or hear from you again?'

'I'll ring, but it might take six months to have my affairs in order.'

'Ooh, get you,' she mocks, but I'm serious.

'I don't want to return to my old life. It's not the place for me any more, but I can't leave certain things as they are.'

She nods, and I suspect she realises I'm talking about people, not Peterborough. She looks cute in her café uniform and I realise I'm still drawn to her. She holds out her hand.

'Good luck, Logan. Stay in touch.'

I shake her hand and we both hold eye contact. She turns and crosses the road, looking around once. I'm tempted to glance upwards in thanks, but there's a long path ahead, and a lot could still go wrong. It's tempting to return to my tent and rest, but it makes sense to get on with things. I might be on the news soon. First, I need to stop at Grantham on the way back to leave the hard drive I took out of Zanthos's PC with an old friend. Luckily, it's on the same train line. I've decided to leave the cash I found at the Zanthos house there too. I'll peel a couple of fifties off for expenses, but that money is bad news.

I have to visit Archie Spencer next. It's better if he doesn't know I'm coming. We'll have to see what he has to say for himself. Forgiveness could be difficult for me when I spent so long thinking about how I should hurt him.

## 38

DI BARTON

Everyone was in bed when Barton arrived at home last night, and they were asleep when he let himself out of the front door in the morning. It was still dark, but the moon was out and the ice and snow reflected the light beautifully. He got in the Land Rover and sat thinking as the heater did its job on the windscreen. Barton had a feeling that there would be bodies found today.

The papers would instantly become hysterical when they found out the type of people involved. Barton wondered what sort of person they were dealing with. Would they stop whenever they felt they had taken their revenge? In his experience, killers got a taste for it. They needed to be caught before the urge overtook them again.

Nothing insightful had come to Barton this morning when he woke, so perhaps four hours of sleep weren't enough for his brain to work its magic, but there was something niggling away at him.

He put his wipers on and cleared the windscreen, then pulled off the drive. Mrs Zanthos, Pfeiffer and Ballanchine were all missing. Barton reckoned he would only need to locate one of them, dead or alive, to get the investigation moving in the right direction.

Unsurprisingly, he was the first in the office, but Zander arrived a few minutes later. Barton had texted his sergeants the previous night that Pfeiffer's sister had been in. Zander plonked a McDonald's coffee carton in front of Barton.

'Did they stop selling Sausage McMuffins?'

Zander shook his head and tutted in disgust, then revealed the bag he had concealed behind his back and gave his boss a McMuffin and a hash brown.

'Any thoughts?' asked Zander as they both tucked in.

'My brain hasn't woken up yet. Let's send someone out to see Pfeiffer's sister. I'll get Family Liaison around there. It'll save time in the end because I don't think he'll be going home.'

'Good idea.'

'I'll get the media involved too. It's possible Pfeiffer got lost in the snow. He could still be sitting in his car. When all this melts, we'll have a much better chance of locating that. It can't have just vanished. I'll check the number plate cameras this morning, but they won't have been working perfectly in that weather. We might at least narrow down the search.'

'What did his sister say?'

'He went out in the afternoon. She had his salmon on the dinner table at six, but he never showed. She was very upset. I asked her a few looseners on Pfeiffer's criminality and if he had any enemies. She acted as though he'd spent the last twelve years on a world cruise, and it was nice to have him back.'

'Weird how people can stick with someone after doing what these three arseholes did.'

'That was Pfeiffer's first offence. Reading between the lines, I'd have said that the other two mongrels were the ringleaders. That's why I reckon Zanthos's wife was in on it. I've got an itch in my head about her.'

'That's probably just the hamster on the wheel in there needing some more cheese.'

Barton laughed. 'You're right. Get him some biscuits as well, please.'

The rest of the team trooped in at eight, by which time there was a real hum of action in the room. The ANPR cameras had picked up Pfeiffer's car on the Longthorpe parkway and again on Oundle Road near the Botolph Trading Estate. Barton knew the area and asked Malik to check the location of the park where the abduction of the child occurred.

Barton thought of Mrs Zanthos again. He wanted to go through her life with a fine-tooth comb. After a few minutes of pondering, he fired an email off to the department who handled the sex offenders in the city to see if there was even a whiff of any involvement from her.

Uniform had been instructed to sit outside the three perps' properties until further notice. Barton also called the armed response vehicle that was operating in the county that day and updated them. After all, it was likely they were dealing with a killer and would need backup at some point. At 8:25, while he was waiting for everyone to finish what they were doing for the meeting, Barton stared out of the window. The ice on the roads was turning to slush. He didn't have to wait long to discover what the melting snow had left behind because just then his phone rang. He listened for a minute.

'Stay there,' he replied. 'Do not let anyone near the scene. I'll have a CSI there as a priority.'

Barton turned round with a grim face to find his team all seated and staring at him.

'That was the officer at Zanthos's place. There's blood on the table at the rear of the property. Quite a lot, by the sounds of it. Too much for it to be an accident.'

'So do you think someone's taking them all out, then?' asked Strange.

'Yes, without any further intel, that's the route I'm going down. Strange, I want you to visit Pfeiffer's sister. Go at the same time as the liaison officer. Butter the sister up. Say you met Saul in the prison and he seemed like a nice guy who made a terrible mistake.'

'It's not my first rodeo, boss.'

Barton smiled and nodded. The pressure was getting to him. The incident room would allocate lines of enquiry, but he wanted certain things done immediately.

'Leicester, speak to the child's family in California. God knows what time it is over there, but I'm pretty sure it's the middle of the night. I want as much as you can get on the relatives. Who was the angriest, that sort of thing?'

'Yes, boss.'

'Malik, gen up on the abduction case itself and email everyone a summary. Something might pop out as you're doing it.'

Malik gave him a thumbs-up.

'Zelensky. These people are missing. Let's treat them as such. We need to start looking at their bank accounts and phone records. I'd hate to find that they're all booked in at the Travelodge.'

'Zander, I say we assume Zanthos was killed in prison, so—'

Barton's mobile rang again. His face fell as he listened to the update.

'Okay, I'll be right there.'

'Zander, ring Mortis. He won't want to miss this. Then you and me are off to the park near Candy Street on the British Sugar Estate.'

'Who have they found?' asked Zander.

'It's unconfirmed, but judging by the location off Oundle Road, it's got to be Pfeiffer. A bunch of kids were throwing snowballs on the way to school. A lad scraped some snow off the window of a parked car and got a surprise. An old man was inside, staring at him, and the kids realised he wasn't moving. They told a teacher when they reached the school, and he returned to the vehicle and managed to open the door.'

'Dead?' asked Zelensky.

'Dead.'

# 39

## DI BARTON

Barton instructed the others to carry on with their tasks, while Zander and he got in Barton's car and drove towards the crime scene. The traffic was terrible. They passed two accidents, and a bus that had given up the ghost outside The Cross Keys pub, which added to the chaos. Barton had so many things flying around in his head that he was finding it hard to focus while Zander was prattling on about last night's basketball.

'Have you had a chat with Kelly about your mysterious night together?'

Zander froze mid slam-dunk gesture.

'Any reason you're bringing that up now?'

'Holly wanted to know.'

'Hmm. We had a quick coffee yesterday and pussyfooted around the topic. She kind of laughed it off, so we're cool.'

'I can buy you a bottle of tequila each and a bag of pretzels if you'd like to recreate that special moment.'

'Funny. I'm not sure what to do. We're back to normal now, and I missed our laughs at work when we were being weird with each other. I really like Kelly, though. I reckon she'll return to her way of keeping everyone just out of reach and I'll accept that, if it's all I can have.'

'Very brave. If they gave out medals for courting, you'd receive a VC for that attitude. Ask her to dinner, or take her go-karting.'

'Go-karting?'

'Yeah. Kelly's sporty and fun. Do something different and show her how exciting you are. Woo her.'

'Right. I appreciate the gesture, but I don't want dating advice from a donut-eating cop who's scared of his own wife.'

'I'll tell Holly you said that.'

'Please don't.'

They both chuckled.

'I know what I'm doing. I'll strike at the right moment.'

This time only Barton laughed. He turned into the British Sugar estate and indicated right towards Candy Street. The road was cordoned off and a tent had been placed next to an old green Jaguar. Barton parked up on a nearby driveway and waved at the woman who peeked from her curtains.

This estate was one of the nicer areas in town, with no social housing. There weren't many homes on there worth less than a quarter of a million, which was plenty for Peterborough. Most of the workers were white collar and there was a heavily oversubscribed school. It was considered a safe place for children, at least until Pfeiffer, Zanthos and Ballanchine struck twelve years ago.

PC Rivendon was manning the barrier and let them through.

'Anything to report?' Barton asked him.

'No. It's like something from a gangland movie, but he's frozen solid so it must have happened yesterday.'

Barton and Zander reached the car. All four doors were open. Barton saw an ornate handle sticking out of the rear of the driver's seat. And when he looked at the driver, he saw over an inch of blade protruding from his solar plexus area.

'That'll do it,' said Zander.

'Very much so,' replied Barton with a frown. He didn't like this development one bit, and he said so.

'I agree,' said Zander. 'There's no doubt what the perpetrator's intentions were here.'

Before Barton could comment, Mortis appeared in full CSI suit.

'Morning, lads.'

'How did you get here before us?' asked Zander.

'I used Waze. It took me through town. Handy piece of kit, that. You two dinos should haul yourselves into the twenty-first century.'

PC Pignatiello was also on the scene.

'I was first here,' she said. 'The car was fully covered in snow, and, seeing as it stopped snowing early evening, you've pretty much got a time of death if you combine that with the trigger from the ANPR camera.'

Barton, Zander and Mortis all smiled.

'Anything else?' asked Zander.

'No signs of a struggle in the car. I would say the victim knew his killer, or they knew of each other at least. It feels a very personal way to kill someone. Brutal, too. Merciless, even. The fact there was no attempt to hide the body is concerning. That could be cockiness, overconfidence, or a person hell-bent on causing as much havoc as possible before they get caught. They want the world to understand this man was killed for a reason. They think he deserved to die.'

'Nice work,' said Zander. 'Ever thought of being a detective?'

Barton rolled his eyes as Pigs and Zander grinned at each other.

'Mortis,' he said. 'Preliminary findings.'

'Well,' said a beaming Mortis. 'It's lovely to not be the only one with a brain at a scene for a change. Everything this clever young woman said. Dead yesterday evening. No bruising around the face or hands. Anyone would die quickly with this type of wound, even though it would have probably missed the heart. Massive internal bleeding would still occur. Obviously, I'll do a full PM, but it's unlikely to reveal much else.'

'Bollocks,' said Barton. 'When I heard he had a knife in him and he was by the playground where the girl was taken, I kind of hoped it was self-inflicted. It's interesting, then, that he's died here of all places, and yet it's not suicide. Why would he come here? Surely, if he was spotted, he would most likely end up back in jail. And how would the killer know he was here?'

'Maybe he or she was following him,' said Zander.

'Isn't it more likely that the perpetrator drove here with him?' said Pigs. 'If the killer wanted to make a statement, where better than the location of the abduction? He could have stayed in the rear seats and driven the knife through when they arrived. There would have been poor visibility at that time. He could have just got out and walked away.'

'He?' asked Barton.

'Nearly all murderers are men.'

'Yes, but not all, so it's best not to assume. Very good, though. You've passed the entrance exam.'

Pigs blushed.

'Two down,' said Zander.

'Ballanchine to go,' replied Barton. 'Maybe it was Mrs Zanthos.'

Barton stared at the ornate knife handle. It looked expensive. He put a plastic glove on and rested his fingertip on the point of the blade, which was deadly sharp.

'It's possible, I suppose. It wouldn't need superhuman strength to threaten an old man into his car, then run him through with a knife this sharp. She might have been involved and decided to kill Pfeiffer so he couldn't ever talk.'

'No, she's too elderly for this, surely,' said Zander. 'And she can't have been responsible for the prison murder, if it was one.'

'Maybe she plotted with Ballanchine,' said Zander. 'You mentioned he was feisty.'

'Yes,' replied Barton. 'I can imagine Pfeiffer going meekly to his death, but Ballanchine wouldn't want any involvement in this. He'd know he'd be the first person we'd speak to after discovering it. I think Pigs is right. Pfeiffer was driven here and killed, or was forced to drive here. The link is obviously the fact the original crime was committed here. We need to find out who would want Pfeiffer dead so much that he would go to all this trouble and not be too concerned about getting caught.'

Barton stayed at the scene until lunchtime. Zander and Pigs set out on foot to ask at the neighbouring houses if anyone had seen anything, but unsurprisingly, considering the weather, nobody had. CSI were doing their thing and had released the body to Mortis. Zander and Barton said their goodbyes to Pigs, and Barton noticed her grinning at Zander. As they drove off Barton turned to Zander.

'I really like Kelly,' mimicked Barton.

'Shut it,' said Zander.

'Ever thought of being a detective?'

'I mean it, shut it.'

# 40

## THE COLD KILLER

The train pulls into Peterborough station at 3 p.m., two hours late. The sun has disappeared, and there's a wet gloom to the concourse as I meander along it. There'd been no trolley service on the train, and I'm starving. The Pumpkin Café at the exit looks expensive, but I push through the double doors and give the young woman a tired smile. I ask for a panini and an Americano, then take a seat. She brings it over and places a piece of cake next to it.

'We're closing soon, and it'd only go to waste.'

My hangover is still lingering, which shows how out of practice I am with alcohol, and it strikes me that I've lived my entire adult life feeling a little hungover, apart from when I was in prison. I was quite enjoying being clear-headed and the last thing I fancy doing is seeing Archie Spencer when I'm not at my best.

The coffee, cake and panini hit the spot, but it's an effort to get out of the seat. I leave the girl a quid tip and wave at her on the way out.

The town centre is reasonably busy with people. You can't miss the homeless, though, everywhere you look, in the doorways of boarded-up shops. They look desperate and defeated, having long given up on praying for a miracle to occur, but am I so different? How long would I need to live in the woods until I became one of them?

I wander over the town bridge and head to Westwood Park Road. I've known where Archie's lived for years but never got around to visiting him. I suppose it was something that I liked knowing I could do one day, like seeing Brenda again, even if I never did. It's a day for progress. He owns numerous properties over the city. I dug the foundations for a conservatory at one of them, but didn't tell the foreman that I knew him.

I stand outside the electric gates to his huge house. The laurel trees conceal the ground floor, but I'm impressed. I wonder how different Archie's life would have been if he'd gone down with me. Would he still live here? Perhaps I'd live in the nice house instead.

I think Archie would have done well even if he'd been in the nick as a kid. People who don't care about the rules are tough to keep down. While his competitors would have been worrying about the law, Archie would have been already ruthlessly breaking it.

Weird how he came back to Peterborough to run his business. It seems to be a place you can't easily escape from – a bit like quicksand. Still, Archie has to pay for leaving me high and dry. He passed me that knife. I wouldn't have done the damage I did otherwise. I allow myself another small smile. I didn't have to use it, of course, and there's no point blaming anyone else for my stupidity. My crimes are on me. His real mistake was not to do what he said he would, namely look after me inside. I press the buzzer.

I stand there for a minute, stamping my feet and hugging myself. Someone had thrown a paper away on the train, which I read and, apparently, it's going to be ten degrees tomorrow. It's hard to imagine when you're shivering. I step to one side and analyse the tall fence round his property. Years ago, I'd have just vaulted over it, but I don't like the look of the barbed wire on top. Then the gates start to open.

I stride down the drive with a confidence I don't feel. Archie was king of the ambush when we were growing up. He didn't ask questions either. Well, not until it was already over. My eyes widen when I get to the front of the building. There's a huge porch and a swinging seat and Archie's on it, smoking a cigar. I walk over, climb the steps, and stand a metre away from him. He leans back, resting his elbows on the chair arms. We eyeball each other for a few moments until Archie breaks the silence.

'You took your time coming to visit.'

He's aged badly. Some men seem to last forever. Archie is a man who wore himself out early. I let out a breath, realising I'd imagined him still to be how he was as a youngster. All fists and fury. Rage and thunder.

'I didn't want anything until now,' I reply.

'Yeah. What is it you want?'

'Some money.'

'Oh, any amount in particular? Fiver for the bus? Tenner for a taxi.'

'Ten grand. Cash.'

Archie frowns, then tips his head back and lets out a deep rolling laugh.

'No problem. Do you need it in used notes?'

'I figured you owed me that much for letting me down. I never mentioned the knife was yours, and you got away scot-free.'

'Fuck's sake. We were kids.'

'Yes, and this kid went to prison.'

'I'm not giving you any money.'

'If I'm honest, I didn't think you would.'

'Why bother coming, then?'

'I wanted to give you the opportunity.'

'The opportunity for what?'

'To say sorry. Make amends. Do the right thing.'

'Yeah, well, I don't do that.'

'Shame. For you, that is.' I gesture up at the big building behind him. 'Life's treating you well.'

'Can't complain.'

I didn't come here for chit-chat. It's time to unsettle him.

'I hear you had a boy.'

Archie's eyes narrow. He never could hide it from me when his devious thoughts were churning through his devious brain. He spits over the white picket fence next to him.

'Meet him in prison, did you?'

'Yeah. Chip off the old block.'

'Very funny. The boy's an idiot. I cut him off. He can rot for all I care. Don't think I don't know about you, Logan. I've kept an eye on you over the years, thinking you'd be after something sooner or later. It's just a surprise it took this long. It made me laugh knowing you were working on that conservatory for me.'

I can't help scowling.

'This is my city. That's why I came back. I know all the roads, and all the toads, and I control them. I've got my fingers in every little pie in town.' He pauses to waggle his fingers at me. 'And I've become rich and powerful. Now, normally, I'd have you killed for coming here like this, but I'm going to let you live. For old times' sake. That, and I also enjoy the fact you're a fuck-up.'

'You don't look to be the kind of man who's able to take care of business any more. I bet you could eat plenty of pizza, though.'

Archie can't help losing his cool, but he winces as he leaps to his feet. Nothing like bad knees to make you feel like a pensioner. When he's balanced, he keeps his distance, which is further proof he's a spent force.

'The last man who came to my house and was rude to me left about three pints of blood on my lawn.'

I turn around and marvel at the gardens and the two sports cars parked near a large garage.

'We used to be the same, but now we're different,' I finally say.

'Yeah, why's that?'

'You have a lot to lose.'

Then I hear an ominous click that sounds like the barrel of a shotgun closing. Sure enough, Evie steps out of the front door. She looks meaner than ever.

'Listen to you two idiots. You're like a pair of camp cowboys. Logan, fuck off. I clean any scum off my porch the permanent way, so let's not find you here again.'

'Nice to see you've mellowed with time, Evie.'

'Piss off, or stay and argue. Don't matter to me.'

I step back down off the porch and walk ten metres away, before turning.

'One day, Evie, someone will close your nasty mouth for good.'

'Well, it won't be you.'

Archie flicks his cigar stub at me, but it falls short.

'Don't say you never had the opportunity, Archie. The moment for apologising is over, and there'll be no begging for another chance.'

'What's that supposed to mean?'

I smile at him and walk back up the drive. Just before I'm out of sight behind the trees, I stop and spin round. They are both in the same position, looking concerned. Evie has the gun raised.

'Everyone pays eventually, Archie. Your time is coming.'

# 41

## DI BARTON

The rest of the day was a frustration. The team cracked on with writing reports and updating files. Ideas and thoughts were thrown about the incident room as the team speculated on who they thought was responsible. But really it just felt as though they were all waiting for Ballanchine's body to turn up. All afternoon, the niggle that had been in Barton's head wouldn't go away. Just before the 6:30 p.m. meeting, he realised what it was.

He stood and walked to the front of the room. The team gathered around, except Zelensky, who was on the phone after saying she had one last important thing to check. Barton summed up the facts.

'Still no sight of Mrs Zanthos or Ballanchine. I don't think either of them are suspects. I'll tell you why after we hear an update from each of you. I have an idea. Let's see if your intel leads us to the same conclusion. Malik, what have you learned?'

Formal as ever in a sharp suit and gold tie, Malik stood up.

'The abduction was a nasty case, but the girl seemed unscathed, so it could have been a lot worse. Even so, the guilty parties were clearly extremely dangerous men who were likely to reoffend. The judge rightly sent them away for a long stretch. This was Pfeiffer's first charge, but the judge still sentenced him to the same amount of time as his co-defendants. I'm guessing that the judge assumed that was right because they were all involved to the same degree. Or the judge may have suspected that it was just the first occasion Pfeiffer had been caught.'

'I take it the other two's records were extensive?' asked Zander.

'Yes, Ballanchine is, was, a committed sex offender. His record goes back to being a juvenile. No rapes, but indecent exposure, sexual assaults, multiple breaches, mostly from going near schools and playgrounds. He's been to jail on seven separate occasions. No chance of rehabilitation. The file suggests he's known Zanthos for decades, but he didn't go down when Zanthos went down for abusing his own children.'

'So Ballanchine will have a list of angry people after him a mile long.'

'Yes. As for Zanthos. I hadn't heard of the earlier case concerning his own kids, which sounds especially tragic. To keep it short, he interfered with one of his kids when he was young, and then moved onto the younger brother. The older brother threw himself off a pedestrian bridge in front of a coach after sending a letter to the police. He said he couldn't protect his brother and didn't deserve to live. That letter sent Zanthos down for eighteen years, of which he served nine. He would have been inside when Ballanchine was for a couple of his stints, so if they didn't know each other before, they could have connected then. I'm checking their records to see if they were at the same establishment together. If they were, it gives them plenty of time to concoct their later scheme. Although, after Zanthos came out, he kept his nose clean until the abduction.'

'What happened to the brother?' asked Strange.

'He was little more than a toddler. The social took him and he was eventually adopted. Obviously, that information isn't readily available.'

'There's motive there,' said Zander.

'For killing Zanthos maybe, not the others,' said Barton. 'But it's a lead. Fill in the paperwork for access to the adoption records. We'll need authorisation from up high. Would the kid have been told that one of his real parents was a sex offender and he was abused? Who'd want to know that? Leicester, any joy?'

Barton smiled as Leicester came and stood at the front with a notebook. He and Malik were now in their thirties, but they still seemed young to Barton. They were true professionals, though, and they were becoming vital cogs in the machinery of his team. They'd called Leicester 'Red' a few times as a nickname, but it hadn't stuck.

'I spoke to the mother of the child who was taken at her new home on the outskirts of San Diego. She was quite teary. It seems she still blames herself, even after all this time. The little girl involved is fine, though. She doesn't remember anything about it, and that's the way they'd like to keep it. When I asked her if she knew of any family members or friends who might want to take revenge, she said no.'

'You believe her?'

'Definitely. She was a nice lady. They had only just arrived in Peterborough for her husband's job after being in Norwich. They hadn't time to make acquaintances, let alone friends. She's American and wanted to go home, anyway. She said she retrained as a psychologist.'

'Good work,' said Barton.

'I had a chat with her husband too. She didn't want me to, but I explained it was necessary. I got hold of him at his office. He confirmed everything she said, but he was still very angry about it.'

'I don't suppose he paid for a bounty hunter to do the job or flew here for a quick holiday,' said Barton.

'No, but he did say to let him know when we found out who did it, because he'd like to send him a bottle of champagne.'

'I see we're saying *him* again, but I agree we're likely looking for a male. Zander?'

'Well, if we're assuming it's one killer, then they're very different methods of killing. He might be escalating in violence.'

'Perhaps, but that comes to my idea. If this is the same person who killed Zanthos, then he was in prison recently. The prison said that they had a lot of inmates being released soon off that wing. Maybe one of those people killed Zanthos. It's hard to get hold of weapons in jail, so he used one of the oldest methods there are: suffocation. He also wouldn't have wanted to get caught because he probably planned to attack the others when he was released. If he'd killed them all inside, it would have been too suspicious.'

Strange clicked her fingers.

'Nice. And now he's out, he doesn't particularly care about getting caught, because he's done what he set out to. That's why he left Pfeiffer to be discovered. Ballanchine's got to be dead already.'

'Do you reckon he's going to hand himself in afterwards?' asked Barton.

'Maybe,' she replied. 'Or go down in a blaze of glory.'

'Yes, that's a concern. Although, perhaps he or she plans to vanish afterwards,' said Barton. 'They could think they're cleverer than us and they'll get away with it. We need to speak to the prison and find out who's left that wing since Zanthos died in his cell.' Barton checked his watch. 'I'll have to wait until the morning for that. I have some of the names from a MAPPA email, but this seems very personal. I can't see Crannock or Drummond throwing their futures away over very old sex offenders. Celestine, yes, but he isn't due to be released yet.'

'What of Mrs Zanthos?' asked Zander.

'Got to be dead as well, surely,' said Malik.

'Not so fast,' said Zelensky, scooting her chair over. 'I've been going through their bank and phone records. I've just received the final piece of info, and it's important.'

'Please don't tell me she's spent the afternoon shopping in Queensgate.'

'The records for Pfeiffer and Ballanchine were dead ends. Then I checked Mrs Zanthos's. There's been two withdrawals in the Millfield area for £250 each at a Barclays ATM within a minute of each other last night. That's the maximum per transaction.'

There was a hubbub of noise as everyone started talking at once.

'Quiet, please,' said Barton. 'That's a turn up. So perhaps Mrs Zanthos is still alive.'

'Unless the killer stole her card,' said Zelensky.

'Ah, good point. Don't Barclays usually have CCTV looking at their ATMs?'

Zelensky nodded. 'I think they all do now.'

'Get onto it straight away, thanks,' replied Barton, but he could see from the expression on her face that she had more. 'Something else?'

'Yes, I also noticed that the balance didn't match the available funds. There was an authorisation amount from a recent transaction that hadn't had time to appear on her statement. I rang Barclays retail just now to find out what it was for.'

Zelensky smiled.

'And?' asked Barton.

'It's for a room at the Bull Hotel.'

# 42

## DI BARTON – SUNDAY 15TH DECEMBER

Detective Inspector Barton was deep in the land of nod when his phone woke him. The previous evening had been fruitless and frustrating. The team had raced to the Bull Hotel and spoken to the manager, who had confirmed the booking for a Mrs Zanthos for a room that night. Her description matched. Zelensky had also got hold of the footage from the ATM she used, and it was definitely the woman they were looking for.

The only problem was that Mrs Zanthos hadn't returned to sleep in her room. Leicester had kept an eye out outside in an unmarked car while the rest had waited inside. At ten, Barton had told Zander and Strange to go home, and he himself had left at midnight. The armed response team were parked up in the car park and had also agreed to stay until midnight. They were local men on call, so they could return fast if necessary, but Barton suspected they wouldn't be called out.

He was getting the feeling that Mrs Zanthos was a smart cookie. She'd only have to watch the news to see what was happening. It wouldn't take a genius to work out that the killer might be after her as well. And perhaps she would think the authorities were as dangerous to her at this point as the killer on the loose. The fact that she wasn't rushing to the safety of a police station told him a lot about whether she was an innocent in all this.

The car registered to the Zanthoses had triggered the cameras over near Eastfield in the early evening, but then nothing more, and the booking at the Bull was clearly a red herring. They would check all guest houses and hotels over the next few days, but if she was shrewd enough to lead them astray, it was likely she would be paying in cash using a fake name at one of the less salubrious motels Peterborough had to offer. If she hadn't already left Peterborough, that was.

Barton reached over to the nightstand, where he'd left his phone each night ever since they'd moved in nearly fifteen years before, and stared at the blurred screen. Bloody hell, he thought. I'm going to need glasses soon, too. He swiped the screen to stop the jangling sound waking everyone in the house and staggered through to the bathroom and closed the door. If he held the phone at the end of his reach, he could just about make out his sergeant's name. He put the handset next to his ear.

'John, are you there?'

'What time is it?'

'Six.'

'Okay, Zander. Give me a second.'

Barton rested his phone on the cistern so it didn't slide into the toilet – he didn't want to make that mistake again – and splashed cold water on his face. Early morning phone calls were always important, so he'd need to be at least semi-conscious. He grimaced to stretch his face out and picked up his phone again.

'Did the team pool win the lottery?' he asked.

'Nope, sorry, it's not good news. Uniform have found Affoot.'

Barton frowned at the name.

'Who the hell is Affoot?'

'No, not Affoot. A foot.'

'A foot of what?'

Barton heard a growl down the other end of the line, but Zander remained polite.

'You know, the thing that's usually on the end of a leg, but this one isn't, hence me ringing you so early.'

'Ah, right. Whose is it?'

'Come on, John. If I'd have known that, I would have said, "We've found Bob's foot."'

'Okay, so it's a man's foot.'

'I don't know that either, or—'

'Yeah, yeah, I get it. Where was it found?'

'Nine Bridges, Northborough.'

'Okay, you driving?'

'Fifteen minutes, bring the flask.'

Barton cut the call off and sat on the toilet. Ballanchine lived in Glinton, the village next to Northborough.

# 43

## DI BARTON

As Barton's brain grumbled into action, like an ancient boiler, he knew the prison had to be the answer. Opening his email account on his phone, he checked to see if Monty had replied to his message asking for a list of who had been released since the death of Zanthos. With any luck, it would give them a lead. The prison usually took a release address. Maybe Barton would be really fortunate and they'd find the culprit at their home cleaning their knife collection.

Barton was still sitting on the toilet yawning when the door opened. His seven-year-old son, Luke, sized up the scene in front of him.

'You've been a while. Are you having a poo?' he asked.

'No, I was having a wee, but I was trying not to make any noise.'

'Good, because I need a wee, and I don't want to do it in here if you've made it smelly.'

Chuckling, Barton rose, rinsed his hands, and lumbered back to the bedroom. His wife, Holly, was spread out on the bed. For someone who wasn't much over five feet tall, she'd done a good job of filling it. He smiled at her. They were both mid-forties now, but she'd aged better than he had. It was a Sunday morning, so he dressed in jeans, shirt and a thick roll-neck sweater. It'd be nippy up at Nine Bridges.

He sat on the edge of the bed, making sure he didn't break one of Holly's feet in the process, and pulled on a pair of thick socks. By the time he returned to the bathroom, Luke had finished his wee so Barton took a few pieces of toilet paper and cleaned up the spillage. Luke had gone back to bed, which was brilliant. He'd tortured Barton and Holly since he could walk by getting up at 5:30 a.m. every day, demanding breakfast. Maybe the sticky teenage years were starting early, and they'd rarely see him again.

Barton brushed his teeth and washed his face. He'd accepted his baldness, so a flannel over the top of his shaven head was an easy start to the day. There was, however, a certain lived-in look appearing on his chops. He could just about recall thinking that thirty was old.

Lawrence's and Layla's doors were shut, but he had another room now to look into. In some ways, it was like having a fourth child in the house.

He trudged downstairs and turned the kettle on. While it boiled, he walked to what used to be his office, where the door was open, and peeked in on his mum. She looked frail but peaceful. He noted with a wry smile that she'd got up in the middle of the night and put the light on. He picked up the toy rabbit she'd taken to carrying around and rested it next to her pillow. 'Oh, Mum,' he said under his breath.

He grabbed the flask and dumped in four big dessert spoons of Douwe Egberts and filled it two-thirds with boiling water, one third milk. No sugar, or the others would bellyache about it. Taking hot coffee to crime scenes was a trick he'd learned from his old boss, DCI Naeem. Happy detectives solved crimes. He had five minutes until Zander arrived, so he peeked in the pantry. There were a few new packs of cereal, which was excellent news because he liked them best when they were crispy. The kids and Holly never closed the tops, so they soon became soft. Mind you, what the hell was milled linseed? Slender granola didn't sound great either.

With a furtive glance behind him, he filled himself a big bowl of his favourite, opened the fridge, and poured on plenty of blue-top. His belly growled, which sounded remarkably similar to applause.

He was happily munching away when his wife came and stood next to him with her arms crossed. Her eyes were wide, despite the fact she was scowling. He lowered his spoon.

'John, what the blazes are you eating Coco Pops for?'

'I was hungry.'

'Your pancreas will explode at your age.'

'I needed sugar.'

'Couldn't you have had some fruit?'

The doorbell sounded. Barton got to his feet with an apologetic smile. He grabbed an apple from the bowl, picked up the flask, then bent down and kissed Holly on the cheek.

'Saved by the bell,' he said. 'Good idea about the fruit.'

'Is it serious?'

'Let's just say something is afoot. I'll probably be late again.'

She shook her head, but waved at him as he yanked his warm winter coat off the hook. He left feeling pleased with his little pun, especially considering how tired he was.

Zander, wearing black jeans and a black ski jacket, was leaning against the new love of his life; his new-to-him, sky-blue, MR2 sports car. Zander raised an eyebrow. Barton went back into his house, tutting, and got the keys to his Land Rover. He returned, and they clambered in. The 4x4 fired up and Barton drove through the quiet streets of Orton Longueville village with the beam from his lights cutting through the darkness.

'What's the latest?' he asked.

'The foot was found at five this morning by a farm labourer cycling to work. It was in the centre of the track.'

'I assume it's a male foot.'

'Yes. Strange was on call and confirmed that it was highly likely to be from a man. She's gone to the scene. The responding officer said he'd set up a perimeter and had a brief look around for the rest of the body.'

Barton grimaced, but he was very pleased the foot didn't belong to a child.

'No sign of anything else?'

'Nope. Not even a couple of fingers. I've spoken to Strange. She got lost herself going there, so passed the phone to the PC. He said take Paradise Lane, then it's just off the pedestrian bridge across Maxey Cut, which apparently is a kind of stream, and doesn't appear to be on my phone's satnav.'

Barton laughed.

'No, problem. I know where it is. We'll drive through Glinton and turn right on Mile Drove. We can park up and walk through. It's farmland with a few copses. This snow is probably covering the remainder of the body. It wouldn't normally be too difficult to bury someone out there, although the ground must be hard now.'

They hit the parkway and Barton put his foot down, taking the car to over a hundred. There was very little traffic at this time of the day. To their surprise, it took a while to catch up to a Toyota Celica. Barton drew alongside it and slowed down as the Celica slowed down. Zander wound down his window. A young lad peered out at them and blanched at Zander's stern face and the displayed warrant card. Zander pointed at the next slip road off, which the youth went up. The detectives didn't have time for speeding tickets, so they carried on, hoping the shock would be enough to teach the racer a lesson.

'What are you thinking? It must be Ballanchine?' asked Zander.

'Yep, although Mrs Zanthos could have had big hairy feet. Might be someone unconnected, but unlikely. Depends where it was found. It's not easy to cut someone's foot off without them being still.'

Zander frowned as he considered how the foot got separated from the owner's body. As they slowed entering the village, Barton gave Glinton's McDonald's an affectionate glance as they passed. Glinton was a small, popular place with a good school. Holly would have liked to have moved there, but even fifteen minutes away from Peterborough was too much for Barton, who preferred to be in the thick of things.

Once he was through the village, he carried on along the road towards Northborough, but at the first bridge he turned right and drove down what was little more than a thin concrete strip splitting the farmland. The surrounding fields seemed sinister with the light mist and eerie twilight just before dawn.

Barton pulled up on a patch of dirt and killed the engine. There was silence apart from the clicking of contracting metal. They both steeled themselves for what lay ahead. Opening their car doors disturbed three rooks, who left their trees cawing. It felt like bleak midwinter, even though Barton knew the temperature was due to rise significantly later.

'How do you know about this place?' asked Zander as they left the car.

'It's a great spot for walking the dog. There's no traffic, and it's only busy during the weekend.'

'Dogs, eh? Considering you haven't got one, is there something you're trying to tell me?'

'It's a bit too early for those kinds of jokes,' said Barton with a smile. 'An old girlfriend used to have a beagle,' he explained.

They could just make out the emergency lights in the distance through a row of trees. After a minute's walk alongside a ploughed field flecked with half-melted snow, they trudged over a bridge, which swayed perilously under their heavy stride. The water was so still that it looked like ice. They traipsed round a corner to a lane next to another ploughed field where they found a woman in uniform.

'Morning, sir.'

The officer wrote their names down and let them through the tape. The rest of the emergency vehicles had arrived from the other end of the field. There was a small tent set up, which Barton guessed would cover the foot. Strange and Mortis were outside it, laughing with each other.

Mortis, the pathologist, so nicknamed because of his interest in the stages of decay, could be amusing, but was not often prone to this current state of heightened mirth. Strange, a diminutive, fiery Londoner who'd been with the team for over two years, didn't chuckle like that often either.

Strange turned to them.

'Starsky and Hutch have arrived.'

That set Mortis off again.

'Which one am I?' asked Zander, who was six feet four and black.

Once Strange and Mortis had calmed down, Mortis explained.

'My wife received the results of her scans, and they think they got it all. She has some radio to go through, but it's more than we hoped for. I found out last night and have been feeling decidedly jolly ever since. The second reason for my amusement is that Miss Strange here asked me if I'd get paid full whack for the post-mortem.'

With that, Mortis pulled back the tent flap and revealed the foot, which looked very lonely and which was still encased in a very sensible men's brown shoe.

# 44

## DI BARTON

Barton stepped towards the body part and was surprised by the lack of blood, and said as much to Mortis.

'Yes, that would indicate that the foot was likely cut off a dead person.'

They all digested that fact for a few moments.

'I've got two uniforms doing a quick search along the perimeter of the surrounding fields,' said Strange. 'In case other bits, or persons, are near here. I've spoken to Control. There are no missing people or reports of disturbances in the area for the last forty-eight hours. We know Ballanchine, who we suspect to be the owner of said foot, lives nearby on his own, so I waited for you to arrive before we made the next move. His house is only a short walk from here.'

Barton cursed. They'd had a watcher on the property until late yesterday evening. Typical that the moment they needed the manpower elsewhere, something happened. Strange looked behind her and beckoned over one of the search team who had returned.

'Ah,' she said. 'Here's PC Brown, who was first here and has been remarkably stoical about it.'

A short, muscular man strode over and shook everyone's hand. Zander poured everyone a cup of coffee.

'So,' said Barton to Brown. 'Talk me through it.'

'Not much to say. We received the call and drove straight here. We were only a few minutes away.'

Barton smiled, guessing they were at McDonald's. He nodded for Brown to continue.

'I grew up in Peakirk, not far from here. The labourer was waiting when we arrived. And that was it. There was a foot on the path. I touched it, just to see if it was still warm, which might seem gruesome, but I trained as a butcher before joining, so this kind of thing doesn't faze me.'

'I take it that it wasn't?' asked Zander.

'Wasn't what?'

'Warm?'

'No, sir. Very cold.'

'Where's the guy who found it?' asked Zander.

'I let him go,' said Strange. 'His ID checked out, and he was late for work. He said he'd come to the station after his shift finished this afternoon.'

'Fair enough,' said Barton. 'Who's to say whoever did this isn't hiding in the undergrowth nearby?'

They all looked over at the row of bushes directly behind them. Barton chuckled and turned his stare to Mortis.

'I haven't moved the foot,' replied Mortis. 'But I've pulled the sock down to take a look. There is plenty of swelling, which is common in elderly people with weakened circulatory systems. The skin appears lacking in moisture, although that's perhaps not surprising. The shoe is old and has no unusual markings. It's bigger than my size nine, which would point to a male, and that matches with the style of shoe.'

'The man we've been looking for is seventy-seven and isn't in great health.'

Mortis nodded, grimly.

'Any signs of bitemarks, animal or otherwise?' asked Zander.

'Like in the case of the Snow Killer?' replied Mortis. 'No, I'd need to check with the microscope, but it seems to be a very clean cut. I doubt it was dragged here by a fox and it's definitely too heavy for the birds.'

'Possible weapon used?'

'Has to be something sharp. Axe, maybe a sword, or a very heavy knife swung by a strong person. Guillotine perhaps.'

Barton frowned as they heard more vehicles arriving in the distance and the clunk of car doors slamming.

'Okay, CSI can do their job, but we have to search for the rest of the body at the same time while respecting the integrity of the scene. Make sure you assess the situation from the outside, because it looks like there's a maniac on the loose. I'll ring for the armed response vehicle and notify Command. The public will need to be warned.'

Barton looked down at the foot and wondered out loud.

'How did a lone foot get to be in the middle of a path?'

'Maybe our killer had the body parts in a wheelbarrow, and it dropped off,' said Strange, with the look of a woman who couldn't believe what she was saying.

'Perhaps it was left there deliberately,' said Zander.

Before they could process that possibility, a shout came from the edge of the field next to them. The PC over there sprinted back to them. When he arrived, he looked Dracula white.

'Did you find the rest of him?' asked Barton.

'No, sir. Just the head.'

# 45

## DI BARTON

Barton told the others to wait while he walked up the path to the edge of the field. He decided not to put boot covers on. There was already a myriad of footprints, and he knew what he was going to ask everyone to do. He was getting warm in his thick coat when he reached the spot, so he pulled down the zip.

Barton had felt slightly out of kilter ever since his mother moved into his house. Staring at a butchered head in an icy field wasn't helping. The snow had melted to reveal the front of the face, which was a mess, but there were two eyes and about half the nose still intact. It looked a little like the man Barton recalled interviewing on the wing. Even in death, the skin had a tinge of yellow. Ballanchine deserved scant sympathy, but who would do this to another human and why? What kind of statement was this killer trying to make?

Barton had no doubt they would solve the case and fairly soon, but would it be quick enough? Were there more people on the murderer's list? He checked his emails on his phone. *Come on, Monty, I need that released-prisoner information.*

Three men had taken that child all those years ago, now those three were dead. Things were moving too fast for Barton to let the snow melt and reveal any more of the remains, which could be spread out all over the field. Barton had to search it now, which was a gruesome task, but he had the manpower. He needed to know if there was only one head in this field. They might get lucky and find the murder weapon. It was a chilling thought on a warming morning that whoever did this remained at large.

As Barton walked back to his team, he analysed what needed to be done immediately. Someone would need to inform Control. A risk to life for the public required special handling at many levels, including the press. That, luckily, was for others to deal with. His job was to narrow down the suspects until only one remained. But first, who else could be at risk, if anyone? The three men were dead. He suspected the woman, Mrs Zanthos, was in hiding, unless the killer had found her.

Were there other people linked to this case who were about to be attacked? Maybe whoever was responsible had an MO to clean up all the perpetrators of one case, then move on to the next.

He updated the uniform sergeant on the areas he wanted searching. They were to leave cones where they found *anything of interest*, a phrase that covered benign to grisly. Barton sent up a little prayer that there would be no evidence of more than one human's remains. He regretted parking on the other side of the river now, but it wasn't the end of the world. Zander had gone to Ballanchine's house in PC Brown's vehicle. At least, Barton could discuss everything with Strange as they strolled back to his car.

Even in the short time they'd been at the scene, there'd been a considerable melting of snow and ice. Barton's brain was firing on all cylinders now. He'd need to ramp up the investigation, ask for extra resources, the works. But there was always a chance at the start of a case that the answer was staring you in the face and could earn you a quick result. Barton decided he would stop at the prison on the way back to the station. He told Strange and she nodded in agreement.

'Okay, Kelly. Tell me who you think killed these three old men.'

'The victim, now grown up?'

'Who is a girl, living in California, still only sixteen.'

'Okay, how about her parents, or family friends?'

'Unlikely after twelve years. Border control has no record of them visiting here since they left. Friends wouldn't be motivated enough to murder.'

'Fine, let's assume someone strong did this because they transported the body and hacked it to pieces. I would start at the first death in the prison and look at our interviewees to see who fits.'

'Agreed. I think the jail is key, but if Zanthos was killed inside, why wait until just before the three of them were released? Why not kill all of them in the jail over time and be done with it?'

Barton's phone rang. He raised an eyebrow at Strange.

'Yes, Zander.'

'We got to the house, but it seemed undisturbed. The snow's melting fast here with no shade from the sun, but there were no footprints that we could see. I've been thinking about the body parts. The killer would have had to do their butchering somewhere. I was going to give the door a little muscle, but first I took a look in the back garden. There's an old wishing well, which looked intriguing, but it had been filled in, so the hole was levelled off. The partially melted snow on it was a dirty red colour. There was a handle visible. It looks like how I imagine a sacrificial altar would after a busy weekend.'

'I'll be there in five minutes.'

Barton carried on walking and brought Strange, who by now had undone her jacket as well, up to speed.

'The weapon was sticking out of the snow?' she asked.

'Looks like it.'

'Shit.'

Barton had to agree. Someone who couldn't even be bothered to hide the murder weapon was too frightening to comprehend. A person doing that had nothing to lose.

'Okay, John. I'm thinking about the prison. The murderer kills one victim in his cell. Gets away with it because it looks like a natural death. Maybe they planned to kill the others too, but us turning up put paid to that. But they weren't too bothered because they knew they were leaving shortly anyway.'

'That works. The killer was probably on the wing, but Zanthos still could have just died from natural causes.'

'Drummond was only recently put on that wing.'

'That's true.'

'Although, we met a lot of violent types on there. You said there were more than is normally on that type of wing.'

'Yes, but they weren't necessarily killers. It could also be two or more of them.'

Strange gave him a look.

'That doesn't bear thinking about.'

'Indeed, there's real planning here. It's possible the three of them just annoyed one of the other inmates and he decided to do away with them, but these feel like emotional kills.'

Strange got her notebook out of her pocket.

'We had six main suspects. I know who my money's on.'

Barton got in the car with a brief surge of confidence. They might be able to contain this and get the perpetrator back behind bars before anyone else got hurt. He started the engine and put the heater on to demist the windows.

'Still, there are other possibilities,' said Strange. 'Who's to say this is connected? Maybe Zanthos's death was natural, and this is another beef. The person responsible could be aiming to kill everyone on that wing now he's free. Perhaps it was to do with something that happened a long time ago, that we don't even know about. You understand how people's allegiances and thoughts change over time. There could have been more people involved in that child's disappearance twelve years back.'

Barton smiled at Strange's analysis. She was right to muddy the water. Yet, Barton was convinced that he had met the killer a week last Saturday in prison. Which one of them had stared him in the eye with a mind full of murder?

# 46

## DI BARTON

They pulled up outside Ballanchine's house, where Zander was waiting, leaning against a gate with his face turned to the sunshine. Barton couldn't help thinking the world was going mad. Heavy snow and ice for two days, then sunny, clear skies. It was no wonder people were doing weird things when even the weather could be so unstable.

His phone beeped as he got out of his car. It was a message from Zelensky, who was focusing on Zanthos's first conviction for abusing his own family.

Just had a weird thought about the adoption case. Also struggling to get information fast with BRC. Call if you aren't in later.

BRC stood for Back Record Conversion. Around the year 2000, the people who held the purse strings realised that if they scanned all the millions of case files that had been put together over the years, and input them on the computer, you could do away with most of the filing staff. It worked reasonably well, but there were often problems. Pages could be missing, sometimes even complete files vanished. Usually, they could be located elsewhere, but it took time. Time that Barton did not have.

Zander said nothing as Barton and Strange got out of the car. He just walked around the back of the cottage and they followed. When they reached the wishing well, two centimetres of the handle of a knife were clearly visible, sticking out of the snow. The snow had a dark red tinge underneath it and Barton was annoyed this hadn't been noticed earlier, but he guessed it might have been covered still. Mistakes would always be made. Early opportunities missed.

He put on a plastic glove, gripped the handle, and removed the knife from the snow. It was surprisingly heavy, about a foot long, and had a curved blade.

'Wait,' he said. 'It's the same handle as the weapon that killed Pfeiffer. And it's not a normal knife. What are those Arabian swords called?'

'It's a scimitar,' said PC Brown, who gloved up and took the blade from Barton and hefted its weight. 'I said I was a butcher in the past. A scimitar is a butchering knife. The weight makes it extremely efficient, especially if it's been sharpened properly.' He touched the edge and nodded. 'Did you say that the weapon used in the Pfeiffer murder was the same?'

Barton took a picture of the weapon, then put it back where it was.

'Yes, I think so. Are they rare?'

'Two ornate ones like this would be. There's a stall on the market that sells trade equipment for butchers, bakers, that sort of thing.'

'You can buy these off the rack?'

'Yes, you need to produce ID and be over eighteen. The stall-holder takes a photo of the ID, in case there's any fallout. He has to order most items in. The guy on the stall opposite does key cutting and tool sharpening.'

'Okay. When you get away from here, pay him a visit and ask the necessary. Show him a picture. If he or the knife sharpener recognise it, ring me immediately.'

'Yes, sir. The market isn't open until tomorrow, when I'm off, so I'll go then.'

Barton gave him a thumbs-up while his brain whirred. This was getting to be a complicated case requiring extensive personnel. CSI would need help from the surrounding counties, but it would still take them weeks to go through this area and get the results back. Zanthos's house would also need putting through the process. Barton crouched down and peered at an object resting on top of some snow at the side of the well.

'Is that...?'

'Yes, an ear, by the looks of it,' said Zander.

Barton looked around. He considered commenting about whether Mortis would get paid his full fee for that one too, but the time for jokes was over.

'Come on,' he said to Strange. 'Let's head to the prison. If Monty can't help us, I'm sure someone else there can. I'll try him again now it's gone nine.'

Barton pressed dial as he returned to his car. Monty picked up, so Barton signalled for Strange to drive while he brought Monty up to date. A minute later, after a couple of 'bloody hells' from the man on the other end of the phone, Barton finished the call.

'He'll be ready for us,' he said.

Strange pulled out of the country lane, and they were soon motoring along the parkway. There were snow drifts at the edges of the roads, but all the black tarmac was visible. Barton updated Strange.

'The most important info we need are addresses, current and

historic, for any inmates released in the period we're after. There are issues with data protection, so that might take a while. Monty also said he'll talk to prison security and see if they've received any extra intel on the three who are now dead.'

'Do they have to give release addresses?'

'They have to if they're under probation, and they are likely to for forwarding post that might turn up at the prison after they've left. They'll have at least an idea where they've gone to, even if it's just informally. I'll find out who the offender managers are for any suspects, and we'll ring them straight away.'

Strange nodded in agreement. They were making good progress to the prison when Strange cleared her throat.

'You all right, John? You seem distracted of late. Is it your mum?'

Barton let out a big breath.

'I am a little distracted. Holly joked yesterday that I might be an orphan soon, but that's kind of what I feel like, which is pathetic at my age. It's as though an element of my life is out of control and could change at any minute, or go on for years. It's unsettling.'

'I think I understand. My parents are getting a bit doddery, but they have each other. I suppose I've never thought about what might happen if one dies. I always reckoned growing up was something you did in your twenties, but perhaps it really happens when your parents need your help, when they come to rely on you instead of the other way round.'

'That's very perceptive, Kelly. What are you after?'

Strange chuckled. 'That's better. Humour will see us through, especially with all this crazy killing. These crime scenes could be from a Freddy Krueger movie.'

She wasn't wrong.

As they soon took the turning for the jail, Barton again appreciated that he lived in Peterborough. The population of 200,000 was surrounded by a circular road system. Even in the middle of rush hour, you could get to anywhere in the city in thirty minutes. They were soon parked up outside the jail and walking to the entrance.

Five minutes later, they had gone through the gatehouse and were sitting opposite Monty in his office. He had a young officer with him. Her name badge said Ella Brannigan.

'Right, this is Ella from Resettlement. She's collated the information for you. All departing prisoners have numerous appointments with the resettlement department before they leave to make sure they're ready for civilian life,' said Monty.

'To help find jobs and accommodation?' asked Strange.

'Kind of. Normally, we'll try to arrange job interviews for when they're out, but we also get their benefits claims set up. They're less likely to reoffend if they have money straight away.'

'Do they need to give an address for their claim?'

'Yes, sometimes they will explain they're homeless, but then use an address of a day centre for their claim to be set up to. I've compiled two lists for you,' said Ella. 'One is for those who've been transferred, which might not be important. There are seven others who have been discharged.'

Strange had her notes out. Barton took the release names and read the first one out to her.

'Pfeiffer.'

'Deceased,' said Strange.

'Ballanchine.'

'To be confirmed, dead.'

'Balchunas.'

'The foreigner with one arm. Unlikely,' said Strange.

'He was another of mine,' said Ella. 'He was a good guy with an unfortunate conviction for exposure.'

'He could be assisting in some way. Is this the address he gave where he was planning to live?' asked Barton.

'Yes, it's a shared house provided by the council. He was very pleased to get it.'

'Okay, we'll check him out, anyway.'

'Grace?'

'I'm afraid he's dead, too,' interrupted Monty. 'He returned to St Ives and froze to death on a park bench a few days ago.'

Barton thought back to the crazed but harmless man who believed he was in a fast-food restaurant.

'Khan.'

'Wasn't he the one crying at his own shadow?' said Strange.

'Yes,' said Ella. 'Khan crashed his car, killing his girlfriend. It broke him. His parents picked him up the day he got out and took him home to Birmingham.'

'Drummond,' said Barton with emphasis.

'He's one of our suspects,' said Strange. 'Violent record going back years.'

'Unfortunately, we have him NFA,' said Ella.

'No fixed abode?' said Strange. 'With his record?'

'Yes. It's the sad truth that many leave prison like that. We normally house men like him, but if no one wants them or there isn't space, we still have to release them. He may have said he was homeless, but some have somewhere to go and just don't want to tell us where they're heading.'

'Then he could still be in the city, getting up to no good,' stated Barton.

'Yes, he has a history of violence, but nothing sexual. He was only on the VP unit after a fight on the mainstream wings.'

'Could he deliberately have tried to get on that wing?'

'No, he didn't want to move on there at all.'

'I can believe that. Maintaining their reputation is very important for men like Drummond.'

'He served three of a six, so Probation will have seen him by now. If he's homeless, they'll still have a clue where he's staying. They'll also have previous addresses for him, which is often where they end up returning to, even if it's sleeping in a cupboard.'

'You'll love this,' said Barton. 'The last name on the list is Crannock.'

'Do we have an address for him?' asked Strange.

'Yes, but it's up north. Newcastle,' replied Ella. 'He was also released on licence, so he'll need to liaise with Probation, but he had a train warrant to Newcastle. It's not a cheap trip otherwise. Assuming he went, it's unlikely he would come back here.'

'Unless he has a connection we don't know about yet,' said Barton. 'We need to find Drummond and Crannock fast. If they haven't got watertight alibis, we'll run a fine-tooth comb over them. Can I chat with Raja or Green, to see if there has been anything they've noticed on the wing?'

'Green's on nights, so he'll be sleeping at home by now,' said Monty. 'I'll talk with him this evening when he comes in. If he has some intel, I'll let you know. Raja's called in sick today with a migraine, so I'll try him at home. He's due in tomorrow.'

'Crannock and Drummond both have the same offender manager, June Agyepong, although if Crannock was moving up north permanently, he'll have been assigned someone up there. This is June's number,' said Ella, handing Strange a slip of paper.

'Thanks,' said Barton. He racked his mind for any other avenues. 'I don't suppose that Charles Celestine has somehow got out? He seemed very capable of something like this.'

'No, he's gone back to the open prison. Although someone made a complaint about him, saying that Celestine said he was going to kidnap them and chop their hands off.'

'Will he still get released after that?'

'Yes, the person who made the complaint is a pathological liar, so it didn't hold much weight. I'll check that he hasn't just wandered out of the D-Cat. I dread to think what Celestine will get up to when he does get out.'

Ten minutes later, HMP Ford open prison confirmed that Celestine was in his cell. Monty got them all a coffee, and they discussed Drummond and Crannock's prison records. Neither seemed to have any connection to the three dead men, or had anything so gruesome on their records. Barton and Strange said their farewells and returned to their vehicle. Barton glanced at the clock on the dashboard: 10 a.m. He rang the number he'd been given for Agyepong and she picked up quickly despite it being a Sunday. They were all in a business where there was often work at the weekends. There was a pause after he explained what he wanted and why. He put her on speaker so Strange could listen.

'Great. He's due to see me tomorrow morning at ten. I'd like to say it wasn't anything to do with him, but I had the impression something wasn't right with Drummond when I came to visit him just before he was released. He also seemed wired on his last day. We let him down for housing. He said he's slept rough before, so I'll check his file. We might know the general location. They tend to return to where they've stayed before.'

'And Crannock?'

'I was glad he was going back up north because he doesn't give a shit who he hurts. He's capable of most things, but this is extreme, even for him. If he's done this, I'd be worried because he's the type to get a taste for it. I passed the file on to Probation in Newcastle. I'll see what they say. Hopefully they'll have met him by now, but he might not have reached there until late with the trains and the weather. Obviously, he could have the perfect alibi if he's two hundred miles away.'

'Can you come in this afternoon to Thorpe Wood Station?' asked Barton. 'We'll have a meeting where we decide next steps, but if they know where Crannock is, he'll need to be picked up and returned here for questioning.'

'I'm seeing an arsonist at one o'clock in Bretton, so 2 p.m. would suit me.'

'Agreed, see you then.'

Barton terminated the call and Strange turned on the ignition.

'Still think it was Drummond or Crannock?' she asked.

'That's what the old Barton belly is screaming. That one or both is involved somehow, at the very least. We're missing something, though.'

'I agree. To kill in that way usually needs a personal connection. When we find out what that is, the picture will be clearer.'

'Yes, but it's the organisation and planning that I don't like. It's almost military.'

Barton rubbed his chin. The newspapers would have also caught on by now, which would give the killer the exposure he clearly wanted. Barton had the sinking feeling that to really grab the world's attention, there would be a grand finale.

## 47

### DI BARTON

When Barton walked into the incident room, Zelensky came straight over, enthusiasm written all over her face. He nodded for her to start talking.

'Mr Zanthos interferes with his son. That child kills himself when Zanthos begins to touch the younger brother. That story really made an impact. The case was all over the papers back then. Leicester is reading through some articles from that time for me. The weird thing is that the mother wasn't convicted of anything, so why would the other kid end up being adopted?'

'Can you get that information?'

'I'm struggling, but I spoke to a very helpful bloke at the council's department for adoption, and he reckoned their records will be more detailed. Failing that, because it was only thirty years ago, he said the person who dealt with the case is probably still alive. It's not as though you'd be able to forget the details for something like that.'

'When did he say he'd get back to you?' asked Barton.

'Tomorrow lunchtime.' She smiled at him. 'We're going to solve this fast, aren't we?'

Barton gave her a reassuring nod, then went to see his boss, DCI Cox, in her office. She shouted, 'Enter' as she saw him approach, so he walked in and sat down. The DCI's job had been a straight fight between Barton and Cox. She'd won fairly, so their relationship was good, albeit strictly professional. She had a lively green dress-suit on, but her demeanour, as always, remained cool.

'Update, please, John.'

'The team is more or less of the same mind. It's too much of a coincidence that Zanthos was killed in prison just before he got out. Therefore, we're confident our suspect was on the wing. Two violent prisoners were released after that event, and now the other two men who took that child are also dead. We believe one of those two is responsible. We hope to pick them up today or tomorrow. Hopefully nobody else will die in the meantime.'

'Motive?'

'Maybe something as simple as them being child molesters, but we think there's a more personal link, which we haven't found yet. We have a few different avenues to explore. We have a meeting at two with their offender manager. One of them is likely sleeping rough in the woods around here. I'm looking for resources.'

'What do you need?'

'We must find Drummond as soon as possible. It'll be dark by four, so if the OM gives us a heads up where he might have pitched his tent, we'll head out. The easiest, but not the cheapest, way will be to get the helicopter up. There can't be too many people in there sleeping rough at this time of year. Thermal imaging cameras will show the location of anyone in the vicinity. Then we can just walk right to where he is and grab him.'

'Do you reckon he's a danger to the police?'

'No, I don't think we're on his target list, but to chop up someone like that means whoever it is has probably lost their mind, or all hope. We'll need to be cautious.'

'I agree, either out of control, or perhaps just very angry. I'll find out whether we can have the helicopter, and I'll check the availability of Tactical and the armed response vehicles.'

'Okay. I'm struggling for manpower to look for Mrs Zanthos. She can't have vanished.'

'Agreed. I'll have the other detective team track her down.'

The incident room was a beehive of endeavour until they broke for the 2 p.m. meeting. Agyepong turned up with a minute to spare. Cox arrived on the button. They were waiting for Leicester, who was gazing at his screen. Barton was about to say something when Leicester looked up.

'Holy shit. I wasn't expecting that,' he shouted.

Barton noticed Cox frown, so he stifled his smile.

'Explain,' said Barton, gruffly.

'I've been looking through the front pages and other media from around that time, some of which are pretty detailed. When Frank Zanthos killed himself, it opened up a complete media storm to do with mental health issues and vulnerable children. He leapt from the bridge and was instantly killed, but he wasn't alone. He was with two friends.'

'Jesus, don't tell me it was Drummond and Crannock,' said Barton.

'Almost! One was Logan Drummond. You won't believe the other.'

Barton braced himself.

'The other was Archie Spencer.'

Silence fell in the room as they attempted to knit the pieces together. It seemed everyone's head was spinning. Strange tried to summarise it first.

'Okay. Frank Zanthos dies. His father goes to jail and serves nine years of an eighteen stretch. He's out for quite a while, then receives a further twelve for the abduction. Drummond somehow ends up on the same wing as him thirty years after the suicide, and Zanthos senior dies. Pfeiffer and Ballanchine are also there at the same time. Drummond, Pfeiffer and Ballanchine, and Crannock are released on the same day. Pfeiffer and Ballanchine are murdered a few days later. Got to be Drummond.'

Barton drummed his fingers on his forehead while he organised the information in his mind.

'Yes, it gives him a motive, and explains how he could be that violent. Ms Agyepong, anything to add?'

'June, please. I've asked around the whole department and even reached some of the people who have since retired but were involved with these two in the past. The first thing to mention is Crannock didn't turn up for his first appointment with Probation in Newcastle. He was supposed to attend as soon as his train arrived. Because of his record, he was immediately recalled to prison. The police up there have been searching for him since the evening after he missed his appointment.'

'No joy?' asked Zander.

'Well, they haven't caught him yet, but he's all over CCTV. They have him leaving the station the day he got out, then on numerous cameras as he made his way to one of the rougher housing estates. He's there somewhere, drunk by the look of the images of him staggering around from Saturday. It's a run-down place, but they know where the squats are and they're hoping to pick him up tonight.'

'What do you think of him as a killer?'

'He told the handler before me he'd do anything for a thousand pounds. Literally, anything.'

'He sounded like a bullshitter to me when we interviewed him in the prison. There's often considerable distance between saying something and doing it,' said Barton.

'And if he is drunk in Newcastle, that means he can't have been involved in the demise of Pfeiffer or Ballanchine,' said Zander.

'No,' replied Barton. 'It's highly unlikely that he managed to fit seven hours on a train and a load of killing into his busy drunken schedule. This isn't his type of crime at all. Robbing isolated old people in their homes perhaps, but not this organised carnage.'

'Drummond it is, then,' said Strange.

'Looks that way, although he didn't strike me as the type for wiping out old men, whatever they might have done,' said Barton.

'Maybe he snapped in prison. It must have been a shock to see Zanthos again after all this time,' said Zander.

Agyepong broke the following silence.

'The good news is that I spoke to the others in the department who knew of Drummond, and it was widely known that when he camped out before, he stayed down by the river.'

'Which part?' asked Barton.

'There's a crossing over the Nene Valley Railway line not far from the Botolph pub and through the housing estate. It leads onto a small wood next to Woodston Ponds. Quite a few of my clients have had to sleep in there over the years. I had a Lithuanian who lived there for over a year.'

Barton looked across at Cox and raised an eyebrow.

'Sorry,' she replied. 'I can't get a helicopter or Tactical until tomorrow at the earliest. There's been machine-gun fire at a housing estate in Hitchin and a high-speed pursuit in Stevenage. If we had stronger intel, I could push harder, but the ARV can be here within the hour. It's Cureton and Smith. If you want to go in now, it's your call. I'll support your decision.'

Barton gave a little smile. Yes, but it would be his neck on the line.

'Okay, we do it,' he said. 'Cureton and Smith will cope fine with Drummond, armed or not. He's mid-forties, and he hasn't got a gun, as far as we know. We can put on PPE, take batons and PAVA spray, and back them up. If he's in there, he won't be able to escape because the river traps him in.'

He looked around at his team.

'Are we up for this?'

Leicester, Malik, Zander, Strange and Zelensky all stood up.

'Right, we leave at 3:15. Two cars. I'll ask the ARV to meet us here at 3 p.m. to run through how they want to handle this. Get ready, both with your equipment and your heads. This guy is dangerous, but if we have a chance to get him into custody right now, we should try. Let's bring him in.'

The team dispersed quickly. Barton shook Agyepong's hand and thanked her for coming in. When he got back to his desk, he saw that some letters and a small box had been placed on it. His name was on the box in scrawled writing. He shook it, and something inside rattled.

As he searched for a way through the excessive Sellotape, Barton started thinking ahead. What would happen if they confronted Drummond in the woods? Drummond would spend the rest of his days in prison with his record and the brutal nature of the kills. That his victims were sex offenders didn't come into it. His days of freedom were over. Ballanchine had been cocky and full of it, but perhaps it was a front for getting old and frail. Many would consider Ballanchine's offences unforgivable, but no one deserved to be chopped up, and judges tended to frown on vigilantes.

Cox had confirmed that Mrs Zanthos's face was going to be on the news that night and there would be a reward offered for further information leading to her being located. Barton couldn't help thinking that this was what the murderer was after. Drummond would never get away with committing careless crimes such as these, so perhaps he wanted publicity. Mrs Zanthos would be named and shamed. The public interest would spread like wildfire.

A madman slaughtering sex offenders would be front-page news, and the killer would even be a hero to some.

Barton grinned as he finally got into the box. His smile faded as he looked inside and took the item out. It was a pen. The same one he'd lost in the prison.

## 48

DI BARTON

At 3:10 p.m., the ARV team of Jules Cureton and Al Smith arrived at the incident room. They approached Barton, who shook hands with both of them. Cureton was in his fifties now and Al was in his thirties. Barton had trained Al as a new PC, which made him feel his years whenever he saw him. Barton explained the situation to them and after some qualifying questions, Cureton bobbed his head confidently.

'I know Woodston Ponds well. An ex lived nearby, and we used to walk that way to the pub. Al and I got called to a disturbance there some time ago. Nasty business.'

'How so?' asked Barton.

'Two Lithuanians were having a knife fight when we turned up,' added Smith. 'But people soon calm down when a loaded weapon is pointed in their direction.'

'And he has nowhere to run to,' said Cureton. 'It's winter, so there'll be little foliage cover. If there's a tent in there, we'll find it. If he's in it, he won't escape. If it's an empty tent, we can discuss further options then. I take it we have uniform to help with perimeters?'

'We have plenty of bodies,' replied Barton. 'We can have four of them close the path off at the Wharf Road turning and we'll shut the path where it crosses the railway line behind Botolph Green. DCI Cox will be there with a further team to respond to any changes. Any pedestrians and cyclists can easily re-route down Oundle Road, so we're not in any rush. There'll only be a few souls around there at this time of the year. It's quite sinister at night, and everyone knows people live in there, and that they might be desperate.'

'To sum up then,' said Cureton. 'We have a single path which you guys will cover, leaving us a small wood to walk through, followed by the big pond area. The man we're after is violent and dangerous, but he's in his forties and we don't believe he's armed. He's not special forces or a fitness freak?'

Before Barton could reply, his mobile phone rang.

'Just a sec,' he said.

He pumped his fist as he disconnected the call.

'The other incident has cleared. The helicopter is on the way, but they will only have about thirty minutes of fuel when they arrive. Another ARV is en route, but won't be here for an hour.'

'If we wait for the other armed unit, we'll lose the helicopter,' stated Smith. Years of working together meant Smith and Cureton didn't need a discussion. Smith continued. 'We go in quietly, get in position. The bird can fly over and, with thermal imaging, anyone in there will stand out like a sore thumb. If the threat changes, for example, the suspect is not alone, or is armed in some way, we'll look to retreat and contain. We'll have the radio on talk-through, so listen in. The situation could change rapidly.'

Five minutes later, a series of cars and vans was bumping down the slope out of the station car park. Barton drove with Strange beside him in the front passenger seat and Zander in the rear. Barton realised that all of them had sacrificed another weekend and no one had complained. He also realised it was another weekend leaving Holly to look after his mother.

It was still daylight as they turned onto Oundle Road but the shadows were drawing in. With the sun now hidden, the temperature was plunging. Zander and Strange seemed subdued.

'You two okay?' asked Barton. 'You're quiet.'

'Just focusing. This could be a dangerous situation. I was just thinking the same thing about you,' said Strange.

Barton hesitated.

'I was pondering what happens next, other than the hours of paperwork.'

Strange smiled. 'Nothing else?'

Barton grinned. Strange didn't miss much.

'Is it that obvious?'

'Yes. There's a lot that could go wrong here, but you don't seem that fazed. Is your mind on your mum?'

'It feels like my mum is fading away fast. I have the feeling there's little time left, and I should be at home.'

'I doubt she'll realise you aren't there. Holly and the kids will be with her. She's surrounded by affection, and hopefully you've put the heating on.'

Barton laughed loudly. 'What does that mean?'

'Holly said you keep turning the thermostat down, so the heating often doesn't even come on.'

'It's not so chilly that we need to maintain temperature and moisture levels similar to an African jungle. I rarely feel the cold inside.'

'Yes, but look at your size and insulation. You're like an elephant seal, happily lazing on the sea ice, despite it being minus fifty.'

'I can imagine that scene,' said Zander from the rear seats as they drove past the Botolph pub and parked up behind the ARV and one of the response vehicles.

'I'm going to take some holiday when this case is finished,' stated Barton. 'Spend time with Mum before she can't remember who I am.'

'Good for you,' said Zander.

'Right, then,' said Barton. 'Game time.'

Strange stepped out of the car with a smile.

'This is exciting. It's been a while since I was involved in anything like this.'

Barton gave her a reassuring grin as he pulled on his stab vest. Drummond was outmatched and outgunned. This should be simple, but Barton had been doing this job long enough to know things rarely turned out the way he expected. Perhaps, this would be one of those exceptions. After all, Drummond couldn't evade semi-automatic rifle fire.

Ten minutes later, the path was closed and any pedestrians on it had been sent away. The uniform team were in position, and the detective team had both ends of the wood covered. Strange, Malik and Leicester at one end, with Barton, Zelensky and Zander at the other. Cureton and Smith were at the edge of the wood with Barton. Cureton was speaking to the helicopter pilot through a pair of headphones. Barton and Strange wore similar equipment and the pilot's voice was loud and clear.

'Okay, ground team. As discussed, we'll take a run over now from east to west, passing over the target area, including the ponds. We'll be quite high so as not to draw attention, but if he's there, I suspect he'll hear us.'

They stood still for less than a minute, then the helicopter's whirring blades could be heard in the distance. Barton looked to the east where the sky was now full of clouds. When the helicopter appeared and approached, it seemed as though it was pulling a dark blanket behind it as daylight disappeared. Barton had a sense of foreboding that matched the horizon.

Thirty seconds later, the helicopter peeled away, and the pilot resumed communication.

'Visibility is poor at the ponds. There's a surface mist down there, but no signs of life. The wood has one heat source. The trees down there are thicker, but we could clearly make out a green tent with what I would say was a male next to it, looking up. He's a hundred metres to your left, thirty metres from the river. His face was covered, but he's wearing a big dark parka coat. There's nothing else in there but rabbits and foxes. Get your target. We'll be seconds away if he evades and flees.'

'All received,' said Cureton. 'We're going in.'

'Wait,' said Barton. 'I almost forgot. You asked about his training. There were rumours he'd been fighting in wars abroad, maybe the Legion, but we don't know for sure. You mentioned it earlier.'

Cureton stared hard at Barton for a moment before nodding twice. He turned, whispered something to Smith, and moved off.

Barton watched the two men stride into the wood. He walked after them to the first line of trees and looked inside. It wasn't a thick wood but there was a light fog, which had settled around the trunks. It lit up eerily when the torches on the riflemen's weapons passed over it. Now the helicopter had gone, it was deathly quiet until a squawk from a startled bird put him further on edge. As Cureton and Smith got further away and closer towards the river, the mist consumed them. Barton swallowed and removed his baton from the holder.

# 49

## THE COLD KILLER

When I fought in various war zones, you could often sense a change before it happened. Unnatural sounds might echo your way, or the jungle would go quiet. Nowadays, they send a massive helicopter overhead so you can't miss it. I bet they think that I'm just a tired, cold, old man, and not up to much. Although Barton's more on the ball than I thought. I wouldn't have expected them down here for a few days yet, and then not with all this backup.

I pull the mobile phone out of my pocket. I've tried ringing my contact but the number rings out. There have been no replies to my texts. I've met men ready to implode or explode before and perhaps he already has. I wonder who'll go down with him. I snap the sim card and launch it and the phone as far as I can into the passing water.

It's annoying that they have already located my base because Archie was supposed to be receiving a visit from me tomorrow. I've done nothing today but think. I'm tempted to let Archie go, but there's a part of me that won't rest if Archie doesn't pay for his sins. I suppose there are other ways. The crack of a snapping twig echoes through the trees. I know little about the UK's police resources, so who's coming is a mystery, but I'm guessing they're armed. Let's hope they don't have twitchy fingers.

I crouch with the river splashing against the bank behind me. I checked it earlier, and it's a rapidly flowing torrent with all the melted ice and snow. It's chilly, too, but probably my only chance because they'll count on it trapping me in. I pick up the heavy-duty torch I bought and walk towards the men. The mist is a godsend, meaning I can get close. One of them sees me, but I step back and I'm soon out of sight.

'Armed police! Stand still,' a man shouts in a deep, slow voice.

I hear them clearly now, scraping past bushes and crunching through the debris underfoot. They're good, methodical, and they swiftly approach. I take up a position behind my tent. These men may be armed police, but even if they know I'm ex-forces, they won't expect my surprises. It's one of the first things you learn. If you're on your own, you'll need to sleep. Guard your perimeter. Earn yourself time.

The first one steps into the small clearing with his rifle trained my way. He's mid-fifties and walks forward with a measured confidence. He doesn't say anything. Instead, he crouches and keeps his weapon pointed at me. To my right, another man appears, weapon raised.

'Stay where you are,' he orders.

They are both exactly where I want them.

## 50

DI BARTON

Barton listened to the ARV team's shouted commands over the radio. It was obvious that they had their sights on the man they suspected to be Drummond but he wasn't complying with their orders, as Cureton again repeated his demand for Drummond to show his hands.

'Suspect has now extended his arms,' declared Cureton. 'He's moving closer. Possible weapon in his right hand, but it looks like a large torch.'

The radio buzzed. 'Place the torch on the ground. Argh!'

Barton's ears strained as the radio crackled and broke up. Then it echoed loudly as Cureton asked Smith if he was okay. There was silence again for a few seconds.

'Smith is down. It looks as though a branch above him snapped, but he's getting to his feet. My rifle is still trained on the suspect, who hasn't moved. Kneel, now! Hands behind your head. Drop the torch. I'm heading in.'

After a few seconds of silence, Barton didn't need his radio to hear Cureton's scream as the woods seemed to amplify it. A flock of crows scattered from the treetops. Something large and loud was moving in the woods, crashing through branches, shifting fast, and coming their way.

'Jules, give me an update,' shouted Barton into his mic.

Static came back. Barton, Zander and Zelensky stood three metres apart at the end of the woods, batons drawn. There was a rotten fence dividing them from the ponds leading up to the river. The only exit was through the officers.

A dark shape hurtled out of the mist and gloom.

'Stop!' roared Barton, but a torch beam shone in his face, blinding him.

The figure cannoned into Zelensky, sending her flying. It dodged Zander, sprinted, then jumped onto the top of the fence, slid over and out of view. The radio burst into life. It was Cureton.

'I stepped in some kind of trap, lower leg injuries, but Smith is on his way. Get the bird back and have them confirm the suspect's direction of travel. Follow if you can to keep the suspect in sight. Don't engage until Smith is with you. This man may need taking down to stop him.'

Zander flew past Barton and hauled himself over the two metre fence. Barton checked Zelensky was okay, gave an update over the radio and ran towards the fence. It was rotten, so Barton put his head down, imagined himself charging the back line in a rugby match, and smashed straight through it. He found himself in a gloomy field. Zander was fifty metres ahead and running along a wooden walkway set around the central marshy pond area. Zander stopped and looked into the marshes. Then he stepped off the raised platform and disappeared into the mist.

Barton ran hard round the edges of one of the ponds, but slowed when his feet were sinking up to his ankles. The helicopter raced overhead, much lower now, with its beam on the marshes. Barton reached the walkway and clambered up, soon reaching the spot where Zander had gone in, but he couldn't see anyone. He could hear plenty, though.

There were the grunts of a desperate struggle, and curses Barton recognised as Zander's. But the mist had covered the ground in front of him, and the sound from the helicopter made it hard to get a direction from the shouts.

Barton glanced to the other side of the walkway and spotted Drummond clambering onto it. Drummond stood, lit by the downward beam of the helicopter. He held up his torch and waved with it. Then he turned and peered behind him, towards the river. Surely, he wasn't going to try to swim across. The struggling cries of Zander had changed. There was desperation and panic threaded through every syllable now. Barton stepped off the boards and walked forward. His boot sank in the mud up to his calf and he almost lost his balance. He could see very little, but he was closer to Zander's choking sounds.

The helicopter came lower, and the blades dispersed most of the mist. Barton's eyes roamed the centre of the marshes. It seemed to be a muddy, watery pool. Zander had turned on his back, with only his head and one arm visible out of the thick liquid.

'Help,' he spluttered.

Barton took two steps and sank down to his knees. He felt the mud hungrily sucking at his boots.

'Do not move, or I will shoot,' Smith bellowed out behind him.

Barton stared at Zander; whose chin had sunk lower in the water. Eighteen-stone Barton was the last man you'd want to attempt this kind of rescue. He tried to recall if he had rope in his car, but suspected it'd be too late by then. The walkway was a big circle. Zander was nearer to Drummond's side than his. How had Drummond got through it? If Barton went round the other side, he'd be closer. He'd have to run, but even then, Zander could have gone under by the time he made it.

'Take another step forward, and I'll shoot,' hollered Smith again.

Barton looked up and saw Drummond edging back towards Zander. At the same time, Barton noticed a row of logs and a plank that had been laid in a row to create a safe route along the edge of the pool. It still seemed bloody precarious, but explained how Drummond had got across. Drummond took another step down. What the hell was he doing?

'Final warning,' bellowed Smith.

'Wait,' said Barton, realising what was happening. He put his hand up and turned to Smith. 'Drummond's rescuing Zander.'

Sure enough, Drummond returned to the edge of the pond. He picked up a long branch and held it out towards Zander, whose arm flailed in that direction. Barton heard footsteps thundering behind him. Zander got a good grip on the wood and Drummond pulled on his end. A minute later, after a lot of effort, Drummond stepped forward, grabbed Zander's jacket, and heaved and yanked him out of the mud and onto his back. Barton could see Zander's heavy breaths puffing into the chill air. Drummond collapsed to his knees, staring at Barton. He put his hands on his head. Smith came out of the fog next to him.

'Do not move!' he thundered at Drummond, with his rifle held high.

Zelensky appeared beside Smith and quickly cuffed an exhausted Drummond's hands behind his back. Barton breathed a huge sigh of relief. It was over.

## 51

### DI BARTON

It was 10 p.m. by the time Barton started the interview with Drummond. Zander had been sent home to warm up after his ordeal and Cureton was in a lot of pain at A & E. He'd fallen through some disguised twigs into a wide trench, which had a solid wooden bottom with upturned nails sticking out of it. His falling weight had driven those nails into his knees.

Smith had taken a step forward when they first apprehended Drummond and a branch had dropped on him, knocking his weapon from his hand but not hurting him. It had been hard to see in the dark whether it had also been a trap, but Barton assumed it was.

Now Drummond sat before him, staring directly into Barton's face. They'd given him a shower and a clean seventies-style blue tracksuit with white stripes. It would have looked comical on most other men. But there was nothing funny about what Drummond had done, and what he appeared capable of if the cuffs were removed.

'I'm stating for the third time, for the benefit of the recording and complete clarity, that Mr Drummond has again denied representation. He also doesn't want any advice from the duty solicitor prior to this interview. Is that right, Mr Drummond?'

'Aye. I don't trust anyone here.'

Barton rubbed his temples for a few moments. Drummond was unlikely to tell him anything, even though everything he'd done up to now seemed to be about making a statement. Barton decided he'd try a different tack.

'What is it that you want society to understand?'

Drummond smiled at him. He flexed his cuffed hands and inhaled deeply through his nose. Barton felt Strange tense next to him, but Barton was rarely wrong when it came to the threat of violence. Despite what the movies would have you believe, only someone who wanted to break bones in their wrists or arms started a fight in handcuffs. The reason they were used all over the world was because they were the ultimate handicap.

Drummond wasn't the type of man who took lives for nothing. The men who got Drummond's unwanted attention were people who he felt deserved it. By some measures, his judgement was proportionate. People who bullied got the kicking they'd bestowed on others. Men who thought they owned pubs were taken down next to the bar for everyone to see. That was Drummond's way. You only crossed him once. These murders had to be connected with the suicide of his friend all those years ago. His friend died, so those responsible would too.

'I'm not telling you anything you want to hear, John Barton. You set me up.'

Barton frowned. He remembered the case against Drummond six years ago. It was a pub fight, instigated by Drummond, where, even though outnumbered three to one, Drummond had put his foes in hospital. One for over a month. It was a brutal attack without mercy, and he explained all this to Drummond.

'Rubbish. I'd never been in that pub before and had only gone in for a couple of beers with a woman I'd met. They made a few comments at the bar. I told them not to. They persisted, so I got in their faces, and called them out. One of them swung. The CCTV showed as much. They lost. That should have been the end of it.'

Barton placed his hands over his face and rubbed the bridge of his nose. He took his hands away.

'Do you feel hard done by? You nearly killed them.'

'I didn't though, did I? They got what they deserved.'

'This isn't the wild west. Why not walk away? Look where you ended up.'

'Would you walk away?'

Barton considered that. His twenty-year-old self wouldn't have done. He imagined a scrote giving Holly some grief when they were out. What Drummond had done was understandable, if not acceptable.

'You'll be fifty before you know it,' he said. 'Aren't you tired of this life?'

Drummond's shoulders drooped.

'I am. But I didn't deserve six years.'

'Perhaps not. But you've led a life of violence. Society doesn't want people like you in it. You're always a hair's breadth from lashing out. It's not for you to judge, nor be the executioner. Someone getting killed or seriously hurt was inevitable.'

'Pub brawl to an almost ritualistic killing is quite a leap,' said Drummond.

'That's why I wanted to understand what you want the world to know.'

'You don't deserve my help.'

Barton leaned back in his seat. Clearly reason wasn't working.

'I hear you were in the French Foreign Legion.'

'That's right, I was.'

'I assume you were trained with guns and knives, to take lives, quietly and effectively,' said Strange.

Drummond barked out a laugh. He smiled at Strange, then looked at Barton.

'I like her. Sneaky like you. I bet she'd enjoy pinning these recent events on me, just as you would. Get me out the way.'

'We are aware of your connection to Zanthos,' said Barton. 'Is that why you did it?'

Drummond sneered. 'Ooh, nice question. Never assume, Barton, you know that.'

'You have a motive, and you have the skills.'

Drummond's fists tensed. He rose from his seat, leaning forward. 'I was a soldier. Yes, I took the lives of many men. In fact, they called me The Cold Killer, because I was ruthless and efficient. Soldiers died at my hands. It was war.'

'Is that why you killed Zanthos, Pfeiffer and Ballanchine?'

'They weren't men, they were cockroaches,' Drummond shouted while jabbing a forefinger on the table.

'Who made you the judge?' provoked Barton.

'People who abuse children don't deserve justice. They deserve a painful death.'

'Is that your message?' asked Barton.

Drummond visibly relaxed and retook his seat. His face softened. 'Don't you think that these events send a strong message to other sex offenders? That the punishment will now fit the crime,' he said.

'You know you can't go around making up the rules and killing people,' said Barton.

'I never said I did.'

Strange shook her head. 'You have three years left of your sentence. You're going straight back to prison to finish that sentence having assaulted police officers this afternoon. Then, add on a sentence for a triple murder. You'll die in jail. We know those men did terrible things to children and I can understand how you might think justice hasn't been done. If you confess, explain your reasons, then a judge could show leniency.'

Drummond looked for a moment as if he was going to spit on the floor in disgust. Instead, an unusual expression came over his face that Barton couldn't read.

'Come and see me in the morning. I'll give you a confession.'

# 52

## DI BARTON – MONDAY 16TH DECEMBER

Barton had a troubled night. Usually, after a case was solved, he would sleep like the dead, but he'd thrashed around so much that Holly had got out of bed at some point and slept on the sofa. There was a steaming cup of coffee on his nightstand, so she couldn't have been too annoyed. He got dressed and went downstairs. The only thing on his mind was Drummond's confession.

Holly had made him a big bowl of porridge. Lawrence and Layla were nowhere to be seen, but Luke sat beaming at him from the other side of the kitchen table. Barton plonked himself down and Holly joined them.

'We're the three bears,' said Luke.

Barton reached over and squeezed his son's hand. Luke happily spooned his cereal in, before pushing the bowl away. He started to look at the cartoon on the back of the cereal box. If only Barton's life were so simple.

'Papa Bear needs to spend some time with Momma Bear,' said Holly. 'Or she's going to skin him.'

Barton smiled. 'Apologies. It's been a crazy few days. How's Mum?'

'Odd. She seems content but barely eats anything. The doctor's coming out again to see her. If she stops eating, they'll have to take her in and feed her in another way, but she is at least still drinking.'

'I'm sorry you're having to deal with all this on your own. I'm hoping we'll put the case to bed today with a confession.'

Holly paused the spoon at her lips. 'Oh, dear. I've seen that look before. You're not convinced.'

'Not completely. Drummond, the suspect, is definitely involved. He's right in the middle of it, but I don't think he's acting alone. If he confesses, he might be protecting someone else. Maybe the person who actually did the killings will then get away with it.'

'Why would he confess if he didn't do it?'

'I'm not sure. During the interview I couldn't read his expression, but I think I get it now. He didn't say it, but I reckon he wants to go back to prison. Murders like these would get him a life sentence, probably thirty years at least. He'd be nearly eighty when he got out, if they ever let him out.'

'What's the word? Institutionalised?'

'Perhaps. He's done a lot of jail time. Sometimes people give up. Others decide that life in prison is easier than life outside. Maybe he thought that he'd kill the men he believed were responsible for the death of his friend and that was him finished.'

'Thirty years in prison doesn't sound appealing.'

'No, that's the other thing. He had the relaxed demeanour of a man who'd made his choices and to hell with the consequences. I wouldn't be surprised if he killed himself inside.'

'I saw the news. What he did was appalling. Dangerous men like him deserve to be off the streets. I doubt he'd be missed.'

Barton spooned the rest of his porridge into his mouth and pushed the bowl away. He'd barely tasted it.

'My brain isn't happy with how this fits together. It's as though I have a finished jigsaw puzzle, but a few of the pieces are in the wrong place. You know what's weird? I always kind of liked Drummond.'

'You like serial killers now?'

'He wasn't one before all this. I sort of respected his no-nonsense, gung-ho attitude to life. Drummond enjoyed fighting, and he didn't take any shit. His problem was he was too good at it.'

Holly glared at Barton, but luckily Luke hadn't heard.

Barton pulled his coat off the back of his chair and kissed his wife on the top of her head.

'Hopefully I'll be home at a reasonable time. We can have a proper conversation with Mum, or we'll chat about what the future might bring.'

'We need to organise Christmas, too, John. I hope you've already invited Kelly and Zander.'

Barton cringed because he'd forgotten, but was saved by Luke.

'Daddy,' said Luke. 'Layla says she wants a pony for Christmas.'

'Turkey is more traditional,' replied Barton. 'But once it's covered with cranberry sauce, it all tastes the same.'

'Your dad's pulling your leg, Luke. And he eats so fast, he could be eating anything.'

Barton put his shoes on and opened the front door. He heard Luke ask Holly what 'shit' meant, then ran to his car.

When he reached the station, there was an almost celebratory atmosphere in the office. Cox gave him a card on his desk and congratulated him.

'Any luck tracking down Mrs Zanthos?' asked Barton.

'No, sorry. Even if we get her now, without someone talking, we wouldn't have a strong case.'

Zander was taking the banter well about his unorthodox arrest technique.

'I could have got out at any point,' he shouted to the crowd, 'but I could see weakness in his eyes.'

Leicester, Malik and Zelensky all let off a party popper in Zander's direction, then threw the containers at him.

Strange was waiting for Barton.

'Drummond is in interview room three. He's still declining any representation. You're the only one he'll speak to now. He said he has four words to say to you, which will make you understand. Then his mouth is closed. The next time he'll open it will be at the trial.'

Barton frowned.

'Doesn't he mean when he's sentenced? If he's confessing, there won't be a trial.'

'I think we should prepare to hear something that complicates everything.'

Barton nodded. He wholeheartedly agreed. After a conversation with the CPS solicitor, Barton followed Strange to the interview room and they took seats opposite Drummond. With the formalities completed, Barton looked him over. Drummond had been through a trying experience, but even with stubble and bags under his eyes, he exuded strength and purpose.

'Let's have it,' said Barton.

'First off, Zanthos died in his cell of natural causes. I'm here to confess about the savage deaths of the other two paedophiles, Pfeiffer and Ballanchine.'

'Fair enough,' said Barton.

'I'm telling you this in all honesty.'

'Go on, then.'

'I didn't kill either.'

## 53

DI BARTON

Barton and Strange stared at Drummond, then looked at each other and closed their eyes in unison. They tried to get more information out of Drummond, but he leaned back in his chair, stared at the ceiling and said nothing. Another minute later, and Barton gave up. He'd already spoken with the CPS and Drummond was charged with the murder of Zanthos, Pfeiffer and Ballanchine. Barton returned him to the custody suite. It was just before nine, so Barton asked Strange to ensure Drummond was at the magistrates that morning and to attend the court and observe. With any luck, Drummond would be back in prison by lunchtime.

Barton walked into the office and almost booted his bin up into the air. To his surprise, he quickly felt his anger subside. There was something else at play here. Zander came over for an update and merely shrugged afterwards.

'Let him rot in jail. His offending days are over.'

'Yes, hopefully so. But get this – I'm inclined to believe him.'

'You don't think he did it?' asked an incredulous Zander.

'I could accept that he killed Zanthos in prison. Drummond confessed to being a cold killer. That fits. Pfeiffer maybe, but his death was kind of staged, and I can't see Drummond chopping up Ballanchine and spreading him out over the fields. That's a different motivation and end result.'

'Yes, but Mortis and CSI have confirmed what we suspect. The knives were the same. Someone killed Pfeiffer and left the knife in him, then chopped up Ballanchine and left an identical knife to be found with the pieces.'

'Has Mortis got a time of death for Ballanchine?'

'No, he said it was impossible under the circumstances. When he put the remains that were found in the field together, he had the full complement, so there wasn't any trophy keeping. If pressed, he would say that Ballanchine died more than twenty-four hours before we found him. It has to be Drummond. He was there on the wing for Zanthos, and he was released at the same time as Pfeiffer and Ballanchine.'

'Right,' replied Barton, absorbing the information.

'Although,' said Zander, 'it does beg the question as to how he knew where to find both of them.'

'Prisoners talk. Perhaps they told him where they lived. Maybe he looked on the Internet or at past papers. He might have followed one and tortured him to get the information for the other. Otherwise, who helped him?'

'No idea. And if Drummond didn't do it, then who did?'

Barton clicked his fingers. 'I still like Crannock for some involvement. Did they pick him up?'

'Yes, an inspector from up there rang in last night. Crannock was arrested and his licence was revoked. He didn't even go to court. They just returned him to prison up there. He has a year left, so he's not going anywhere for a while. With so blatant a breach, I expect he'll serve at least another six months before they give him another opportunity. I'll arrange for him to be transported here when I get a minute.'

'Why not get him back immediately?'

'They questioned him and checked CCTV. They have him getting off the train on the day he was released. He told them he'd been staying at a mate's house on the high street, drinking and taking drugs ever since he got out. Around the time we think Pfeiffer was killed, Crannock is on CCTV at Tesco buying booze. He was seen so regularly in the local area that unless he has a doppelgänger, his alibi is watertight.'

Barton looked at the bin again. He tensed his jaw to stop himself from swearing. The phone on his desk rang.

'Barton.'

'Morning, sir. It's PC Brown here. You remember I told you about the stallholder on the market who sold those types of knives?'

'Yes, did you talk to him?'

'His stall wasn't open. The guy opposite said that he'd been away for a wedding, but he gave me his mobile number. I got hold of him, and he remembered selling them a few months ago.'

'Did he know the person?'

'No, but he said he would have taken ID. He's back tonight and is happy to come with his records to the station.'

Barton chewed his lip for a moment.

'Did you get a description of the person he sold the knives to?'

'He said the man had a hat and scarf on, so he would struggle to recognise him again, but he did say he was white, middle-aged, large and serious.'

Barton finished the call and stood up. Drummond fitted the description, although he wasn't particularly tall. Obviously, that would depend how big the stallholder was, but maybe the answer had been staring him in the face from the beginning.

He pondered whether the motivation for this case went all the way back to the suicide of that young man, Frank Zanthos, nearly thirty years ago. Drummond or Crannock couldn't have bought the knives as they were in prison, but there was always someone else involved in this story and he was free, and there was no doubt that Archie Spencer was a big, tall man.

Barton told Zander to keep everyone motivated and get the paperwork entered onto the system. He was going to speak to Archie Spencer in person. Malik was at the next desk to his.

'How's your paperwork?'

'Nearly up to date.'

'Come with me. We're giving Archie Spencer a visit. I'm going to offer him a couple of nights' bed and breakfast here.'

Malik signed out a grey Vauxhall Insignia. A businessman's vehicle suited Malik. He put the car into gear and turned to Barton.

'Any rush?'

Barton shook his head. He needed time to think. His initial enthusiasm over Spencer's involvement had faded. It was true that Spencer might be pleased about the deaths of the men, but Spencer had never been to prison. Why would he risk everything for such a scant reward? Barton supposed Spencer might be a sick man. He had looked ill. Maybe he wanted to settle some old scores before he died. Barton growled at the lack of clarity. He just couldn't see Spencer getting his hands this dirty.

The system they used to investigate, HOLMES, would find connections for them to explore, but it took time as it needed the data to work with, which was why getting the paperwork done was so important. But Barton had all the knowledge rattling around in his head already, and it was as they pulled up that a piece of information slotted into place like the hint of a new dawn.

Barton and Malik got out of the car at Spencer's mansion and checked the gates, which were locked. Barton pressed the call button on the intercom and grinned at Malik.

'I was pretty sure the murderer was on the wing,' said Barton.

'Aren't you now?'

'I think I was close. I still think the killer was in the jail, but maybe not resident on the same wing.'

Barton watched Malik's calm face.

'So the perpetrator was an inmate on a different wing.'

Barton raised an eyebrow, waiting for the penny to drop. Finally, Malik's expression turned to one of shocked realisation.

'Archie Spencer's son is in the prison.'

# 54

## DI BARTON

Barton tutted at the lack of response from the intercom but Malik was still trying to wrap his mind around it all.

'This is making my head spin,' he said finally. 'You think Archie Spencer had his son take out Zanthos as revenge for something that happened thirty years ago. How could he do that if they were on different wings?'

'I'm not sure, on either count. It's just another connection which brings us back to the jail. I've seen Drummond's prison record. He was on main location until shortly before Zanthos died. I'd put money on Drummond and Boy Spencer having known each other inside, maybe they even shared cells. It's possible Drummond and the lad concocted a plan to have Drummond moved to the VP wing to reach Zanthos.'

'His son hasn't been released, has he?'

'No,' replied Barton. 'Spencer Junior inherited his father's principles and most of his mother's charm. He was born a ticking crime bomb. They could have put pressure on another inmate to help them out. Maybe there's a different person we don't know about yet that's involved. Perhaps Drummond got on the wing to get rid of

Zanthos, but someone else was involved from one of the other wings.'

'Good thought, sir. Drummond could have pulled the strings when he got out, but the killer was someone else they'd met in the jail and they were leaving the establishment soon.'

'Yes. Where better to meet someone with no money and loose morals? They probably had a choice of whom to contract any kills to. That person would have had no connection to the victims, hence us struggling to find the link. Archie Spencer is a rich man, and it seems people kill for very little these days.'

Barton walked back to the gates and looked through the railings but all he could see were thick laurel trees. He stared up at a camera on the top of the gate and wondered if Spencer was watching him. The railings had spikes on them, which Barton didn't like the look of. He also wouldn't put it past Spencer to be lurking in the bushes with his chainsaw and a prepared defence that he didn't know anyone was there.

A posh voice caught his attention. A woman was encouraging her reluctant dog to leave the house on the opposite side of the road. Barton crossed over to her.

'I don't suppose you know if the Spencers are in? Or where they might be?'

'She could be at home, but he's out gallivanting on a golf day with my husband.'

Barton smiled at her cut-glass accent, while clocking her Barbour jacket and Hunter wellies.

'When are they due back?'

'Early evening.'

'Is he a friend of yours?' he asked.

The woman looked behind her, then back at him.

'If Mr Spencer wants to be your friend, he's hard to say no to. Although, he is generous and helpful. We had a problem with some noisy neighbours a while ago. Archie said he'd sort it. I haven't seen them since. Good day, sir.'

Barton watched her try to march away, but she had to drag the dog with her and he wondered whether he should find out any more about that particular story. First things first, he decided. Malik was pressing the intercom button again when Barton rejoined him.

'Malik, knock around the immediate neighbours. Ask a few general questions, but also check if anyone has noticed any visitors lately. Especially one that resembles Drummond.'

Barton looked up at the top floor of Archie's house and saw movement. He didn't fancy a run-in with Evie right now. It was Archie he needed to speak to.

'I'm going to walk back to the station,' said Barton. 'I need a few quiet moments to think because I think we're on the right track. When I get back, I'll request a search warrant for this place. I should have it approved so we can come back tonight. I'll be happy to drive through Archie's gates myself if he doesn't open up.'

'What's the plan this afternoon?'

'I'll ring Monty in the prison and go in, if I can, to look through the records. He'll be able to tell me how easy it is to enter a wing that isn't your own. I reckon when I hear the name of whoever's responsible, I'll know them. At the very least, I'm going to question Archie's son. It's still possible it was Drummond, but I just don't think he would kill that way. I don't believe the soldier in him would approve of it. I'll see you in the office in an hour or so.'

Barton strode towards Thorpe Road. It was only a twenty-minute walk, but it was a biting day and so were Barton's thoughts. He'd arrest Archie Spencer tonight, whatever he said. There was still something not quite right about everything that had occurred. He took his phone out and rang Monty at the prison. Unexpectedly, Monty picked up and Barton started to explain.

'Steady, John. I'm just leaving the office. I have a meeting with some of the service providers who help when the residents get out. Is it urgent?'

'I'd like to come in and talk to one of the prisoners and look at who's been released from the other wings since the Zanthos incident. I've got a few queries about how prisons work too.'

'Okay, I'll be back at five. I'll meet you at the gatehouse then. My secretary will run the reports so they're ready when you arrive, and she can get the prisoner's file printed out for you. Who is it?'

'Gilbert Spencer. Do you know him?'

'His name doesn't ring any bells. He can't have been too badly behaved, or I'd have heard about it. Does he need moving for his protection or anything like that?'

'No, I don't think so. The picture isn't clear yet, but he might be involved with the Zanthos death. We've caught Drummond as well. He's at court today, so you should have him back in the nick by this afternoon at the latest.'

'Right. Do you reckon he was responsible for the recent murders?'

'I suspect he was involved, but as to what extent, I'm not sure. When Drummond arrives, which wing would he be allocated to?'

'He'll get risk assessed upon arrival. If he was on the VP wing, he'd normally return there, but for obvious reasons that isn't a good idea in this case. The block and healthcare are both full at the moment. We had a near riot on an exercise yard this morning, but he should be fine on the induction wing.'

'Would it be possible for him to wander the prison and get on other wings? Visit Spencer, for example?'

'No, not a chance. New arrivals don't leave the wing for anything but healthcare appointments and induction meetings. They're escorted by wing officers in that case. Even if he got off the wing and went to another, the staff on that wing wouldn't recognise him and so they wouldn't let him on. Let me check which cell Spencer is in.'

Barton carried on walking as he heard Monty tapping on his keyboard.

'Spencer is on a completely different houseblock from the induction wing. I can't see how he could get over there. I'll let the reception staff know to put Drummond on the induction wing or even keep him in reception if he kicks off or his behaviour makes them suspicious. We'll have a chat when you get here and go from there.'

Barton said he'd meet Monty at five, and cut the call. He found himself walking fast. The clock was ticking.

His phone rang.

'Yes, Malik.'

'Two doors down, a neighbour saw what she described as a dodgy-looking fellow leaving Archie's property. She considered ringing the police because he looked like he was up to no good, but he wasn't the first criminal, her words, that she'd seen visiting that house.'

'Did she describe him?'

'Yes. It can only have been Drummond.'

# 55

## THE COLD KILLER

It's 3 p.m. when I'm finally taken into the dock at the court. The presiding magistrate coolly stares down at me.

'Please tell the court your name and address.'

'Logan Drummond, homeless.'

After the formalities, she reads out the charge. She double checks with the legal advisor that I'm also a licence recall, then clears her throat.

'These are serious offences where bail would rarely be considered. That fact combined with the breaches of your licence means you are immediately recalled to prison. I am obliged to ask if you'd like to give an early plea, but I would urge caution considering you have declined counsel.'

It's a small court. There have been no leaks from the police station, so the only observer behind the plastic screen is the short blonde in a sensible suit who was one of the detectives present when I was arrested. Her keen gaze is right on me. I wink at her.

'I'd like to enter a plea.'

The magistrate pauses for a few seconds, then nods.

'Not guilty.'

Her left cheek twitches. 'Plea accepted. You will be notified at the prison when your next court appearance will be. The door behind you will shortly open. Anything else you'd like to say?'

I shake my head, and I'm soon heading back to the court cells, which are now empty. The guard down there is waiting for me.

'Room for one more on the bus, Drummond. At least you aren't hanging around here until tonight. Hold out your hands. We need to cuff you for the journey, but we'll be there in ten minutes.'

'Fair enough.'

I step onto the bus, which seats eight in tiny compartments with just a moulded seat to rest on. The guard nudges me in and closes the door. As he leaves, the man in the compartment in front of me clears his throat.

'Drummond, that you?'

It sounds like Riggot.

'That you, Chimp?'

'Yes, bruv! We must love it.'

Riggot, or Chimp as he's called by everyone who knows him, is a prison officer's worst nightmare. I'm not sure what condition he has, or maybe it's just a surplus of energy, but he can't keep out of trouble. He also can't do his bang up. He's only five feet tall, and weighs nothing, so he has a habit of climbing things. Chimp scaled the building once and sat on the roof for an hour. He only came down because there was a good dinner that day. My mind ticks over. He might be a useful asset when we get to the nick.

The van idles outside the entrance for twenty minutes, then we're in and soon parked outside reception. They take me off the bus last of all. The screws know their regular visitors like me, and obviously they will have heard why I'm back. The SO is a big black guy called Odom. He's sound.

'Will there be any trouble today, Drummond?'

'No, sir.'

'Remove the cuffs,' he says to the transport staff.

The van driver cautiously removes the handcuffs. Odom takes a scan of my index fingerprint, then an officer ushers me over to the new body scanner to see if I have a weapon up my arse or drugs bagged in my stomach. There's neither. Odom is staring at the computer when I return to the front desk.

'You've been charged with the murders that have been on the news.'

'Yes, but I'm innocent until proven otherwise, and it's a set-up.'

Odom seems to analyse my face for a few moments.

'Isn't that what they all say?'

'Not me. Those men deserved to die, but it wasn't by my hand.'

He studies me again.

'You seem different. Happy, even.'

'I have something to live for.'

'Or is it because you've given up?'

I've known Odom for years. He's always been a perceptive guy.

'I almost did.'

He lowers his eyes and continues reading whatever's on my record.

'You were on the VP wing last time. Why was that?'

'I had a rumble with a few lads on the main wings just before I was due for release. They put me on there so there weren't any repercussions. It's all sorted now.'

Odom taps his pen on the desk while he thinks.

'There's a note to say that the people you *rumbled* with are still here.'

'As I said, it's fine. I bet you don't want to house me with the VPs.'

'No, I was considering sticking you in the block, but it's full. Do I have your word that you won't cause trouble?'

'Well, obviously I'll defend myself if I have to, but the last thing I'm looking for is more bother.'

Odom considers my answer. He gave me the benefit of the doubt years ago for a scrap that I hadn't started but had finished. A bit afterwards, I paid him back by having a word in the ear of a prisoner who was causing chaos on the wings. That message didn't get through, and I had to drive it home, so to speak, but it means Odom and I share a level of respect. Anyway, he hasn't got much choice in where to put me if everywhere's full.

'I'll allocate you to the induction wing with the other arrivals. We'll look into something more permanent in a few days. Keep your head down.'

I give him a tiny nod even though, unfortunately, it's a promise that I know I will break. He prints out my ID card and takes me along to the property desk.

'Why?' he asks me.

'Why what?' I reply.

'Risk coming back. You're wasting your life here. There's a decent person inside you somewhere.'

I smile at him but keep my mouth shut. I had to return. I've come for my boys.

# 56

## THE COLD KILLER

It's half four by the time they march us fresh meat to the induction wing. We're a lively bunch. There's a Romanian I've met before who could pass for a young Marlon Brando and doesn't take any shit; Chimp, who appears to be high, and a skinhead with army tattoos who looks as if he could attack anyone at any moment. The officer walking us over sensibly keeps behind us.

On the induction wing, I get a single cell on the top landing. I tell the screw that I've got a really urgent healthcare appointment soon because I'm on Subutex. He asks to see a movement slip, which a prisoner needs to leave the wing, but I explain to him that they said they'd collect me later today or this evening. He's flat out busy and doesn't care, but this conversation will register.

Subutex is the new heroin inside. It's supposed to be a drug to replace heroin, like methadone, where a pill is placed under the tongue to dissolve. If you crush it, though, then snort it, you feel a buzz, followed by a long monged-out state. It keeps prisoners chilled and seems to make a sentence go quicker. As a result, it's gold dust and highly restricted by healthcare. If I'm able to get off the wing and he can't find me, he'll think I'm at the appointment and it might buy me some time.

At 5 p.m., the workers come back from industries and Chimp and I lean against the gate, watching them go past. I'm looking for a weak officer I can tap up, or maybe even Grayson or Kevin themselves returning from work. All I need is five minutes, preferably ten. Grayson, I think, would be cool. Hopefully, Kevin will calm down when I tell him my story and about how I went to see his mum. In my experience, prisoners are quick to excuse others because they've made mistakes themselves, although perhaps forgiving an absent father is a different matter.

As the last few prisoners filter through, two officers appear: Raja and Green. They were on the VP wing when Zanthos died. They look over.

'Back from the gates, please,' shouts Green.

He says something to Raja, who laughs and leaves. Green walks towards me.

'Give us a minute,' I say to Chimp. 'If you create a disturbance down the bottom, I'll make it worth your while.'

Chimp doesn't need much encouragement, and he slips away.

'What are you doing back so soon?' asks Green.

In five minutes, the food trolleys will come over with the returning kitchen workers. It's the busiest period on the wings and my best chance. One screw has to supervise the food being taken out of the trolleys or the choice bits will vanish, while the other one will have to run around sixty cells letting the returning inmates back in their kennels. They'll have little idea if a busy officer allows me onto their landing.

I tell Green my latest news. He knows my story from before, including the revelation about Kevin Reed being my son. As I'm talking, I realise that everything I set out to do has been done, apart from Archie Spencer, who has escaped justice. They do say that the devil looks after his own. When I'm finished, Green seems confused.

'What are you asking?'

'I need a ten-minute chat with Kevin and Grayson, hopefully in their cell. I might not get the chance again. They could ship me or them out at any moment.'

Green looks dubious.

'You know you aren't supposed to be on any wing but your own,' he says. 'You'll get nicked for it if they find you on there.'

'I'll blag it. Say I was chatting to a mate and someone let me on.'

'If they find out it was me, I'll be in the shit.'

'Look, this needs to happen now. The detectives are all over these murders. They've got me. Then they're going to start looking at how I ended up on the VP wing. It's over. I need to warn Kevin and Grayson to keep their mouths shut about our connection. This has nothing to do with them. I'm not sure what they'll do if they hear from someone else that I'm back inside for a triple homicide. They won't know I'm innocent. Please, this is my only chance.'

There's a huge cheer behind us. I turn and spot Chimp break-dancing on the pool table. Green stares hard at me for a few moments, then opens the wing gates.

'Follow me, they're upstairs.'

We trudge up four sets of stairs in the quiet with only our foot-steps tapping on the concrete. When we open the door to the hub area, it's heaving with prisoners and noise. Perfect. I keep close to Green as he heads for X2 wing.

'I'll let you on,' he says, 'but then I'm out of here. I'm on general duties downstairs, so I need to get back and open the doors for the trolleys.'

He pauses before he opens the gate. Whatever he considers saying, though, stays unsaid, and he lets me on. He vanishes through the throng of milling inmates, while I slip down the wing.

As I thought, one of the officers is in the servery waiting for the food trolley, and the other is on the top landing.

Green didn't tell me which cell they're in, so I'll need to start at X2-1 and go to each one. I feel someone's eyes on me and look up to the top of the stairs. It's Spenny, my old cell mate, staring below. His gaze follows me, calculating, but I ignore him.

I keep my head down and wander along the rows of cells, staring at the door cards, which have the mugshots of the occupants on. A door near the bottom opens and Grayson steps out. I speed up and put a hand on his chest when I get there. I push him into the cell. Kevin is watching *Countdown* on the small TV.

Grayson laughs at me.

'Couldn't keep away?' he asks.

Before I can reply, Kevin has scraped his chair back. He rises from his seat, chin forward, eyes blazing. He clenches his fist in front of him, then steps towards me.

# 57

## THE COLD KILLER

Kevin attempts to stride past Grayson, but Grayson slams an arm across his chest.

'Let him talk,' he says. 'Assuming that's what he's here for.'

Kevin grabs Grayson's wrist and throws it down, but he stands still. Seeing Kevin again, I can spot how similar his features are to mine in so many obvious ways. Even his eyes smoulder the same as mine and I return his stare. My mind empties as I try to remember what I planned to say.

'I was a troubled soul.'

Kevin shakes his head, but I realise that this might be my only chance and I blurt it out.

'I was a troubled soul. I left your mother because I thought she and Grayson were better off without me. She hadn't told me she was pregnant. I fled to London, where I eventually ended up getting a hefty prison sentence. When I got out, it felt like there was too much water under the bridge. I've lived a life I'm not proud of. Bad things happened to me when I was young, and, instead of dealing with it, I took it out on everyone I met. My reward has been a lonely existence with nothing to show for it, except you guys.'

Kevin shakes his head but keeps quiet.

'I appreciate it's late in the day, but I want to make amends, or maybe just help out in some way.'

'You're twenty-five years too late, mate,' says Kevin.

'Yeah, we don't need your advice,' adds Grayson.

I look from one hard face to the other.

'I can see that you're doing well for yourselves.'

Kevin takes a big stride forward, knocking Grayson onto the bed. He raises his fist. My military training, and years of life experience, urge me to strike first, but instead I raise my chin.

'I owe you at least one free hit.'

Kevin's jaw bunches. He flexes his hand, then shoves me in the chest.

'Get out of here,' he snarls.

I step back, wondering what else to say.

'I went to see your mother.'

Grayson gets up off the bed, and they both look uncertain for a moment.

'And?' Grayson finally replies.

'She was hopping mad. She wanted to hit me too.'

I sense a small grin from Grayson, but he stops it blossoming. Even Kevin's shoulders relax a little.

'We had a talk. A long one. I told her about prison and all the rest. Explained how I'd never have kept away if I'd known. If I'm honest, we had a laugh. It felt a bit like old times.'

'Sneaky,' says Grayson. 'Our hands are tied in here, and you slip into the house and slide your feet under our table.'

'Your table?' I quietly ask.

They both have the grace to look away. These boys might have done stupid things, but they aren't daft. Anyone would understand that raising them would have been a challenge, especially alone. I sense it's time to leave, but I haven't got my message across with any clarity.

'Your mother's close to giving up on you. She wants a quieter life, with no aggravation. She wants to look out for herself, or be looked after. Did you plan to go back home when they let you out of here?'

It's clear they had both contemplated doing exactly that. I can also tell that now is the only time they've considered that maybe they wouldn't be able to. It's a form of rock bottom. There comes a moment in your life when the choices or mistakes you've made will mean you're completely on your own. It's called growing up. You realise the world doesn't revolve around you and what you want. It's a particularly tough lesson when you realise you haven't got a home to return to.

Grayson looks worried, but Kevin responds how I would.

'I'll be fine,' he states firmly.

I grin at him. 'You will. I don't reckon your mother is the type of person who'd quit on you, but perhaps you have some time now to think about the person you want to be, and what future you'd like. Don't do what I've done.' I hardly recognise the words coming out of my mouth. Who am I to give advice? Is this what fathers do, or haven't I earned that right? I puff out my cheeks. 'Look, I'll see you.'

I hold out my hand for them to shake. They stare at it for a few moments but don't take it.

'Why are you back?' asks Kevin.

'I had stuff to resolve. There were things that needed sorting from long ago. And they're trying to pin three crimes on me, but they won't stick.'

'Will we talk to you again?' asks Grayson.

'Of course. I got recalled for missing probation, too. I reckon I'll do another six months or so. I'll write if they transfer me.'

Grayson grins. 'Is this one of those "do as I say, not as I do" conversations?'

I can't help laughing out loud at that and Kevin joins in.

'You're right. Maybe I am full of shit, but I'm telling you, this is it for me. I'm planning to change. When I get out I'll move up near your mum. Perhaps we could be friends, possibly more, or there might be nothing, but I'm going to try. If we can build something between us, and that includes you, be a family of sorts, then that's more than I've had before, and I'll take it.'

'Will you be taking us to McDonald's when we get out? Or football matches?' said Kevin with a small smile.

'No,' I say, in a stern voice. 'I'm an old man. You have to take me.'

Kevin studies my face and I can see there's a lot going on inside his head. He needs space to think. I lower my hand, but Grayson reaches over and shakes it. I look to Kevin, who stares down at my open palm, but doesn't take it.

'You need to earn that,' he says.

'I will,' I reply. And for the first time, in a long time, earning someone else's trust is the most important thing to me.

The door squeaks behind me. It's slowly pushed open and nudges my back. I expect to see an officer there and I'm ready to blurt out my excuse for being in here, but it's only Spenny. I smile at him and step out of the way so he can come in.

'All right, mate. We're all cool here,' I tell him.

I turn round to the boys with a grin. They both have a look of horror on their faces, as though it's a set-up and they're about to get attacked. But then their gaze drops and I realise I've been a fool.

I should know better. I was stupid not to suspect the worst. Haven't I learned anything these past few days? I'm an idiot to have believed Archie when he told me he had nothing to do with his son any more. Dads don't desert their children if they can help it. Especially if they're useful.

I must have lost my touch if I haven't guessed that Archie would strike first. I've walked straight into his trap. Even though I know it's already too late, I fling my elbow backwards towards Spenny's chin, but I'm only halfway through the movement when the weapon he's holding in his left hand pierces my body above my left hip. My back arches with pain, but it's just a distraction. I know what comes next.

I'm stuck against the metal frame of the bed, so there's little space to manoeuvre. It doesn't matter, he's too quick. Out of the corner of my right eye, I see Spenny's right hand and in it something that looks like a piece of file, but there's a glint from where it's been sharpened along the side. He presses it hard against the side of my neck as I desperately flinch away. A roar of 'No!' from one of the boys echoes around the room. Then a sharp bite as the blade is slid firmly across my exposed skin.

There are a few seconds of numbness, then warmth as blood pours down my body and agony sears into my back and neck. A fist flies over my shoulder and I hear an almighty thud. Then it's a foot that flashes by, followed by a howl of hurt as more blows rain on the man behind me. Yet, it's as if there's a thin barrier between me and the others in the room, which deafens the sounds, softens the pain, and I slide down the wall to my knees.

# 58

## DI BARTON

DI Barton left his desk at 4:50 p.m. and nodded at Strange to indicate that it was time for their visit to the jail. Barton wondered whether Drummond had arrived there yet, and, if so, where they had put him. There were murderers on many of the wings, so he guessed he could be anywhere. That was the prison's call.

Barton had spent most of the afternoon with his head in his hands, trying to create a story in his mind that fitted all the parties concerned. Was Archie Spencer working with Drummond, or were they enemies in some way? Someone else had to be involved. What was he missing?

As they were leaving, PC Brown was just arriving. He had arranged to meet the stallholder from the market shortly.

'Ring me as soon as you find out if it's important. Talk to Zander when you're done.'

Zelensky was returning from the coffee machine.

'Did you get that information from the council about what happened to Zanthos's remaining child?'

'I chased half an hour back. He's received everything and was reading through it. He told me to give him an hour and ring him again.'

'Call me when you hear.'

'Will we be able to get hold of you in the prison?'

'Good point. Call the gatehouse. Tell them we're with Montgomery. They'll contact him on his radio.'

Barton drove as fast as he could through the busy streets. It was always hectic past the hospital at rush hour and he cursed his choice of route. Why hadn't he gone through Longthorpe and the back roads?

'You're quiet. What's up?' asked Strange.

'I really don't like Drummond for these kills.'

'Why not?'

'People tend to be certain types. They rarely meander too far from who they are, especially the older they get.'

'Didn't Drummond say he'd killed before?'

'Yes, but, morally, he thought he was in the right. He was a soldier. Our dealings with him have always concerned violence, but he was brawling with other men who were looking for trouble. In his head, they were fair fights.'

'And none of them died.'

'No, I believe he knows that killing is not the answer. Not in civilian life, anyway.'

'I think I agree. Even though he was there when Zanthos's son jumped and he was his mate, that wouldn't be motivation enough to wait all this time and finish them so up close and personally.'

'Exactly, it's about motive. People need a strong motive to commit murder. I can't see any money angle here, and it's not sex. It's revenge. Someone wanted to punish them. Now, who would want to kill Zanthos, Pfeiffer and Ballanchine more than anyone else? Who is most likely to want them dead?'

Strange squeezed her nose as she concentrated.

'The father of the girl who was taken. Or the girl herself.'

'Correct. But I don't like a woman for it, even though she could be a muscle-bound, highly trained commando after this long. But we spoke to the parents. It doesn't fit. And they're in California. I had Leicester check with border control. They haven't returned to the UK since they left. Not under their own names, anyway.'

'There must be bad memories for them here.'

'Correct.'

'Who does that leave?' asked Strange with a frown.

'Who would most want revenge against Zanthos? Forget about the other two.'

Strange glanced over at Barton as he pulled up outside the jail.

'Shit. His two sons. One of whom is dead, which narrows it down.'

'Yes. The child was adopted and might have had a different name. But at eighteen, or even before, they may have been told by their adoptive parents the truth. I don't know what the rules are on that, or if there are any. It'd be a tough conversation.'

Strange whistled.

'That would make you pretty angry,' she said. 'To find out your father went down for molesting both you and your only sibling, who killed himself because of it. And your mother didn't want you afterwards, or wasn't allowed to have you. That would take some getting over. The surviving son would be mid-thirties. If they were going to do anything about it, surely they would have by now.'

Barton let out a deep breath.

'That's what I've been struggling with all afternoon. Something like that could fester, meaning it might be a long time before they did anything. But there's another obvious explanation.'

They reached the gatehouse. Strange pressed her warrant against the glass.

'DI Barton and DS Strange, appointment with Mr Montgomery at five,' she said.

The officer smiled and put a visitor's form in the tray with a locker key for them to put any forbidden items in. Barton passed Strange his phone, and she put it with hers in locker four. Barton filled in the form to confirm they understood the rules about entering one of Her Majesty's Prisons. Strange signed at the bottom and placed it back in the security tray. She clicked her fingers.

'Oh, my God. I've got it.' She looked at Barton with renewed respect. 'We think Mrs Zanthos was involved. She certainly knew about that shrine at the back of the house. That means their children were the product of two sex offenders. Therefore, there's an increased likelihood that their children would inherit some of their sickness.'

'Correct. To have killed Zanthos, you'd probably need to have been on the sex offenders' wing.'

'We'd have spoken to him.'

'Exactly, and he'd be mid-thirties. We need to look back at who was on there and that age.'

They were buzzed through the entrance to another security door, where Monty was waiting for them.

'Why kill the others, though? Where's Mrs Zanthos? Only Crannock was released at the same time as Drummond, and he's too old to be the son.'

'Yes, we're missing something, but I have a feeling it's about to be revealed. Possibly by Brown, or maybe by Zelensky.'

'And Drummond's innocent?'

'No, he's in the mix somewhere. And he failed to comply with his licence by not meeting his offender manager as agreed, so he would have been recalled to prison, regardless.'

Monty stepped forward and shook their hands.

'Come up to my office. You were right about Drummond. He shared a cell with Gilbert Spencer shortly before he left.'

Barton and Strange exchanged a glance. They followed Monty through the busy corridors, fighting against a crowd of white shirts as Monty explained.

'Half the prison employees disappear at five. Nearly all the admin staff leave then, some wing staff, and all the officers from programmes and industries.'

They made it up the stairs where it was quieter, and entered Monty's office. Barton and Strange took a seat round Monty's table while he got the paperwork organised.

'How long were Drummond and Spencer sharing for?'

'Hang on. It's here somewhere. It was a good while. Four months, give or take.'

'They must have been pally to be together for that long.'

'You'd have thought so, but Drummond was attacked by a group of men just before he was put on the VP wing, and Spencer didn't step in to help him.'

Barton looked out of the window across at the expanse of windows that housed nearly a thousand men.

'Could it have been a ruse to get Drummond with the VPs?'

'It's unlikely. People were severely hurt, Drummond included. No one talked afterwards, so we're in the dark about the cause of the argument, but in a place like this it doesn't need to be much. Disagreements get blown out of proportion. The ringleader had only just got here. Drummond considered himself the alpha male, so he often had chats with the new arrivals. Not all of them back down.'

Monty's radio sprang to life.

'Personal alarm, personal alarm. Officer Vallance, last known location, Royce two wing. First Response, please attend.'

Barton rose from his chair.

'What does that mean?'

'It means there's been an incident. Relax, we get five of these a day on average. It's most likely a fight, but it could be a suicide, or threats to staff. We teach the officers to be cautious. If in doubt, call for backup. First Response will attend within seconds. That's spare officers from other wings. There will be a nurse en route too, in case it's something serious.'

Barton stared over at Strange, who also looked uneasy.

'Could this involve Drummond?' she asked.

'No, Royce wing is on houseblock five. Drummond is on the induction wing, which is houseblock three. There's no way he could have got over there.'

Barton felt the silence in the room closing in on him.

'Where is Gilbert Spencer's cell?' he asked.

Monty checked on his PC. Barton watched him slowly swallow.

'Royce two.'

The radio crackled again.

'Personal alarm. Personal alarm. Officer Batley has reported a code red and all outstations at his location. Royce two. I repeat, First Response, Second Response, Hotel 1, and all available outstations, please attend Royce two wing.'

Monty stared at Barton for a second, then punched in four numbers to his phone.

'Houseblock five,' answered a female voice.

'Who is that?' asked Monty

'Hotel 1, the nurse.'

'What's happened?'

'There appears to have been a fight. The officers are clearing the wing now and putting everyone behind their doors. They're struggling to hold two of them down. Another inmate is being given first aid. Oh!'

'Oh, what?'

'They've signalled the wing is safe for me to enter, so I'm going on. Please make sure at least one ambulance is on the way, and if the doctor is still here, ensure he attends immediately. Everyone's drenched in blood.'

# 59

## DI BARTON

Monty terminated the call and stood up.

'The staff on duty will deal with what's happening, but I'm going to go over and make sure everything is watertight. Usually in these cases, it's all over in a minute and it's just a case of cleaning up.'

'And letting the ambulance in?' said Strange.

'Right. Again, that's not unusual. Last summer we had them queueing up outside when a rogue batch of spice found its way into the prison.'

'Sounds as if a crime has been committed,' said Barton. 'Can't I come with you?'

Monty shook his head.

'Non-prison staff are always evacuated from the area if anything like this occurs. The proper steps will be taken. I'll make sure any evidence is secured in the right manner.'

His phone rang again. This time he picked it up as opposed to answering it on speaker.

'Victor One,' he replied.

He listened for a minute.

'What do you mean, they think it's Drummond? Surely the wing staff must know who's on their wing.'

He listened again for another minute, tutting frequently. He finished the call by snarling down the phone. 'Ring me in five minutes. I'll be in Security. I need to know how this has happened.'

After slamming the phone into its cradle, he looked up at Barton, his mind obviously churning. The radio crackled.

'All available outstations, male side, clear the route for the ambulance. I repeat, open the gates to houseblock five.'

Monty placed his palms on the table and leaned back.

'That was Oscar One. She runs the operational side of the prison. It seems Drummond got on the same wing as Spencer. Exactly what happened is sketchy at this point. There's been a fight in a cell occupied by two brothers. Kevin and Grayson Reed. Spencer has attacked Drummond, wounding his neck with a bladed weapon. Spencer has taken a severe beating at the hands of the brothers, who look like they were protecting Drummond. Spencer is missing an ear.'

'Is Drummond critical?' asked Strange.

'Yes, they think they've applied adequate first aid, but there's blood everywhere. As you heard, the ambulance is on the way. They'll have plasma on board and will hopefully keep him going until they reach the hospital.'

'You don't sound confident,' said Barton.

'We have a lot of suicides caused by deep cuts. If a person bleeds too much, their heart stops. Come on, I'll take you to Security, so we can watch the footage from the wing. I'll leave you there and the officer will show you out. Oscar One is opening a command suite, and I'll need to be there. Ring me first thing in the morning, when I'll have a clearer picture. The inmates who go to the hospital will have a triple escort, so they'll be secure.'

They left Monty's office and took another flight of stairs up. It felt surreal to have listened to the action but not seen any of it. Events had moved so fast that Barton was only just catching up.

'I thought you said there was no way he could have got on another wing, especially on a different houseblock,' he said.

They reached a door labelled Security and Monty ignored Barton's comment, opened it and walked in. A gaunt woman with a severe grey fringe regarded them from behind a computer.

'Sheila, can you show us the footage from Royce two?' said Monty.

'I've just been looking at it.'

She pressed a few buttons on her keyboard and gestured to the screen on the far side of the room. Some CCTV that Barton saw nowadays was similar to watching a movie. The quality in the prison was considerably worse, but it was clear enough.

'Talk the detectives through it, please, Sheila.'

Sheila spoke a little as if she were doing the voiceover for a nature programme.

'Sorry, there's no sound. Here is the line of cells, from one at the top of the wing, to eighteen down at the bottom. I know Drummond well. That's him, definitely. He's got himself on the wing and walked towards R2-15. You can see him checking the door cards, so he doesn't know the location of whoever he's looking for. He sees who I think is Grayson Reed, pushes him back into his cell and follows him inside. The door isn't fully closed behind him because you can still make out the edge of the toilet inside. Both Reed brothers are in there, as they come out later. Here we are, this is Spencer arriving.'

Barton peered as the grainy footage played on. Soon a man appeared walking towards X2-15. He stopped outside the cell door and removed an item from each of his pockets. He seemed to ease the door open. Then stepped in. A few moments later, the door can be seen slamming shut and opening again, before slamming again. Something was clearly going on in that cell.

Then Spencer hurtled from the cell to escape, but a big man came out after him and spun him around and up against a pool table. Barton let out a little gasp at the ferocity of the punch that then landed in Spencer's stomach. The next blow was an upper cut that straightened Spencer back up, followed by a heavy backhand across his face.

'Kevin Reed,' said Sheila.

'Christ,' said Strange.

'Anti-Christ, more like. Okay, Spencer is getting a considerable beating. Now, if you look back at the door, the darker skinned of the Reed brothers, Grayson, is about to pull Drummond out of his cell. The first officer arrives at that point. It's hard to tell if he chose to prioritise dealing with the wound on the man's neck, or if he just didn't fancy interrupting the brutal attack against the pool table.'

Spencer appeared to be unconscious, but his attacker had him held up and was punching the same eye repeatedly, like steady hits from a sledgehammer.

'The other wing officer is about to appear.'

A big blur of white flashed across the screen and rugby-tackled Kevin to the ground. Without support, Spencer fell face down on the floor, but he wasn't unconscious and managed to get to his hands and knees. The Reed brother that dragged Drummond out of the cell, Grayson, then proceeded to kick Spencer repeatedly in the stomach.

'Here's First Response,' said Sheila.

A scrum of white shirts arrived, knocking Grayson over. There were so many officers and rubber-necking prisoners that it was hard to see what was going on with Drummond. Spencer struggled weakly with two officers on the periphery, despite the beating he'd had. The Reed brothers were pinned to the floor by four men each.

'Here's Second Response,' said the monotone Sheila.

More officers arrived and the gawking inmates vanished to their cells, where they were locked in. The nurse turned up and rushed over to Drummond, who was still. An officer in a red shirt walked towards the camera. Blood covered his face.

'That doesn't look good for Drummond,' said Strange.

'No,' replied Sheila. 'But as long as they stop the bleeding and get the ambulance in fast, he'll still have a chance.'

'Sheila,' said Monty. 'Drummond shouldn't have been on there. Can you sort out the footage at the gate to see how he got on?'

'Sure. He probably slipped onto the wing with all the returning industry workers or kitchen staff.'

'No, he's only just arrived. He was on the induction wing.'

'But that's on a different houseblock?'

'Yes, I know. You should be able to follow his entire route from houseblock three to five on the cameras. Find out if he was escorted, or if he's managed to just walk around somehow.'

Sheila paused to look at him, the worry clear on her face. The ringing of her phone startled her.

'Security,' she says. 'Yes, he's here.' She passed the phone to Barton. 'It's DS Zander.'

Barton picked up the phone but didn't say anything straight away. What did come out wasn't how he normally answered the phone.

'Shit,' he said.

'Charming,' said Zander. 'Although oddly that's what I just said when Brown gave me a copy of the ID for those knives, and Zelensky told me the adopted name of Zanthos's surviving child. It's the same person and his name features on the report from the visit to the prison where you and Kelly interviewed the entire wing.'

'I told you all along that the person responsible would have been on that wing.'

'Yes, but you didn't tell us he worked there.'

# 60

## DI BARTON

Two minutes later, Barton put the phone down and held up his hand to get everyone's attention. Sheila, Monty and Strange eventually stopped their detailed discussion and stared at him.

'I know how Drummond got on that wing. He was escorted by one of your staff.'

'Why would an officer do that?'

'I'm not 100 per cent sure, but I suspect it's because they've been working together.'

'On what?' asked Monty.

'Killing Zanthos, Pfeiffer and Ballanchine,' said Barton.

'Who is it?' asked a scowling Strange and Monty simultaneously.

'Peter Green.'

'You're kidding me,' said Monty. 'I only walked past him this morning.'

'Nope,' said Barton. 'You're aware of the history. Zanthos has two children. Frank and Ivan. Frank throws himself off a bridge, Ivan ends up in care. He's then adopted and given a new name. Peter Green.'

Monty's mouth opened and closed, but no sounds come out. His eyes glazed over as he tried to recall Green's prison history.

'Well, that's the theory,' said Barton. 'Although, didn't you say he was a weak officer?'

Monty's eyes refocused.

'Yeah, but weak as in a bit useless. He doesn't give a damn about the prisoners, where they are, or what they're up to. There have been regular complaints concerning him not getting people out for healthcare and dentist appointments, or even sending them to work, but there were a couple of incidents which showed he was no pushover.'

'When were they?'

'Let's see. Six months ago, when he'd only been in the job a week, a tough prisoner with the nickname Ridgeback refused a direct order from Green in front of a big group of inmates. Green didn't have the interpersonal skills to handle it at that point, and the guy was a heavy unit, so Green walked away. Two days later, Ridgeback's face is black and blue. We heard a rumour that Green was responsible. Then last week, an extremely unpleasant fellow on the VP unit, Thompson, I think his name was, had to be escorted to hospital to get his ribs checked out and have a splint put on his arm. He didn't talk, but we had a security form from another prisoner on the wing saying Green did it.'

'Did you follow it up with Green?' asked Barton.

'It wasn't from a reliable source. We decided to see if anything else came through, but nothing did. We did have intel that Green was having trouble with Crannock, but Crannock is hard as nails.'

'He's sounding like our man on the inside. Didn't anyone question Thompson?' asked Strange.

'Yes, but Thompson said it was another inmate who he wouldn't name. The prisoners understand there's little value in being a grass, especially on a staff member. If Green is here for revenge, then a large guy like him could do some damage. He and Drummond would be quite a force combined.'

'Too right,' said Barton. 'If Drummond got to Pfeiffer and Ballanchine, then he'd need to have known where they lived. Who would have given him that information? It had to be Green. I reckon one or both of them killed them all.'

Sheila cleared her throat.

'Green shoved another officer at lunch yesterday. I don't know what it was about, but Green was different from how he normally is. He seemed non-confrontational before, but this week he just exuded menace. The bloke he pushed in the queue backed down sharpish.'

Barton's brain was now running at Warp Factor Ten.

'At a guess, I would say he found out who his parents were, and that's messed him up. Maybe it took years for him to decide that he couldn't stand the not knowing all about his past, so he went to find his parents, only to discover Daddy Zanthos in prison and his mum cold and uninterested. He decides to do something about it and gets the job here. You have a fast turnover of staff, so there are always opportunities to join. He deliberately acts weak and finishes up on the easiest wing in the jail.'

'With his dad,' said Strange.

'Yep,' said Barton. 'Perhaps he had doubts, but Zanthos's release date was fast approaching. Green decides to strike at one of the three while they're still inside. Then he resolves to do the other two in when they're released.'

'I don't get Drummond's interest,' said Strange.

'He knew the brother, remember. It sounds as though it was just chance that he got a kicking and ended up on the VP wing. Perhaps he chose to help Green after they discovered their shared history. Maybe Drummond was the final push to encourage Green to act.'

'Okay, but it's a shit plan if you both end up in chokey. Green and Drummond will go down for decades,' said Strange.

'We have to prove all this first. These men aren't fools. We might need a confession to convict if we don't get concrete evidence from CSI or CCTV.'

'Who the hell would confess?' asked Sheila.

Barton shook his head in disbelief.

'All along, I've felt that someone was making a statement with these kills. We need to find Peter Green and ask him. I think he'll tell us. There's no way he's getting away with this, and he knows it. Monty, did he finish at five today after his unauthorised move of Drummond from the induction wing?'

'Hang on,' said Sheila. 'I get the detail sent to my email every day.' She also shook her head as she clicked away on her PC. Barton looked over her shoulder as she brought up a busy-looking document that obviously covered the entire prison. 'It's hard to believe that the killer was in our prison all this time,' she said. Her finger moved along the screen until she got to the male houseblocks, then her eyes narrowed.

'You're in luck. He's still here.'

# 61

## DI BARTON

Barton could feel his pulse picking up. He wasn't sure if he could assume charge now they were in the midst of a murder investigation, but Monty knew the jail. They needed to get to Green with the minimum of fuss and slap some cuffs on him. If he clocked them coming after him, he could prove very volatile, because he wouldn't be able to escape. Monty was staring at him.

'How do you want to play this?' asked Barton.

'Let's find out where he is. Sheila, start looking at the cameras. What's his role on the detail?'

'General duties, houseblock three. He'll be around, or in, the hub.'

They watched the big screen as she linked the camera to it. From the queueing men, it looked as though meds had just started. Sheila switched through a succession of camera views.

'I can't see him,' she said. 'If he's GD, he'll probably be supervising in the med hatch and be out of sight.'

Monty picked up a phone and put it on speaker so the detectives could hear. He got an invalid number tone.

'Shit, Sheila, what's houseblock three hub's number?'

'Five four zero one.'

Monty, sweat collecting on his brow, punched the buttons hard. This time it rang and rang. Barton forced himself to take slow breaths and think. If Green was working, he'd have a radio. He must have heard the chatter about the incident on houseblock five. Suddenly, the call was answered.

'Senior Officer Grant. Houseblock three.'

'Jeff, it's Monty. We need to speak to Green about a delicate matter. Is he in the hatch?'

'No, I'm looking for him too. He's disappeared, leaving us short. I've been in the hatch myself.'

'Any idea where he might be?'

'Not a clue. I already checked upstairs. Get Comms to do a shout out on the net.'

'Cheers, Jeff.'

Monty cut the call and redialled.

'Comms.'

'Hi, it's Monty. Can you tell me if Green is still on the net? He's on the detail as Charlie Ten.'

'That's confirmed. Signed on the net this morning. Still here.'

'Okay. Put a call out asking Charlie Ten to confirm his location, then let me know.'

'Yes, sir.'

The line went dead, and they all stared at Monty's radio.

'Charlie Ten, Charlie Ten. Please confirm your location.'

Barton slumped into a seat.

'My money's on him having left,' he said. 'Green knew there was an incident after he let Drummond on the wing. He also knows that the prison has CCTV nearly everywhere. It wasn't going to take long for us to find out that someone had taken Drummond from a different location and escorted him to another wing. He's gone, and he won't be coming back.'

'Fuck,' said Monty, who was now sweating freely. 'I'll ring the gate and ask if his keys are there.'

Barton wondered if the phone would still work after the pounding it was getting.

'Gatehouse, Paula.'

'Victor One here. Can you check if Peter Green has returned his keys or radio? He took Charlie Ten this morning.'

'Hang on.'

A long minute later, Paula returned.

'His keys and radio aren't here.'

'Have you seen him leave?'

'I don't know who he is. Wait a moment, it's been manic in here. We had a bus from Cambridge court turn up at the same time as the ambulances.'

They heard the handset clunk as she put it down. It felt as if the temperature in the room were rocketing as they waited. Paula picked the phone back up.

'The SO here knows who Green is. Seems to think he left not long after five.'

'Still with his keys and radio?'

'Hang on.'

Barton couldn't sit still as the seconds ticked by. He caught Strange's eye. She mouthed, *Where he's gone?*

Paula returned. 'Maybe. The SO said he didn't queue up. As I mentioned, it was busy. He just assumed he'd already handed his keys and radio in, then nipped back to the changing rooms. Neither his keys nor his radio are here.'

'Okay, thank you. Let me know immediately if you see him.'

Monty cut the call.

'This is a disaster,' he said. He rang Comms again.

'Put out a call asking if anyone is in the vicinity of Officer Green.'

They lost another minute after the request went out, but the airwaves remained silent.

'This is very bad,' said an ill-looking Monty. 'If the keys are misplaced or compromised, then every single lock needs to be changed in the entire jail. It costs a million pounds each time.'

'Okay, we can't do anything about that apart from catch him. Let's focus on his danger to others,' said Barton. 'If we find him, we find the keys.'

'What's his address?' said Strange. 'What car does he drive? I assume you must have the details of his vehicle for him to enter the car park.'

'Yes, we do. I'll need to look at the shared HR file,' replied Monty.

'I know where he lives,' said Sheila. She paused. 'I did occasionally talk to Green. He always seemed sad and withdrawn, lonely even. I felt sorry for him, so I tried to include him if we were sitting near each other in the canteen or I saw him in the gym. His place is in Stamford, not far from the hospital.'

'Right,' said Barton. 'Let's hope he's gone there. I'll ring Zander and get him to check ANPR. The cameras will have picked up Green's number plate if he's taken the A15.'

'He cycles,' said Sheila with regret.

'Really?' asked Strange. 'That's fifteen miles.'

'Yeah, he's got one of those proper road bikes, like you see on the Tour de France. He's surprisingly fit for a big man. And he pushes some huge weights in the gym.'

Barton closed his eyes while he thought.

'Right, Monty. You keep searching for him in the prison in case he's hiding. When are the prisoners locked up for the night?'

'Good idea. Around half six. I'll get the staff to search for Green after everyone's banged up. Make double sure he's not here.'

'I'm going to the gate to retrieve my mobile,' said Barton.

'Strange and I will return to the station. Keep in touch. We've got a real situation on our hands with Green being loose. I'm hoping that because all three of them are already dead, he's finished and is now just trying to make good his escape.'

'What about his mum?' said Strange. 'He might still be after her. Then there's Archie. His son is in hospital after trying to kill Drummond.'

'Can you get me an outside line?' Barton asked Monty.

Monty put a four-digit code into the phone and handed the receiver to Barton, who dialled Zander's number.

'Zander speaking.'

Barton gave him a thirty-second machine-gunning of the facts.

'He must have gone home to fetch his car. It's not easy to run away on a pushbike,' said Zander.

'Yes. And I don't think he planned this today. Green couldn't have expected Drummond to have arrived in the prison this afternoon, so this has happened fast for him. Who's in the office?'

'Malik, Zelensky and Leicester.'

'Have someone check ANPR. See if an ARV or Tactical are nearby. With or without them, we need to be at Green's house, so use any uniformed bodies you can find. Green is the key to this. Let's get him in the custody suite and we can go from there. Update me on the way. I'll be back in twenty and will direct from the incident room.'

'Okay, done. Check your email. The search warrant for Archie Spencer's house has been granted.'

Barton hung up and strode to the gatehouse with Strange following. Monty got them signed out of the prison fast, and they were soon in the car waiting for the barrier to rise.

'Let's swing by the Zanthos house on our way back, just in case he went there,' said Strange.

'Right. I was thinking about what you said. Green wouldn't have known we picked up Drummond and put him back in prison, which also means Gilbert Spencer wouldn't have heard that Drummond was back. Yet as soon as he saw him on his wing, he attacked him.'

'Right. Drummond was seen at Archie's. Maybe he threatened him, or perhaps Archie decided he was too loose an end.'

'Gilbert rings his dad, who immediately tells him to take Drummond out if he ends up back behind bars.'

'Then Drummond arrives on Gilbert's wing like an early Christmas present.'

'There's still a lot here that doesn't stack up. My head's spinning,' said Strange. 'What was Drummond doing in the Reed brothers' cell?'

The barrier rose and Barton revved the engine hard. Five minutes later, he was outside the Zanthos residence, but it looked cold, dark and empty. Barton nipped to the nosey next-door neighbour's house; she opened the door with a big glass of amber liquid before he even got to it.

'She hasn't come back, if that's what you're here for.'

Barton smiled and jogged back to the car. He checked his watch.

'Let's drop in on Archie. He's less than a mile away. See if he wants to shed any light on proceedings. I can give him the good news about Drummond and knock him off balance by telling him his lad's in Intensive Care.'

They raced off down Thorpe Road and Barton was soon indicating to pull into Westwood Park Road. The lights were on in the top windows of the house. Leaning against the closed security gates was an expensive-looking bicycle. One that wouldn't have looked out of place in the Tour de France.

## 62

DI BARTON

Barton left the engine running and got out of the car. He put his hand on the bike seat but it was cold, meaning Green hadn't just arrived. He moved the cycle to the side and checked how secure the gates were. They were solid. Barton looked up at the spikes on top of the railings. He went to the back of his Land Rover, grabbed his baton and PAVA spray, got back into the car and gave them to Strange. She had proven how effective she was with them.

He put the engine into gear and edged towards the gates. When his bumper was touching them, he slowly increased the revs. The gates proved surprisingly strong, but finally, at five thousand revs, there was a cracking sound and they swung apart. Barton trundled along the drive, parked up next to a flash BMW, and they both got out. The front door was open. Bright light shone onto the porch, but no sounds came from the interior. He thought he heard a distant cry and Strange nodded to confirm she'd heard it too.

Barton removed his phone from his pocket and called Control. He quietly updated them.

'That's all confirmed, sir. ETA for the first response vehicle is four minutes.'

As Barton cut the call, he listened to what sounded like a carpet being whacked, then another groan.

'Check the rear,' he said. 'Be careful. Any trouble, make your way back here. Assistance in four. I'll go in the front with caution.'

Strange made her way round the back, and Barton edged through the front door. He could now hear that a TV was on and he recognised the sounds of the local news. Barton considered shouting out but decided against it. He took his jacket off and left it on a chair in the hall. The kitchen was empty, but jangling keys were approaching from the next room.

Green strode through a doorway and pulled up short at the sight of Barton. They were on opposite sides of the island in the kitchen and Barton and Green both glanced at the knife block that was on the surface. It was much closer to Green.

'Stay where you are,' said Barton. 'You're under arrest.'

Green raised an eyebrow, reached over, removed a wicked-looking small knife from the block, and felt its weight. Then Green, still in his uniform, strolled around the island towards Barton. His work boots clumped heavily on the tiled surface.

Green was a different person from the floppy prison officer Barton had suspected him to be. He radiated anger and defiance; a man hell-bent on revenge, a force to behold. And he was armed. Barton stepped around the island, keeping it between him and Green.

'It's over,' said Barton. 'Drop the knife.'

Green looked down at the knife and rested it on the island, keeping his fingers on the handle.

'If you don't want to get hurt, detective, keep out of my way. It isn't over yet, but it will be soon. I'm going to complete the circle.'

Green tensed, then slid the knife fast along the surface towards Barton. While Barton jumped back, Green ran from the house. The knife flew off the edge and bumped harmlessly against Barton's stomach. He let out a sigh of relief, then remembered Strange.

Barton pounded through the hall after Green and watched as he collided with Strange, who had reappeared at the front of the house. He knocked her flat. The baton jarred out of her hand. Green bent over, picked it up and stepped over her. Strange pointed her hand, which still held the PAVA spray, but Green just flicked it from her hand with the baton. He raised his arm, and his eyes narrowed.

'No!' bellowed Barton. 'Don't do it.' He struggled for what to say. 'She hasn't done anything wrong.'

Green paused, then turned his head towards the sounds of the approaching sirens. He had a set of keys in his left hand and the BMW beeped when he pressed the fob. He dropped the baton onto Strange's chest, jumped off the porch, opened the car door and got in. The engine roared into life. Green's window wound down.

'I'd get inside and help Archie. He's hurt himself playing golf.'

The engine crunched into gear, and the BMW screeched out of sight, leaving a frowning Barton in a cloud of diesel smoke. Where was Green going? And what did *complete the circle* mean?

# 63

## DI BARTON

Barton contemplated heading off in pursuit, but helping the Spencers was his primary concern. Uniform would know to follow Green.

'Are you all right?' he asked Strange.

She got to her feet, opening and closing her fist.

'Yeah, check on Archie. I'll ring the car registration through and make sure he's stopped.'

Barton smiled. He'd memorised the number plate too. At that moment, the sirens were on top of them, and two patrol cars drove up the drive, having probably passed Green as he went the other way. Barton left Strange racing towards them and headed back inside the house, collecting his jacket on the way.

Barton found the Spencers in the lounge. Poison Evie was flat out on a big fluffy rug. Judging by the spray of blood and her crushed nose, she'd taken a significant blow to the face. She was unconscious, but her chest rose and fell with a steady rhythm, indicating she wasn't in any immediate danger.

Archie, on the other hand, was slumped in an armchair. His face was hugely swollen and bloody too, but it was his lower half that got Barton's attention. Even though Archie had trousers on, Barton could tell that both legs had been broken midway between the knee and the ankle as both limbs stuck out at impossible angles. Barton walked around Evie and crouched next to Archie. He placed two fingers against his neck. There was a pulse, but it was weak.

'Archie, are you okay?' he shouted.

Archie's breathing rattled in his throat. His Adam's apple moved slowly up and down, then a bloodshot eye opened.

'Piss off, Barton.'

Barton grinned.

'I'm arresting you on suspicion of conspiring to commit murder. Namely, that of instructing your son to attack Logan Drummond. You do not have to say anything...'

As he was talking, Barton hoped that when they listened to the prison phone calls, they would have proof, or otherwise Archie would escape justice again. Although, he'd certainly just had some serious payback. Barton had finished and was getting to his feet when Strange came in with a uniformed officer and two paramedics.

'Are they okay?' she asked.

Barton looked from Archie to Evie.

'They'll both be sore in the morning,' he replied.

'Now what?'

'I assume they haven't stopped Green yet?'

'No, the call's gone out for him to be apprehended. A patrol car saw him flying up the parkway towards the Holiday Inn, but he was gone by the time they reached the roundabout and chased after him. If he keeps to any of the main roads, the cameras will catch him.'

'Okay, we'll head back. Ring Zander and warn him it's possible Green might be on his way home.'

'Let's hope he's not heading to the station.'

'Who knows what he's thinking? He could blame us. He's definitely going to do something dramatic.'

Barton returned to the front of the house, which was now crawling with police. Three ambulances had turned up. He found a uniformed sergeant and made sure he knew to keep Barton updated if anything changed.

Barton and Strange got in his car, and he drove out of the gates back to Thorpe Wood. The traffic was backed up on Thorpe Road after the arrival of all the emergency vehicles, so it took them a while to filter in.

'Green said he was going to complete the circle. What does that mean?' asked Barton.

Strange looked out of the window for a few moments. 'It usually means to go back to the beginning,' she replied.

'Yes, which I can only think means something to do with his youth or his mother.'

'It's a crying shame we can't find her.'

'I've a feeling that she won't show up until we capture her son. Drummond's already in jail. Neither of them will be able to get to her then, and she'll be safe, but I'll have someone outside her house, just in case.'

'Okay. I'm not happy we've got this all straightened out.'

'Nor me. Let's think, what is Drummond's nature?'

'Violent, through and through.'

'What has he spent his life doing?'

'Hitting others.'

Barton chuckled. 'Yes, but his adult offending has been bar fights and pub brawls, street assaults and home invasions. Every single one of the people he's beaten has deserved it. According to him, that is.'

'And he hasn't killed anyone since leaving the Legion.'

'Nope, and he's had a lot of opportunity, and possesses the skills, so he has control. I reckon Green and he made a deal of some kind. We need Green alive to talk or we might struggle with getting anything to stick to Drummond.'

'He breached his licence, missed appointments, so he'll be back inside for a while whatever happens.'

Barton nodded. But for about six months, he reckoned, that was all. Barton wasn't sure how he felt about that. He suspected Green had committed the savage killings alone. It would have been something he had to do himself to avenge his brother.

They were driving past the Woodman pub when Barton recognised Archie Spencer's BMW in the car park for Thorpe Wood golf course. He indicated right and pulled in next to it. They both got out and listened. The BMW's engine ticked as it cooled down, but otherwise everywhere was still, except for the hum of traffic from the parkway. Barton looked around at their location. Green could have run into Ferry Meadows, but what would be the point of that? The thundering vehicles dragged his attention back in that direction.

'He's here, and now I know why,' said Barton.

'What do you mean?'

'The pedestrian bridge over the road to Longthorpe is there,' he said, pointing through the trees. 'That's where his brother fell to his death.'

# 64

## DI BARTON

Barton took a second to conclude that Strange and he were in little danger and raced towards the bank that led up to the bridge with Strange right behind him. Peter Green, who was born Ivan Zanthos, was going to the scene of his brother's death. Strange had only lived in Peterborough for a few years and wouldn't have recognised the location from the file.

'Why has Green come here?' shouted Strange so as to be heard over the traffic.

'I'm hoping he's just come to pay his last respects,' replied Barton.

The bank was too slippery to climb after all the melting snow, so they circled back to the road and ran up the path. It was a shame it wasn't still rush hour because the road below was one of the main routes out of the city and the traffic would have been queueing nose to tail, but at this time of night the roar from fast-moving vehicles filled the air. They saw Green on the bridge, leaning against the hip-height rail. He had his hands in the pockets of his parka, the same style as Drummond's, and was staring down at the rumbling vehicles passing underneath him. Barton stepped onto the bridge but stopped walking when he was twenty metres from Green and in hearing range if he yelled. Strange kept a few metres behind him.

Barton had no idea of Green's mental state, even though he suspected he was suicidal. Up high and exposed, the cold breeze was merciless, and Barton felt it trying to drag his jacket off his back as he took a few more steps towards Green.

'Peter,' shouted Barton at the top of his voice, so the noise of revving engines didn't whisk his words away.

Green turned towards him with a slight smile on his face. He pointed at Barton and beckoned him forward, then pointed at Strange and waggled his finger from side to side. Barton looked back to her, then instructed her under his breath.

'Stop anyone coming near the bridge. Don't let him see you ring for the fire brigade and an ambulance. Get Response or Traffic to close the road further up, on both sides, and get the path blocked on the other end of the bridge.'

'On it,' said Strange, and trotted off the bridge and out of sight.

Barton ambled towards Green as though he had all the time in the world. He wanted to get as near as possible. When he was three metres away, Green spoke.

'Close enough, Mr Barton.'

'I need you to come with me,' said Barton.

This time, Green's smile split his face.

'I'm surprised to see you, but you're a clever guy. If you found your way here, you know what I'm going to do.'

'Don't do it. You're wasting your life.'

The smile vanished from Green's face.

'What life? I've known that I was different from a young age. I can't remember anything from before I was adopted, but I've always been aware of the black hole in my memories. My adoptive parents were small, slight people, which always made me feel like a cuckoo in their nest. I was eighteen when they finally admitted that my parents weren't dead.'

'That must have been hard for you.'

'It was. I ignored it for years, but it became a virus in my system. It spread, until my past was all I was. I didn't need to do much research to find out the truth about my father's crimes, but it was the final blow when I found out my mother had rejected me too. I suspected straight away that she was involved. How could she not have known? And now I have concrete evidence.'

'I'm sorry to hear that.' Barton couldn't help taking the bait. 'What's the proof?'

'You'll see, but there's no rush for that. I want her to understand the fear of knowing it's out there somewhere, aware any day that proof could be shared.'

'Don't do anything daft. You can still have a future.'

Green looked at Barton for a few moments, perhaps wondering if he was being honest. Suddenly, Green's face crumpled up. His shoulders shook, and he closed his eyes. Barton was considering grabbing him when the air horn of a passing articulated lorry startled them. Green wiped his eyes.

'What am I?'

Barton wasn't certain what he was after, so he opened his arms and shrugged.

'A man who's suffered.'

'I'm the product of two evil people. The worst of humanity. How can I be anything but the same as them, when they created me?'

'It doesn't have to mean that,' said Barton.

'It does. I got nature and nurture from them. Everywhere you look it says that if they don't get the child away from the parents while they're toddlers, then it's too late.'

'It isn't too late,' said Barton, but his shoulders slumped.

Green gave him a wry smile.

'The only time I've felt normal since I was young is now, when I know the torment is about to end.'

'Killing yourself won't avenge your brother's death and what was done to you. Your brother took his own life to save yours. He'd hate you doing this. He'd want you to tell your story. If you can't do it for yourself, do it for others who, like you, have been taken advantage of.'

Tears poured again from Green's eyes. Barton wasn't sure if it was through sorrow or the wind chill, but he began to edge along the bridge towards him. Green rubbed his eyes and looked down at Barton's feet, now only two metres away. Before Barton could get to him, Green climbed over the railings so he was on the other side. Barton was one and a half metres away. Another vehicle blasted its horn. With his back to the breeze, Green's eyes cleared.

'It's funny,' he shouted across. 'I wondered why I told you I was completing the circle as I was driving here. Perhaps part of me wants to be saved because I've barely lived. I never kissed a woman. And, remember, I've seen what prison is like.'

A look of determination came across Green's face.

'I'll get life for what I've done, and that's not living,' he snarled.

'Tell your side of things, then. Let the truth be out there.'

'I can't stand it any longer. My whole adult life, I've kept away from children because I'm afraid that something will light up inside me. I can't take any more. The wrongs have been righted, and I've done my bit.'

Barton looked up the dual carriageway. He could see emergency lights flashing in the distance at the slip road up from Orton Longueville. They'd have the traffic stopped shortly. The other access road had a man in a high-vis jacket waving vehicles down, too. Barton peered beneath him, suspecting the fall would kill Green, anyway. He went for a final distraction.

'Did you kill Zanthos, Pfeiffer and Ballanchine?'

Green used the back of a sleeve to wipe his nose and leaned perilously out.

'Yes, I smothered my father, impaled Pfeiffer, and chopped Ballanchine to pieces in a rage that had been building through decades of torment, and do you know what?'

Barton shook his head.

'Afterwards, I felt worse. I'm the child of two paedophiles. There's no hope for me. The blood that flows in my veins is tainted. It's their blood. How could I ever be happy?' Green looked down and started shouting. 'If deviancy is a sickness, then I am terminal. All I've proven to everyone is that I'm no better than they are. That I'll be a danger to others my whole life.'

Green hesitated, then gave Barton a final tired smile.

'I set fire to that fucking room, but I can't destroy my memories, and I'll never change what I am.'

The next words were sobbed, but Barton heard them clearly.

'I can't stay in this world, because it's too hard to live when you deserve to die.'

With that, he released his grip on the railings.

## 65

### DI BARTON

As Green fell backwards, a huge gust seemed to freeze him in mid-air. Barton leaped to the edge of the bridge and seized hold of Green's right wrist and pulled him back towards the bridge. Then Barton grabbed the other wrist. A surprised look crossed over Green's face, then he closed his eyes.

He removed one foot from the edge of the bridge and then the other. He dropped, yanking Barton forward and downwards. Barton's hips banged against the top of the railings. Green's bulk threatened to rip Barton's arms from the sockets as he clung on. He attempted to heave him up, but Green was simply too heavy and swung like a soon-to-be-dead weight. Barton gritted his teeth and snarled and roared, but it was no good. Green's eyes flicked open. He stared up at Barton without emotion and spoke quietly. Despite the traffic, their proximity meant Barton could make out every word.

'Please, let me go. I don't want to be saved.'

Barton heard steps running towards him as his strength faded. He turned to see Strange arriving with a horrified expression on her face as Barton felt himself being pulled over and down. Barton's height had made the railing of the bridge too low for his centre of gravity.

'Let him go,' screamed Strange in his ear.

She reached over and tried to grab the sleeve of Green's coat, but her arms were too short.

'Argh!' yelled Barton as pain and terror ripped through his body. Drool ran from his mouth and his eyes bulged at the searing agony in his shoulders.

Any second, Barton was going to tip over and plunge into the oncoming traffic. He looked up and saw there were only a few vehicles left approaching as the road was now closed, but his grip was slipping. He found his gaze connecting with the wide-eyed driver of a fast-approaching white minibus. Barton gasped for a final time as he teetered on the edge. The faces of his family flashed before his eyes, and he opened his hands.

# 66

## DI BARTON

Barton closed his eyes at the screeching brakes and sliding tyres. He heard a heavy bang as a large object hit something. When he opened his eyes again and looked below, all he could see was the rear of the white vehicle underneath him. Strange was staring down, too. Then both turned round and walked to the other side of the bridge and looked over. Green stared sightlessly up at them, having completely filled the windscreen of the minibus. The driver slowly got out with his mouth open.

Barton's arms screamed with pain. He looked across at the steep embankment, desperate to get down to the scene, but there was no path and the fence was high. He returned to the side Green had fallen from and judged the distance from the top of the bridge to the top of the bus.

'Don't even think about it,' said Strange. 'You'd kill everyone in it.'

They looked back up the road, which now had flashing emergency vehicles approaching at speed. A small sports car was at the front, racing towards them.

Barton ran to the other side of the bridge to shout out a warning to the driver, but when he got there and peered down, Green's eyes were focused on him. Green blinked a few times, then heaved himself out to roll along the bonnet and off the front of the vehicle. He managed to keep to his feet as he hit the tarmac but staggered wildly into the outer lane. The driver jumped back into his vehicle and slammed the door.

The sports car, which Barton could now see was a light-blue MR2, hurtled towards Green. It stopped with a shriek of the brakes. Zander climbed out of the MR2 and approached Green with his fists raised but Green just staggered into his arms and slumped against him. Zander let him drop to the ground and cuffed his hands behind his back.

Barton stared down with mixed emotions. Life never failed to surprise him. All the emotions raced through him as he thought of the decades that had led Green to this bridge. Barton felt like dropping to the ground as the adrenalin drained from his system. Instead, he nodded his thanks to Strange.

They returned to his car, and she drove them to the roadblock, both too stunned to talk. After they'd been waved through, he reached Zander, who'd been joined by an ARV and two response vans. A light rain started to fall. Green would need to get checked out at the hospital, but Barton wanted to have a word with him before he left. He saw Green lying down, with his face sideways on the tarmac.

'Are you okay?' asked Barton. 'Anything broken?'

Green opened the red eye that Barton could see and lifted his head off the floor.

'Only my spirit,' replied Green.

'Let's get him up,' said Barton.

He nodded at Zander, and they lifted Green to his feet. Green's head hung low as they guided him towards the ambulance that had just pulled up. At the doors to the ambulance, Green turned to Barton.

'Thank you, but I didn't want this.'

Barton still detected strength in the man and wondered whether his spirit really had been broken.

'We need to know what happened,' replied Barton.

Green nodded. As Zander helped him in the back of the ambulance and climbed in after him, Barton's phone beeped. He pulled it out of his pocket and read the message from Holly.

You need to come home straight away.

Barton felt his stomach lurch. He showed the message to Strange.

'Just go,' she said. 'This show's over. I'll get the roads open. Leicester can go with Zander. It's finished. Well, apart from weeks of paperwork.'

Barton sprinted to his car. There'd been no detail on the text, but it could only be his mother. What the hell had she done now? Unless it was one of the kids. His big fingers were like bananas as he tried to fit the key in the ignition. He roared away in a puff of black smoke, cut up a van on the Thomas Cook roundabout, and, after jumping the lights at the top of The Village road, was home in less than two minutes.

Holly was looking out of the lounge window as he bumped up onto the drive. She opened the front door just as he reached it.

'What is it? Has Mum had a fall?' he asked, with the words tumbling out of his mouth.

Holly stopped in front of him and put her hands on his chest and spoke quietly.

'She's gone, John. She's gone.'

Holly took hold of one of Barton's hands and led him towards his old office. She pushed open the door. Barton's mother lay on the bed fully clothed. She had placed the rabbit on her bedside table as though she was done with it. Barton edged into the room and looked down on her. He'd seen many dead bodies over the years, and this was one of the better ones.

It resembled his mum, but he knew she was no longer there. Her face was too gaunt, and her body seemed too small on the single bed.

'What happened?' he whispered to Holly.

'She was in the lounge watching TV but had been very quiet all morning. I took her a coffee in the beaker and some biscuits, but she ignored them and got up from the sofa. All she said was, "I'm going to have a lie down." When she reached the door, she turned to me and thanked me. I was confused because she hadn't taken the drink, but she looked so frail that I just smiled. I checked on her a few minutes later and she was fine, but when I went to check a bit after she'd passed away.'

Barton's stomach rolled for the second time that hour. Should he have been here? A part of him thought that saving the life of Green had meant that death had come here, but he knew he was being stupid. Holly stepped out of the room and returned with a kitchen chair.

'Sit down. I'll bring you a cup of tea.'

'Thank you,' he said, but it came out high-pitched.

'It's okay, John. It was a good way to go.'

Barton nodded, waited until she closed the door, and then he started to weep.

# 67

## DI BARTON

An hour later, Barton found Luke and Lawrence watching the film *Home Alone* in the lounge. He called Layla down from her bedroom and paused the TV as they waited for her to arrive. Luke tutted, but his brother read the mood.

The fire was on and, with the TV paused, the room was warm and quiet. The only lights that were on twinkled on the Christmas tree. Layla arrived and sat down so the three kids were in a line on the sofa facing Barton, who stood in front of the fire.

'I'm afraid I have sad news for you,' said Barton.

'Ah, so the rumours are true. Christmas has been cancelled,' said Lawrence.

'What?' said Luke.

Barton shot Lawrence a dirty look.

'Stop it. No, it's about Nanny. She died this afternoon.'

Barton didn't believe in glossing over things and talking about God at times like this. He wasn't expecting silence from the kids, though.

'Are you all right?' he asked. 'It's fine to be upset, or have questions.'

'It's okay,' said Luke. 'Nanny said bye to me a few days ago. She said she was very tired, and it would be her time soon.'

Lawrence nodded.

'She stood in the doorway of my room yesterday morning. It was a bit weird. She didn't stay for long, just said she'd be leaving shortly, and that I was to be like you, Dad. She said you were a good man. I just thought she was going back to her own house.'

The news began to sink in. Lawrence wiped a tear from his cheek. He rose from his seat and walked to the door, obviously not wanting anyone to see him crying.

'I'll miss her,' he said, and quickly left.

Layla was already quietly snivelling.

'She came in my room too, but just sat on the edge of the bed and patted my hand. You know, how she liked to. Was she saying goodbye to me, too, do you think?'

Barton sat on the sofa between Luke and Layla. He started to put his arms around their shoulders but gasped with pain and settled for holding their hands.

'Yes, I think she would have been. She lived a full life on her own terms, and she loved you grandkids more than anything.'

Layla looked up at him.

'Do you know when you're going to die?'

Barton wasn't sure what to say to that. He found himself recalling the recent cases he'd been involved with. The faces of the Snow Killer and Peter Green appeared in his mind.

'Sometimes people decide they've had enough. They believe it's their time.'

'Then they die,' said Luke with a serious voice.

'Not always,' said Barton. 'Life can be mysterious, and there's always hope.'

'I'm not sad,' said Luke.

'Why's that, champ?' asked Barton.

'Because Nanny wasn't sad.'

With that, Luke picked up the remote control and restarted the film. Barton could feel his jumper getting damp where Layla was resting her head on it. He closed his eyes and squeezed his children's hands tightly.

## 68

THE COLD KILLER – A WEEK LATER

I open my eyes and take a few moments to absorb my surroundings. They moved me from the high dependency unit a few days ago because I had improved dramatically, so now I'm on a ward with others, but at least they've put me in the corner. There's not much chance of hiding the two prison officers who are sitting, reading newspapers, at the end of my bed. I'm chained to the bed rails that stop you falling out of the sides, but I've told them to relax. My running days are over.

Five pints of blood drained from me before they stopped the bleeding. I flatlined when I arrived at the hospital, but they got me back. Spenny managed to nick a kidney with the shank, so I've been in the wars. Inspector Barton came to see me a few days ago, but I was away with the fairies on morphine when he turned up. He's coming again this lunchtime. That should be an interesting conversation.

Yesterday's prison officer kindly read the news to me. Green was captured after trying to kill himself in the same spot as his brother. The case filled the first half of the paper, according to the screw. It's a sad story and there are no winners. Only death and sadness. I suppose that pretty much sums up crime. Everyone loses in the end.

Barton's had nearly a week of questioning Green. I wonder what he thinks of it all. There's a big part of me that sympathises with Green and what he did, but he's in big trouble. When the judge comes to sentence him, he's going to focus on what kind of person is capable of doing what Green did to Ballanchine.

I lie quietly trying to get my head around how much I've changed in such a short space of time. One last break is all I need. I hear heavy footsteps and see Barton arrive with the other huge detective.

'Morning, gents,' I say to them. 'Is it my bed bath already?'

'No,' says Barton. 'Green gave us a full confession. We thought we'd come and get yours, then we can all enjoy Christmas.'

A stabbing pain travels up my back as I begin to laugh.

'You don't need to hear anything from me if Green's explained everything. Are you here to arrest and charge me, then?'

'Do you have anything to tell us?' asks Barton.

'I doubt my name came up. Look, John. Do you mind if I call you John?'

Barton shakes his head.

'I didn't kill anyone. I often want to, but I don't. It's not a crime to feel murderous rage, as long as you don't act on it. I had my fill of killing in Africa for the Legion.'

'You said they called you The Cold Killer,' says Zander.

'Yes, they did, but taking someone's life doesn't leave you unscathed. Each death is a weight to carry. Eventually, I knew I couldn't do it any more. As you get older, when life slows down and you weaken, that burden is still with you, and it's harder to bear. I wouldn't wish it on anyone.'

Barton looks at the two prison officers.

'You can have a quick break if you want. Get a drink. He's not going anywhere.'

The older of the two officers shakes his head. 'We need to keep him in sight. We'll give you a few minutes and wait at the door.'

They both leave, and the other detective sits in one of their seats and starts reading the paper. Barton rests on the edge of the bed, making me lean towards him.

'This is cosy, John.'

'Isn't it? What now, Logan? Is it over?'

'It is for me. Assuming no one's pointing a finger at me over the recent deaths, I feel I have one last chance.'

'There's a loose end, though.'

I'm not sure what he means, then realise he can only mean Frank and Ivan's mum. I shrug.

'I told you. That's it from me.'

'There's a missing computer tower. We'd love to have a look at the hard drive.'

I grin at Barton. 'You want her brought to book more than I do.'

Barton stands. 'I don't like loose ends, and I don't enjoy thinking she's escaped jail.'

'Prison is too good for the likes of her. People like her tend to get their comeuppance in the end, but it won't be at my hand.'

'Talking of hands, did you know someone cut her finger off?'

'Did she tell you that?'

'No, seems to be a lot of amnesia around at the moment. In fact, she told us nothing.'

'Well, it's no less than she deserves.'

'What did you want to speak to me about, then?'

'I wanted to let you know that I'm through with the life I've been leading. Blaming you for my predicament was daft. I also wanted to thank you for saving Green. You're an interesting man.'

The two prison officers return, and the policemen stand.

'Get some rest,' says Barton. 'If you feel like a confession, of any kind, here's my card.'

He slips it onto the table next to me. He's halfway down the ward when he stops and returns to the edge of my curtain.

'Will you cooperate at the inquiry into the deaths?' he asks.

I hold my hands out wide.

'Of course not, but don't worry. I bet that missing hard drive turns up.'

# 69

## DI BARTON – 6 MONTHS LATER

Barton and Zander were parked up outside HMP Peterborough prison just after 9 a.m. and Drummond was due out shortly. The case against him, if indeed there was one, had been abandoned with Green's detailed confession at court three months earlier. Green had exonerated Drummond completely, even though Barton was sure that he was involved in some way.

Was Green insane? He hadn't seemed so in the dock. There was no trial because he pleaded guilty, and he gave evidence with times, dates, and methods of dispatch. It was chilling reading, but also partly understandable. At least now Zanthos, Pfeiffer and Ballanchine would never hurt another child again.

The only surprise was that Mrs Zanthos hadn't been pulled into the case. Her name was never mentioned by Peter Green, and she'd said nothing to implicate herself. Analysis of the fire in the garden shelter revealed parts of a computer but not the tower and therefore not the contents. It looked as if she'd escaped justice again. Unfortunately, thought Barton, investigations and life in general weren't perfect. Losing his mother at the same time had made it a tough period. The team had helped him through it, just as his family had. He was a lucky man.

As for Archie Spencer, the surgeons had tried to repair his legs, but there had been complications, and they had been forced to amputate one of his feet. There was certainly some irony in that. Spencer told the police he'd tripped on the carpet. Barton doubted that was even possible, but Green didn't comment on that incident and there was little the police could do. Green was going to get a life sentence anyway, possibly three. An extra GBH with intent wouldn't make any difference.

People like Spencer were old school. They didn't want anything to do with the authorities. Their business was taken care of in different ways. Barton visited Archie a little while after Green was sentenced to hear if he wanted to tell the truth. Barton found him outside on the lawn on a sunbed. He looked older and thinner, and, despite being considerably less mobile, much happier. The word on the grapevine was that he'd retired, and his lunatic son, Gilbert, would be in charge when he got released from prison. Barton suspected it wouldn't be long before their paths crossed.

Powerful men, perhaps all men, tried to hold things together for too long. But Father Time always won. Few got to escape with their heads held high, but at least Spencer could enjoy the remainder of his days, if that was possible being married to Poison Evie. In Archie's line of work, retirement was often instigated by a stranger and a bullet.

Evie's nose had been rebuilt, but the experience wouldn't mellow her. Barton left Spencer's house pretty fast after his charming wife appeared with a bottle of wine and a corkscrew. Classy to the end, she stood in front of him, smiled, and told him to bugger off.

Barton hoped he would leave his job at the right time, but he knew that time wasn't now. It had been a swift investigation, and the team had performed well even if there had been a few grey areas that remained unsolved, and the hard drive had never turned up. That was why Barton was here today. Call it a last roll of the dice.

Drummond had since passed his parole hearing and was a free man this morning. The two big detectives watched two dubious-looking characters almost skip out of the jail. One of them walked past their car and slapped his hand on the roof. Crouching down, he kissed the window, then vanished at a jog.

'That's Crannock,' said Barton. 'I forgot he was leaving today, but he must have received six months for breaching his bail conditions, same as Drummond. The other one is a nutter called Celestine. He must have returned for local release.'

'It's a scary thought that psychopaths like them leave the jail and just slip back into society,' said Zander. 'It will only be a matter of time before they offend again.'

'Very true,' replied Barton, sadly. 'Here's Drummond.'

Zander looked to the entrance and saw Logan Drummond walk from the prison. He also had a spring in his step.

'He looks healthier than we do,' said Zander.

Barton agreed. 'I've told you before. Prison suits some people.'

With what appeared to be new clothes and trainers, Drummond cut a smart figure as he stopped outside the gatehouse and took a brief glance back. He grinned as he walked towards the exit.

'Maybe leaving suits some people too. Still reckon he didn't kill any of the three guys?' asked Zander.

'No, I don't think he did, although he sent me that pen. I wonder if I was in real danger at some point and didn't even realise it. But there are men who can kill in wartime, and men who kill because they feel like it, and I don't believe he was the latter.'

'What kind of men are we?' asked Zander as they climbed from the car.

'Policemen,' said Barton. 'And we're the only poor sods following the rules.'

Zander laughed and Barton joined in.

'I've got a date tonight,' blurted Zander.

Barton beamed at him. 'Nice. Took you long enough. What's it been, eight months since your and Kelly's little sleepover? Holly will be pleased, though. I am too, Zander. I mean it. Good luck.'

Zander didn't respond straight away.

'It's with Pigs.'

Barton looked over for a moment to see if Zander was joking. He wasn't. Nicole Pignatiello had joined their team two months ago after applying to be a detective. Zander had been mentoring her. It looked as though she'd been getting extra attention. Barton gave Zander a wry smile. In his head, he could hear Nat King Cole singing.

Yes, thought Barton, there might well be trouble ahead.

# 70

## THE COLD KILLER

The moment is here. I thank the lady from Resettlement, Bridget, who helped me get prepared for my release. She shakes my hand, holding eye contact, making me believe that this really will be the last time. I'm glad Celestine left quickly. He gave me the largest, most obvious wink that I've ever seen before he went. Crannock was still pretending I don't exist.

It's going to be a beautiful day. There are quite a few clouds in the blue sky, but I can feel the heat on my face as I head towards the exit. The shiny trainers that Brenda sent me for today creak a little with each step. Thinking of her ordering them makes me smile. The staff offered me a taxi to the station, but I'm more than happy to walk. I sniff the air and straighten my shoulders. I'm ready for a new beginning.

I spot two familiar men standing next to a blue Land Rover. It wouldn't have been the biggest surprise to find probation waiting for me, but not these beefcakes. It's fine, though. I did get arrested once as soon as I stepped out of jail, but I'm pretty sure they aren't here for that, and I'll still be a free man. When we're close, I stop and grin.

'Morning, gents, how can I assist, or are you two my welcome home strippers?'

Barton steps forward.

'Kind of. Funds are tight at the moment, so instead of spending the afternoon at Happy Endings strip parlour with an intriguing collection of Colombian beauties, you've got a twenty-minute cold shower with us two at the Regional Swimming Centre.'

'Fair enough. Do they sell beer?'

'You'd need whisky to help you forget.' Barton laughed. 'Perhaps you can give us a few minutes for a chat before you leave. Can we offer you a lift anywhere?'

'It's a nice day, I was going to walk, but you can take me to the station.'

'Railway or police?' asked Zander.

'You two really are a pair of comedians. Railway. I'm off to Northumberland. I'm hoping for a second chance.'

I climb in the rear of the big Land Rover, and they get back in. Barton starts the engine but looks over his shoulder before driving away.

'Good for you. Now, about that pen I got through the post. Off the record, it was you, wasn't it?'

I take my time putting my seat belt on.

'I don't talk to the police, you know that. It's ironic, though. You try to do the right thing and return lost property, and people think the worst of you.'

The railway station is only five minutes away, and we're soon there. I sent the pen to Barton to unsettle him. At the beginning of all this I had thoughts to go further, but I'm glad I didn't.

Barton pulls up at the drop-off point and gets out, leaving Zander in the car. I step out, slam the door and stand next to Barton.

'I sensed a change in you last time we spoke. Is that it? Are you on the straight and narrow now?'

'Fingers crossed. I've some boys to raise and a woman to woo. I hope there's time for both. Tell me, how long exactly did Green get?'

'Life, with a minimum term of twenty-five years.'

'Wow, and he's still alive?'

'Yes, he's ticking along, from what I hear. If he keeps out of trouble, he'll be about sixty when he's released, which isn't much older than we are now. Do we still have something to live for?'

Barton holds out his hand, and I shake it firmly.

'Do you know what?' I reply. 'I'm not entirely sure if I have anything to live for or not. But for the first time in my life, I'm scared, and I love it.'

Barton nods.

'Welcome to parenthood. Good luck, Logan.'

'Same.'

I walk towards the terminal, stopping once at the door to give Barton a final nod. I receive a small one in reply. There's no queue at the desk, and I hand over my travel warrant.

'When's the next train?'

'Platform two, if you're quick, it's coming in now. Or there's another one in thirty minutes.'

I hustle out of the ticket hall, then notice platform two is right in front of me. The train glides in and I get on. I only see a few other people going north at this time of the morning, and my carriage is empty. I choose a seat with a table. I'm putting my bag in the overhead storage when the train jolts to life, and we edge out of the station.

Glancing out of the window through the mesh fence that separates the drop-off car park, I spot Barton leaning against his car. He gives me a single slow wave. Is he praying I don't come back, or is he wishing me well? I suspect the latter, because, even though Barton is police, he's all right.

## 71

### INMATE NO. A1566C – PETER GREEN

I step from my cell onto a noisy wing, nodding to a few of the passing prisoners. It's strange to say it but, for the first time in my life, I have hope. The self-loathing and anger that I felt for who I was has slowly drained away. The scales of my world are balanced now. Those that deserved to, have died, except for my mother, but at least I can pray she lives in fear.

I thought the killing of those responsible would be the end, for them and me. I didn't care if I lived or not, because I had nothing to look forward to. But to my surprise, it was just the end of that journey. A new one has begun.

They sent me here as punishment for murder, but I don't view it like that. My parents and their warped friends moulded me. If you create a monster, do not be surprised if it turns on you. Now, my days of violence are over. The prisoners here don't know that, though. To many, I'm a hero. They avoid my empty eyes and fear the worst, but I've worked in places like these, and my appearance is a facade. I'm calm inside. Finally, there's space in my mind for learning, and room in my heart for friendship, perhaps eventually even love.

As I survey the inhabitants of the wing, I consider those who surround me. There are some in society who don't believe prison is the answer. I'd disagree. Some are born cold killers. I'm right where I'm supposed to be. A place where it's hard to hurt anyone outside these walls. But not impossible.

I wrote to Drummond, who gets out today, and he was kind enough to write back. I appreciated his thoughtful words and encouragement. He'll be a great dad if he gets the chance, although he's clearly not a man to be crossed. Our pact didn't end as we planned, but he thanked me for settling the score with Archie.

I chuckle as I consider the way things have turned out. The young lad with the piercing blue eyes and cheeky grin from three cells up passes by my doorway again. His gaze lasts a second too long. His smile, just a little too wide.

I'm surprised by how my body responds each time I see him. It's as though I'm awakening. I've never felt a connection to another person in any shape or form. How could I be with someone else, when I didn't understand myself?

It's clear to me that this will be a period of change for me. Maybe I'm gay, perhaps I'm straight, maybe I'm neither. I give the lad the tiniest wink back.

At the very least, I have a long while to find out.

## 72

### MRS ZANTHOS – A MONTH LATER

The clock on the wall seemed to tick more loudly than ever once Logan Drummond had been released. Mrs Zanthos frowned at it, then stepped outside with the washing and began to peg the clothes on the line. The sun was up despite it being early, and it was already a pleasant day. She'd been concerned Drummond would come for her after his release, but it appeared not. Even so, the fact he was free had ruined the quality of her life, just as she finally managed to forget about the stolen computer.

From what she'd read on the Internet and in the papers, Drummond had fought in wars all over the world. If he wanted to kill her, he could do it any time with ease. But she was too clever for all these stupid men. Her solicitor had a note saying that if anything were to happen to her, it would be Drummond who was responsible. She'd get the better of him, even if she was dead.

She missed the shrine, though. At some point, she supposed she should fill it in with concrete, but even now she enjoyed standing in it. The pictures of the kids had pleased her, but it wasn't their bodies that appealed, it was the illegality of it all. She liked the planning and the secrecy. Emotions had never been an issue for her. She often read how nothing was worse than losing your children, but she'd easily partitioned it off and carried on regardless.

Mrs Zanthos had fled in the car and driven to Millfield that snowy night she'd escaped from Drummond. She'd driven into town and booked herself into the Bull Hotel in person but with no intention of staying there. Then she'd stayed out of sight at her husband's company flat until Drummond and her son were locked up and she was safe.

When she'd returned to the house a few weeks later, she'd realised she'd been burgled, presumably by Drummond. All the money, jewellery and some of her favourite ornaments were gone. The police had questioned her for days, but she'd stayed quiet, not even mentioning her stolen things. It had soon become obvious that the police had nothing on her.

She hadn't known exactly what her husband and his friends did to the boys, but it wasn't gruesome. She'd heard no shouts of pain.

Well, all that was over now. Her husband, Pfeiffer and Ballanchine paid the price for their perversions and maybe that was just. What they got up to was their business, and she suspected they knew the risk.

She hadn't even been present when that little girl visited, so Mrs Zanthos felt she deserved her peace. All she'd done was organise the photographs on the computer and look after the shrine while the others were behind bars, but apart from that, she wasn't involved at all.

She plodded back to the house, flexing her rheumatic hands. Funnily, the finger that hurt the most was the one that was no longer there. The police had been desperate to know what happened to it, but she wouldn't say. She missed it too, despite the wound healing cleanly. It was surprising how weak your grip was without a little finger.

She shoved the thoughts aside. A nice cup of tea and a chocolate digestive would pick her up. When she got to the kitchen, there was something different about the room. It was only as she filled the kettle that she saw what looked like a piece of computer next to the fridge. A shiver of fear swept over her body as she thought of the missing computer from the shrine. Her ears strained for sounds of movement, then she heard the toilet flush.

The big man who stepped into the kitchen had an impassive face, which evolved into a slow, creepy smile, but Mrs Zanthos recognised the heartless eyes. She saw similar in the mirror every time she looked at her own reflection.

'What are you doing? Get out.'

The man strode towards her, looking down at her hands. Reaching into his pocket, he removed a sealed clear plastic bag with something small, thin and black in it. He placed the bag on the table. She peered at the contents. It was like a dry black slug with a fingernail on the end of it.

'What's the meaning of this?' she asked.

'I wanted to check I had the right person.'

'I don't understand.'

The intruder looked around the room, then returned his piercing stare to her.

'I've been given nearly five thousand pounds to leave this hard drive where the police will find it.'

She stared at him in horror, stepping backwards. That exact amount in cash was stolen from her bedroom. Someone paid this man with her own money.

'I'll double it,' she said.

'Tempting, but now you've seen my face.'

'That computer had nothing to do with me.'

He scoffed as though it were a big fat lie from a red-faced school child.

'I've taken a look at the contents. There's some shocking stuff on there, even for an immoral man like me.'

Mrs Zanthos knew the game was up. Her gaze strayed to the poker leaning against the fireplace. His eyes followed, and he laughed. She edged to the side. Hoping to play for time, she desperately tried to think of ways to distract him.

'Why are you returning my computer to me?' she asked.

'Ah, so it is yours. I assume you know from the news that Peter Green is your son. He gave strict instructions.'

'He's in jail, and he doesn't mean anything to me any more,' she said, sidling closer towards the hearth.

He moved fast and stood right in front of her, putting a hand on her shoulder. Sour breath swamped her as he chuckled.

'Yes, and so was I, but most of us get released, eventually. Open the bag.'

She retreated to the table and opened the plastic bag. She gingerly extracted the finger as if it might move.

'I take it this is mine. Really, you shouldn't have.'

'I'm not returning it,' he replied. 'I'm here for the rest of you.'

Her legs trembled as he removed a weapon from behind his back. It was a small mace. He hefted it in his hand.

Mrs Zanthos jabbed her finger towards the top corner of the room.

'I have CCTV now. They'll find you. You'll die in prison.'

He looked up at the flashing red light on the camera, then slowly returned his gaze to her.

'That's okay,' he said. 'I told the detectives the truth that day. Life's much easier for me inside.' He bared his teeth and spun the mace in a tight arc next to him. 'To be honest, I'd have done this for nothing.'

'Who are you?' screamed Mrs Zanthos, sinking to her knees.

'The name's Charles Celestine,' he replied with the cruellest of grins. 'You can call me Chuck.'

# AUTHOR'S NOTE

A big welcome to new readers of Barton's challenges and thanks to those who have stuck with the series. I enjoy describing these characters' stories. We all need a little Barton in our lives. I find them quite tricky to write compared to my prison books. Linking the two strands together seamlessly takes plenty of concentration, which wasn't easy while home-schooling the kids.

To edit this, I had to book into a cheap hotel during lockdown to get some peace and quiet away from the family. The connecting restaurant was closed, so I barely left the room for three days. It felt like a prison cell, although the toilet was nicer.

For the last year of my career in the prison service, I worked in resettlement. It was one of my jobs to ask the inmates where they were going when they were released. For some, it was nowhere good. Sofa surfing was common. Barns and cardboard under bridges featured, especially in the summer. I often heard people say they had a mattress on the kitchen floor at their parents' house because the sofa was already taken. I felt sad for these people, but it was often tempered by what they'd done to be sent to jail in the first place.

Violent men, like many of the inmates in this story, often have nowhere to go. They have burned their bridges. To be without a home is to be without hope. It was always a surprise when they didn't soon return straight back behind bars.

Please leave a review. If you keep reading them, then I'll keep writing them.

## MORE FROM ROSS GREENWOOD

We hope you enjoyed reading *The Cold Killer*. If you did, please leave a review.

If you'd like to gift a copy, this book is also available as an ebook, digital audio download and audiobook CD.

Sign up to Ross Greenwood's mailing list for news, competitions and updates on future books.

http://bit.ly/RossGreenwoodNewsletter

The next instalment in the series, *The Fire Killer*, is available to order now.

## ABOUT THE AUTHOR

**Ross Greenwood** is the bestselling author of over ten crime thrillers. Before becoming a full-time writer he was most recently a prison officer and so worked everyday with murderers, rapists and thieves for four years. He lives in Peterborough.

Follow Ross on social media:

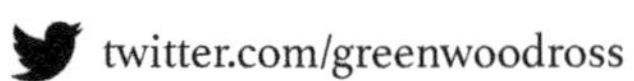

twitter.com/greenwoodross

facebook.com/RossGreenwoodAuthor

bookbub.com/authors/ross-greenwood

instagram.com/rossg555

Made in the USA
Las Vegas, NV
28 December 2021

39742856R00193